LIFE IN A NUTSHELL

Stewart MacInnes

LIFE IN A NUTSHELL

FICTION4ALL

TRANSLATIONS

Irish	English
Fuilteach, Fuilteach, Ifreann Fuilteach! Amadán! Amadán! Amadán!	Bloody, Bloody, Bloody Hell! Fool! Fool! Fool!
Atá tú a fuair fola saill mór asal	You've got a bloody big fat ass
Na Gearmánaigh iad fola ag teacht	The Germans are bloody coming
Fola uafásach	Bloody terrible
Comhlánaigh leathcheann	Complete idiot
Salach muc	Dirty pig
Oscailte suas	Open Up
I ifreann le haghaidh eternity	In Hell for eternity
Ciníochas	Racism
Bitseach	Bitch

Asal	Ass
Fód amach	Sod off
Agus tá tú soith	And you're a bitch
Aindiachaí	Atheist
Aindiachaí é an Diabhal é féin	An Atheist is the Devil himself
Guí mé lá amháin a bheidh do leanaí a bheith ar ais le leat áit a mbaineann siad	I pray one day your children will be back with you where they belong
Peter agus Sally ar ais le leat áit a mbaineann siad	Peter and Sally are back with you where they belong

Chapter 1

Fuilteach, Fuilteach, Ifreann Fuilteach! Amadán! Amadán! Amadán! I mean, Marie Benjamin, what's the matter with you? Show some courage, woman and for God's sake, just look at yourself. You stupid, useless, pathetic, ridiculous, waste of space. I don't want to hear any excuses, I'm not having it. I'm just not having it, you stupid cow. How many times have we been through all this? A lifetimes worth of "how many times" that's what. Idiot! Well, when you've finished berating yourself perhaps you'd like to take a deep breath and calm down. I'm calm now. Good, that's more like it. The fact is you need to stop shaking like a leaf and yes you're nervous, petrified even, but tonight is what you've been waiting for a lifetime. So put all those negative thoughts out of your mind right now and be positive. It's easier said than done there's no two ways about it but, it's already been said, you've been through this a thousand times before. Besides, they're probably just as nervous about this meeting after all this time so stop thinking they won't like you. They're not going to walk out this hotel after only a few minutes. Let's be sensible about this, they're not going to do this after coming all the way from Australia. No, they won't do that, will they? Of course they won't so stop being a silly cow.

At least I'm not the only one here which I'd have hated and the bar's not crowded either which I'd have hated just as much. So it's all good then, isn't it? Just sit quietly, by yourself, in the corner with the sparkling mineral water you've just bought and try not to draw attention to yourself. You can put those silly thoughts out of your mind people might be staring at you. Let's face it, you're no spring chicken anymore and folk don't give a toss about the colour of your skin these days, especially here in London. Why should they? There's so many of us now, you're nothing out of the ordinary. So you can stop feeling self-conscious and realise you're not being stared at. Have you got that? Yes, I think so. More positive, please. Right, yes, more positive. The World is my Oyster, nothing will stop me now. Better? Erm, we'll work on those thoughts.

Will they recognise me from the description I gave them? Oh what if they don't? There you go again you silly woman, doubting yourself. First of all it doesn't matter whether or not they recognise you, does it? You're meeting them on table four, in the restaurant at 8pm, an hour and a half from now. It was silly to get here so early, this hotel is only fifteen minutes on the tube from home. I know I needn't have got here so early but I didn't want to leave anything to chance. What if the tube broke down or if there were cancellations or if I accidentally got on the wrong one and ended up in Barnet or somewhere? You're worrying about something that probably wouldn't happen. Yes, but tonight is too important. Oh my God, what will we talk about? After all, I'm just a dull retired solicitor. What did I just say about being more positive? You've a lifetime of conversation to share and they're going to want to hear about your life as a solicitor. Yes, but when I tell people this they always want to hear about the juicy cases I was involved in. They're disappointed when I say nothing exciting ever happened in my working life; no murderers, no drug dealers or even a bank robber to deal with. You could always exaggerate a little. No, I couldn't do that, I don't want to lie to them. Please yourself. I will. I will tell them despite a lifetime of heartache and despair, I spent my years as a solicitor helping others who had fallen on hard times. That's going to sound dull to them. No, it won't. Tell them about the heartache and despair. Should I? Of course you should. You could start by telling them about Mother. Oh I don't know? After all I disappointed Mother, she wanted so much more for me. Doesn't any mother want that for their daughter? We never spoke for years. These things happen. I'm an alcoholic, they're not going to be impressed with that. Nonsense. You haven't touched a drop in years. They should be well impressed. You deserve a lot of credit. Just as you deserve a lot of credit for all the good you did as a solicitor. I'm just going to make it clear I was never a highly paid solicitor, no big financial rewards and I now live on a modest pension. Yes, but you can also tell them about some of the people you have helped. Mr and Mrs Welland, for example. A hard working couple who were ripped off by those unscrupulous builders who built an extension for them which wasn't fit for purpose. A leaking roof, damp everywhere. Crumbling brickwork. You took those builders to

9

court and won and you found the Wellands a reputable builder to rebuild their extension. I did, didn't I? You helped numerous people who were in arrears with their rents. You negotiated payment plans for them and in some cases you got their rents reduced and debts written off. You were an unsung hero but the point is in an hour and a half you're going to get the reward you've longed for. Besides, it's not all about you. You'll want to hear all about them and their families and friends. You'll want to know everything, won't you?

I do so want them to recognise me, I can't help feeling I haven't described myself to them sufficiently. Oh for goodness sake it doesn't matter. Anyway you're good at describing yourself and other people too. You were always having to describe yourself to clients if you were meeting them on neutral ground. Yes, I remember. I always told them I was black but if they asked, "how black?" I'd say I wasn't black like a dark Irish stout but much paler than that. Hmm, a bizarre analogy comparing yourself to a glass of Guinness but I suppose they got what you meant. I'd then explain that my father was black but my mother was white. No need to explain this to them, is there? But I was proud to tell people this. I still am proud. And they'll be proud of you. Will they? I do hope so.

Have I got the date right? Of course you have. It's Friday 16 October. Your watch says so and that digital clock on the wall confirms it. Yes, but what if they think our meeting is tomorrow? Why should they think that? Look it's your birthday and you're seventy-six today. If you remember rightly when Peter said he and Sally were coming to London and touted October or November you piped up and said your birthday was on 16 October. That settled it for Peter. You'd meet on your birthday. So no, you haven't got it wrong so sit back and relax.

I was so emotional the day Peter phoned out of the blue. I had been late getting home and it was 8pm when I finally managed to get a saucepan of soup onto boil. The phone rang and I remember thinking who that could be as nobody usually rings at this time of night. So anyway, I answered the phone.

"Hello," he said. "Am I speaking to Marie Benjamin?"

"Yes," I said being on my guard.

"Mother of Peter and Sally Brown. Their father, Frank?"

"Yes" I replied, a little worried.

"Hello Mum. It's me, Peter," he said calmly as if this call was a regular occurrence. "We're coming to London," said Peter as a matter of fact.

I nearly fainted, I couldn't believe it. Luckily I keep a chair by the phone and I instinctively sat on it. What a shock! What a delight. Tears of joy flooded down my face. A lifetime of hurt had bottled up inside you. Let's face it, you were an emotional wreck and rightly so. Of course I was an emotional wreck. I'd not known them since they were young children and suddenly after nigh on fifty years I was talking to my son. I could hear my daughter Sally in the background crying joyful tears

11

and she kept shouting "hello Mum" and at some point she came to the phone and by then we were both emotional wrecks.

Before this though Peter had told me six months ago their father died and their step mother decided to tell them the truth. They'd grown up believing I was dead. Frank didn't think I knew about her but I did. Always dressed up to the nines, a bit tarty I seem to recall. Long black hair, bright red lipstick, thick paste of make-up on her face. Long legs and a short mini skirt to reveal more than she should. Are you sure not just being bitter because she was the other woman? No, I don't blame her, it wasn't her fault. If it hadn't have been her it would've been someone else. The problems were between Frank and I.

Somehow Peter had managed to track me down when, despite all my efforts, I'd spent a lifetime trying to trace them. I felt so stupid at my failings when it seems Peter had managed it so relatively easily. You're being too hard on yourself again. Peter knows it isn't your fault you couldn't trace them. His father had done an excellent job in ensuring they were untraceable whereas you wasn't hiding from anyone. Peter also reasoned as he held a senior position in the Australian Police Force and he had, as he put it, certain contacts.

After I'd put the phone down my heart was throbbing with excitement but my joy was tempered by the injustice of living most of my life without them. I was shaking all over. Too right you were shaking. Your body hadn't shaken like that since the dark days when booze was your master. This shaking felt different to when I was on the booze. I was overjoyed at the prospect of seeing my children again but the heartbreak of missing out on most of their life was overwhelming. I sobbed uncontrollably in my kitchen as I remembered those early years I had with them. How Sally used to enjoy me brushing her hair and Peter in particular used to love it when I read him a story. My children and I had formed a bond, a bond so strong not even living on different sides of the World could break. I'd have continued crying all night had my attention not been drawn to the soup erupting like a volcano and spilling onto the hob. The realisation that my evening meal was going everywhere forced me into regaining some control of my emotions and I attended to the mess.

You've not been in a bar nigh on forty years. Being an alcoholic it's best to stay well away from such possible temptation. It's been fourteen thousand, four hundred and ninety-five days since a drop has passed my lips so I think I made the right call. This is a special occasion though and I'm not going to let the demon drink spoil things for me. Nothing is going to spoil it for me. Good that's the spirit, no pun intended. This sparkling mineral water isn't very exciting but it was either that or orange juice which always plays havoc with my bladder, God knows why? The last thing I want is to be in and out of the ladies all night. I just know what would happen and no matter how hard I try I'd have to give in. It would be like King Kanut trying to stop the tide from coming in. Well, then, you've made the right choice of drink haven't you?

I'm going to get bored sitting on my own in this bar. Well, you picked this place. You could have chosen somewhere else. It was convenient for the tube. That's my excuse and I'm sticking to it. Anyway, what shall I do? Do what you usually do in situations like this. Remember what you used to do when you frequented these places? If it was somewhere you hadn't been before you used to have a look round the room and observed what you could see. Yes, I suppose I could do this. Off you go then, observe. Well, let's see, this bar has seen better days by the looks of it. Horrible red patterned carpet. It's a traditional hotel mind and there's a number of original features. Oak beams, lots of brass ornaments and an attractive fire place with an inviting log fire. I can feel the heat from here. Very welcoming, particularly as it's pretty chilly outside for this time of year. There's some interesting looking pictures on the wall including one of Oliver Cromwell, no less. According to the plaque in front of me this building certainly dates back to those times and by the looks of the décor he was probably the last person to apply a paint brush to it. Just imagine, the fearsome Oliver Cromwell taking time off from battle to decorate the hotel. That would be funny wouldn't it? Assuming it was an Inn back then. You're being silly now and stop that silly giggling. You'll draw attention to yourself. When you start giggling you often end up drawing attention to yourself and you don't like this so stop it. Clearly the notion of Oliver Cromwell doing some DIY is somewhat ridiculous. Well, I feel like being ridiculous and at any rate a lick of paint would do wonders for the room. It would make it a much more attractive property. You're beginning to sound like an estate agent. Don't, I'd enough dealings with those lot when I was a solicitor. Now come now, estate agents are in the main perfectly normal decent people. You can wipe that grin off your face. They are. There was nothing decent about that old cow, Miss Marshall. Christ, no wonder she was a Miss. She used to take great delight when some poor soul was evicted from their home. She'd go down the pub and celebrate. Wicked cow. Her aside they were normal hard working people just on different sides to you. Their clients were the landlords whereas you were representing the tenants. I had a duty to these tenants. So did they to the landlords. You've still not convinced me. Billy Meadows. He was all right wasn't he? Yes, I'll give you Billy Meadows.

So what shall I do now? You could assess those two sitting over there. What those two love birds making eyes at each other. Obviously they're hopelessly in love, poor things. What you recon they do for a living? Oh I don't know. What about her? Hmm... Probably sits at a desk all day using a computer. A lot of people do that. Try being more specific. She's probably a receptionist in an estate agents! Oh stop that silly giggling again. Well, I'm not in the mood to try and sum up strangers. I know, I'll go through what I'm going to tell Peter and

Sally. You've been doing that every day, several times a day, each time it's been a bit different. You need to make up your mind what you're going to tell them and what you're not. I need to tell them the truth, that's what. I just need to be clear in my mind what I'm going to say. Oh well, go on then, nothing's going to stop you. Where are you going to start this time? I think actually I should start with my parents, after all, they were here before me.

So my parents. Mother was born Eileen Rafferty in 1919 and Father, Isaac Benjamin two years earlier. I must confess I know little about my father, Mother never told me much. As for Father's parents, my grandparents, I know next to nothing. Mother said they were both dead when she met my father and other than telling me my grandfather was also Isaac and my grandmother was Martha, I got nothing else out of her. What I need is the makers of *Who Do You Think You Are* to invite me to trace my father's family tree. I could do with a treat like jetting off to Africa to find out more but that's not going to happen. Mother, I know much more about. She didn't have any sisters and only had the one brother, Michael. Unusual you might think for an Irish family, especially back then, but Mother said my grandmother had medical issues and having more children would've been a risk. Mother wouldn't elaborate on this.

My grandfather was born in 1898 and he was called Sean. He'd five brothers and a sister and they grew up to have large families. He spoke Irish and Mother learned from him who in turn taught me and

I've never forgotten it. Throughout my life I've often practiced speaking the language as I find it comforting. However, there were some swear words and rude remarks Mother frequently used and I must confess I sometimes say some of these things when I'm in a bad mood. The thing with Mother was she could pick an argument with anyone if the mood took her. There were times when I thought her colourful language wasn't called for but whenever I confronted her she'd say it wasn't in English so it didn't count as swearing. If a man annoyed her she'd usually swear at him and she'd often be rude about his backside. Why I don't know. Quite often her comments about a man would be inaccurate but this didn't seem to matter to her. With regularity she would shout: "Atá tú a fuair fola saill mór asal. This was one of her more moderate outbursts; her language could be a lot worse and I find myself refraining from repeating these even in Irish. Fortunately the people she was verbally abusing usually had no idea what she was saying, ranting in Irish, they just thought she was a crazy mad woman. Occasionally though they'd be someone who spoke the language and I remember, in particular, one man who swore back at her in Irish. She responded by swearing at him and he swore back which went on for a few minutes when Mother suddenly burst out laughing. Fortunately the man saw the funny side too and they both ended up giggling and they parted in the best of terms.

My grandmother, born Mary Carthy in 1900, had four sisters who also had large families. So as a

17

result, Mother had many cousins, far too many to keep track of. Mother also told me when she married my father they were subjected to racial abuse which they did their best to ignore. That was all she would say on the subject but what I do know is she caused a stir amongst her family when she married a Black African who'd been brought up in Britain. She first met Father in Church. Mother was a regular in the choir and one day Father turned up to join having heard through the grapevine the Church Priest was desperate for some more male members. A courtship flourished between Mother and Father from then on. Later, I did try and find out more about their early married life but the newspaper archives had little to say on the subject. The abuse, which surely happened, was swept under the carpet by the press and those in authority alike. Don't get me wrong. Mother could be just as judgmental as the next person. Had Father not been a Catholic she'd never have married him. She wouldn't have married anyone if they weren't a Catholic.

"We're all the same regardless of our colour of skin," Mother reasoned, "your father was after all a devout Catholic; but you sinned when you married a Protestant."

She'd strange double standards did Mother but to be clear, her Catholic views were her own save her life-long friend, Bernadette Carmichael. I've known many Catholics in my life and generally their views are one of tolerance and a live and let live attitude. From what I remember of Bernadette she always struck me as rather strange. Why I thought of her this way is too difficult to define but suffice to say she'd many contradictory views. In some of my more heated arguments with Mother I'd accuse Bernadette of being a bad influence but she'd always defend Bernadette and dismissed anything I said about her. More likely, the truth is they were probably as bad as each other and between them they conjured up a whole list of prejudices. Mother and Bernadette, both aged only twenty, took the adventurous step by moving to London to train as hairdressers and they worked together in the same salon. There was a time when they did everything together and they even got married around the same time. Bernadette married an Irish business man who was Catholic of course and they moved back to Ireland soon after their marriage. Mother kept in touch with Bernadette and when she herself returned to Ireland they resumed their friendship.

You'll need show Peter and Sally what Mother and Father looked like. I've only black and white photos of them but I'll say Mother had red curly hair and freckles on her face especially around her nose. She was tall and slim and held onto her Irish accent throughout her life. I don't recall her accent mellowing over the years but then again I may not have been conscious of any change. It's funny, when I think of Mother I was always think of her as a young adult and not the old lady she became. We'd a volatile relationship Mother and I, always arguing. She'd principles and wouldn't be swayed from them no matter how illogical they seemed to

19

me; thank goodness I was nothing like her. Liar, you were very much like her in many ways that's why you often argued. Yes, if I'm honest, I'm more like her than I care to admit.

Just like Father my hair is dark at least it was before the grey appeared in its place. I can't remember exactly when that happened. In reality it must have been a gradual thing but as far as my memory goes I woke up one day with grey hair. I inherited Mother's curly locks and slim build and that hasn't changed. No matter how ruthless the age of time has been to me my hair remains curly and I've kept a trim figure. When I was growing up some of the kids in the street used to call me Charcoal Locks. I never really minded though. They weren't racist, they were just kids. Not that I really understood what racism meant at that age. Had you been a blonde they'd have probably called you Goldie Locks. That's probably right. Thinking about it, I think I prefer Charcoal Locks.

Father died when I was only a tot so sadly I can only vaguely remember him. Mother showed me photos and clearly he was handsome and a big man. In fact Mother had kept lots of photos and some were of me, many of Mother and Father but I hadn't a clue who some of the people were. Father was always smiling in the photos which I like but it was more of a cheeky grin really. That's about it, although I do have this long lasting memory of this big kind man appearing occasionally with sweets and presents. Yes, he used to bring you a lot of wine gums, didn't he? Yes, he did. He'd always give me a hug and kiss me gently on my forehead whenever he was home. Of the few memories I have of Father, this is the one I cherish most. When I was old enough to understand, Mother told me about the day the official letter arrived bringing news of his death. After Mother had died, amongst some her papers I found this official letter which I intend to show to Peter and Sally. The letter is a little tatty around the edges but all in all it's well preserved. I'd not seen this letter before as although Mother often referred to it I'd no idea she'd kept it. Perhaps she simply couldn't bring herself to part with it? Perhaps, but Mother wasn't one to hold onto things. There wasn't much amongst her personal effects. Birth and marriage certificates but that was about it other than this letter. I've read it a few times but I'll read it again. Yes, it's somehow comforting to read it, isn't it?

Dear Mrs Benjamin.

It is with deepest regret that I have to inform you that your husband was tragically killed in battle on 18th November 1944. I want you to know that Isaac was a very brave soldier and a hero. He died for what he believed in and you can be proud of him. He will be greatly missed by his friends and fellow soldiers. If there is anything I can do or if there is anything that you need, please do not hesitate to let me know. I am arranging for his body to be brought to England as soon as possible and I know you will want to give him a full Christian Burial.

Your obedient servant

Colonel Robert Billings

Mother would never speak about it even when I pressed her for information. However years later I did some research and learned Father was part of the British 43rd (Wessex) Division and for the historical record he was killed whilst part of the Allied Offensive Operation Clipper. I've brought along a whole lot of information for Peter and Sally to take a look at if they wish but any other detail is not important to me. I'd lost my father and the opportunity of growing up knowing him. It must have been hard for Mother to bring me up single handed with little money.

I was only four when the war ended so I was too young to really understand what was going on. One thing I do remember about the war were the Doodle Bugs. I can remember hearing them flying across London and when it was all quiet Mother used to panic.

"Doodle Bugs...Doodle Bugs," Mother would shout. "They're coming. Sweet Jesus they're coming." Na Gearmánaigh iad fola ag teacht. Na Gearmánaigh iad fola ag teacht".

I don't think Jesus had anything to do with it but she'd always say this. Mother ran about the house like a headless chicken but even a headless chicken would've retained more coordination than she ever did. Instinctively though she always managed to pick me up and for some reason we ended up in the cupboard under the stairs with just a little torch providing us with minimal light. Being so young I thought it was just a game and it was great fun sitting almost in darkness. I never really understood what a Doodle Bug was back then. I never knew about the devastation they caused, the homes they destroyed and the lives that were lost. If Mother tried to explain I could never comprehend it. So what was a Doodle Bug to me? Was it some kind of insect? Mother was terrified of spiders so perhaps Doodle Bugs were like big spiders? Indeed on one particular day there was a big spider running around in the cupboard and when Mother spotted it she screamed hysterically.

"Doodle Bugs, Mummy," I muttered as I could hear that familiar sound in the distance.

"Doodle Bugs, or no Doodle Bugs, I'm not going back in there whilst that devil of a creature is in residence," Mother said defiantly.

Mother by now had put me down on the floor and under the kitchen table. Perhaps she thought I'd be safe from the Doodle Bugs under there. Mother then grabbed hold of the broom, ready to beat the spider to death when it came crawling out of the cupboard but it was nowhere to be seen. The spider had presumably decided against entering the kitchen and he'd found his way outside via another route. Perhaps he didn't want to stay in the same house as a mad Irish woman?

Mother's dislike of spiders never left her. Even many years later she turned off the radio every time the Who's song *Boris The Spider* was broadcast over the airways. There was nothing wrong with the tune she explained but just the thought of a spider made her hate it. I burst out laughing when she told me this and eventually Mother saw the funny side of it and we both ended up in a fit of giggles. It was one of a few occasions when Mother and I were happy in each other's company. So thank goodness for *Boris The Spider* and thanks go to Pete Townsend and Co. I've got a CD recording of it now and when I play it I think of Mother which makes me smile. Most of the time you were a nightmare together. We were. The friction began to fester in my teens and after I left home things between Mother and I were never again like they once were. One of us would say something which offended the other and then we'd both say things we didn't mean and then a full blown argument would ensue. The next thing both of us would get hysterical and we'd both end up throwing things at each other. Luckily we were both bad shots. We were as bad as each other if the truth be known but at the time I always blamed her and she blamed me.

The piece of cake incident was a particularly bad one, do you remember? Sadly all too well. I don't know if I should tell Peter and Sally about what happened on this particular day. You must. You promised yourself you'd leave nothing out. Good or bad, you'd share these moments with them. Very well. It was all so stupid and so trivial. I'd invited Mother round for a cup of tea and piece of cake. I was experimenting with cake making and I thought I'd try out my baking skills on her. Big mistake. It was a big mistake all right. I'd cut her a piece of this sponge cake and she sat there quietly chewing away and doing her best not to pull faces. Clearly she wasn't enjoying it but I couldn't leave it at that and I asked her what she thought of it. She tactfully said it was a bit sweet and wasn't going to elaborate. I should've accepted this. You didn't though, did you? You insisted on her saying what she really thought and so she said it tasted lousy. "Inedible. Fola uafásach." That's what she actually said. A few tactless remarks from each of us followed culminating in Mother throwing the piece of cake in the bin. In retaliation I slapped the rest of the cake onto her lap. There was messy jam and cream all over her skirt and she said it was ruined. Things had got out of hand and she smashed the plate the cake was on. I threw a tea cup which missed her and it broke in pieces against the wall. By then we'd both lost it and we picked up whatever was close to hand. Plates, cups, sauces, bowls all thrown and ended up in pieces. She left when there wasn't any more crockery to throw and we never spoke to each other again for three weeks. Frank came home before I'd time to clear up the mess and he said the kitchen looked like a bomb had hit it and he wasn't amused at having to purchase a new crockery set. This wasn't the most shameful thing about it all, was it? Go on, admit what you told Frank. I told Frank, Mother had thrown everything and I was the innocent victim and, as he hated her guts, he accepted my version of things. To be fair the feeling was mutual. From the moment Frank tactlessly admitted he was an Atheist Mother was never going to like him. Mind you, she'd have hated him even more if he'd said he was a practicing Protestant! Now don't laugh, it's not funny. Oh Hell, what will Peter and Sally think of me when I tell them I blamed everything on Mother? They'll think me wicked. It will help if you tell them how ashamed of yourself you were afterwards. Yes, I'd never been more ashamed in my life, it was senseless and so trivial. All the nastiness and all because of silly piece of cake. At least you later apologised to Mother. You did the right thing by going round to her flat and Mother graciously said it was all forgotten. I'm sure Peter and Sally won't judge you harshly. I hope so.

So are you going to leave out most of the first half dozen years of your life? Of course I'm not. Why are you asking yourself that? Silly bitch. Comhlánaigh leathcheann. Admittedly I only have vague memories of my infant years or what Mother had told me but it's important they understand my relationship with her. Sounds fair enough. So what to tell them? Where I lived during the war? Good idea. So during the war Mother and I lived mostly in Hammersmith and for a short while in Chelsea. This may sound posh to Peter and Sally but I'll tell them we were never amongst the elite. Mother could only afford rented rooms in various houses which, to put it politely, were generally in need of some TLC. This was of course Mother's account, as I was too young to remember these places. Typically we lived

26

in only the one room; an adult single bed for Mother and a child's for me. We shared kitchen and bathroom facilities with the other people living at the properties. She told me, with disgust, she used to have to spend hours cleaning the kitchen after other residents who couldn't be bothered to wash up or put utensils and crockery away after use. She often spoke of a Mr Hudson whose hygiene habits left a lot to be desired. Half the time he didn't bother to flush the toilet and he used to leave his dirty shaving water in the sink. He'd walk around the house wearing a dirty vest which looked as if it hadn't been washed in years and his grey beard was stained a dark yellow from his excessive cigarette smoke. His cat was something else. Mother said it stank like a rhino's house. Not that she knew what a rhino's house smelt like but this was her opinion. "Salach muc," she called him.

It wasn't until 1947 when she was able to afford to rent her own flat and only then did I get to have my own bedroom. I remember it well. It was just a box room, just enough space for a bed, a small wardrobe and chest of drawers. But it was all just for me. The walls were decorated with bright flowered wallpaper and Bernard, my favourite teddy bear, sat pride of place on the bed lent against the headboard. Mother had rescued him from a jumble sale, having bought him for just two old pence. She cleaned him up and from the moment I saw him I knew I'd call him Bernard. He was so cute, he'd one brown eye and one black and his feet were tattered and torn. Bernard was passed onto my son when he was born but one day after returning home after a trip to the shops Bernard was no longer in the pram with Peter. I went out and retraced my steps but sadly Bernard was nowhere to be found but Peter was too young to care. I'd like to think someone found him and Bernard continued to bring joy to other children. I must ask Peter if he remembers Bernard.

Living in the flat was a lovely time for me. I used to pretend the flat had a secret passageway and only I knew about it. As an only child you got used to playing by yourself and you had an imaginary friend called Sophie, didn't you? Yes, I remember this vividly. I can't recall why I chose this name, I never knew any Sophie's at the time so I probably just picked it at random. I've often wondered if Sally had an imaginary friend. If she did maybe she called it Sophie. That would be something.

My other companion was a doll I called Dolly, lacking I suppose, the ability to think of something more original. She'd red hair like Mother and she'd a pink dress with pretty frills stitched to the seams. It was the only dress I had for Dolly but I didn't mind. I carried Dolly everywhere I went; the three of us were inseparable. I always took good care of Dolly, keeping her clean and devoid of any damage in all the time I had her. Dolly was given to Sally when she was born and Sally took Dolly to Australia with her. It'd be such a thrill to see Dolly again but I wonder what state she's in? After all, she's an old girl now so realistically she must be worse for wear. I was thrilled to learn Sally has since passed Dolly onto her daughter. Your face lit up at the thought of your grandchild and you're looking forward to hearing about all of your grandchildren. All grown up now. There's sadness in that thought? There is. Not only did I miss out on seeing my children grow up but my grandchildren too. I was denied the pleasure of taking them for a walk in the park or buying them lots of sweets or ice cream even when their Mummy said they weren't to have any. I missed out on the opportunity of spoiling them something rotten like all grandmothers like to do for their grandchildren. I never got to do any of this. All because of their father. That...that... Tut, Tut! Don't say it! You don't want to express your feelings about Frank in front of Peter and Sally, do you? No, I don't. You promised yourself you wouldn't be bitter. Yes, I must think of the positives and Peter and Sally have promised to bring along lots of photos. Peter has two sons, Daren and Paul, whilst Sally has one daughter, Rebeca and one son, Jason. I must remember to ask after Peter's wife, Amelia and Sally's husband, Mark. I've a hundred and one questions which I've written down in my note pad so as I don't forget. Don't let Peter and Sally see that notepad or they'll think it very odd. Would they? I'll try and be discrete.

As much as I loved Dolly and Sophie I wished I'd had a brother or sister. Mother told me I would've done had things been different. They hadn't been married long when war broke out and they saw little of one another before he was killed.

It was difficult to make friends particularly as we frequently moved house. Then when I was eleven Mother took the decision to up sticks and move us both to Ireland. Peter and Sally will be interested to know this was a life changing moment for you. Think how different things might have been if you'd stayed in London? When I was aged about twelve I remember asking Mother why she'd decided to move back to Ireland and she told me it'd been on her mind for several years to return to her homeland. She just needed an incentive to make it happen and this came after a visit from Dr Roberts. As a child I suffered terribly with chest and breathing difficulties and Dr Roberts was a frequent caller to our home. On one particular day I was lying on the kitchen floor gasping for breath and although it was a long time ago, I remember it vividly. Mother immediately sent for Dr Roberts and she was panicking more than usual probably because this was the worst she'd seen me with this condition. It was a relief for both of us when Dr Roberts arrived with his medical bag.

"Thank goodness you're here doctor," cried Mother.

Dr Roberts removed his hat and in seconds he'd placed a breathing aid against my mouth as Mother looked on anxiously.

"Take deep slow breaths," commanded Dr Roberts.

I did as I was told and after a short while my breathing improved.

"Good, good. Now let's get you seated so I can examine you more easily."

Dr Roberts removed the breathing aid away from my mouth and gently helped me to a chair. Meanwhile Mother continued to flap although by now she'd calmed a little. Dr Roberts took his stethoscope from his bag and placed it on my chest.

"Breathe in.... Breathe out."

"Is she all right, Dr Roberts, what's wrong with her?" Mother worried.

"Just one moment, please, Mrs Benjamin. Let me finish examining Marie."

Dr Roberts apparently had a reputation for being abrupt and lacking tact in some instances. Yet Mother recognised he was a very good doctor and better that than to have a pleasant but clueless one. After all, she reasoned, his white hair and a well-worn face suggested he was a mature man with many years' experience as a doctor. Perhaps more importantly I was more at ease with him than I was with that young Dr Bateman, who sometimes called when Dr Roberts wasn't available. There was something about Dr Bateman you weren't happy about, wasn't there? I think it was just his manner. He was always very sure of himself. He was a bit cocky. You didn't like him much, did you? I liked Dr Roberts much better and Mother could see I was much happier with him. Even at a young age I preferred older men.

"Now, Marie, breathe in once more for me.... And out.... Fine!"

31

Satisfied with his examination he returned the stethoscope to his bag and brought out a bottle of medicine which he placed in Mother's hand. He then picked up his hat and placed it on his head.

"Make sure Marie takes a teaspoon of this medicine three times a day," he ordered.

"Certainly, doctor, but what is the matter with Marie this time?"

"Same as always, Mrs Benjamin. I'm concerned that her chest is worsening."

"What can I do?"

"Just keep an eye on her. I suspect the smog we've been experiencing isn't helping and may well be the root cause. Try taking her to the country if you can, the fresh air will do her good."

"Where would you suggest?"

Dr Roberts shrugged his shoulders: "Anywhere you like, as long as it gets her away from the smog for a while; get her away from London that's the important thing." Dr Roberts lifted his hat. "Good day to you, Mrs Benjamin. Good bye Marie."

Mother followed Dr Roberts to the door and bolted it as soon as he left. At that point her mind was made up we were going to live in Ireland. Dr Roberts had prescribed fresh air and Mother said I was certainly going to get it. I remember how excited she was by her plan and she knelt down beside me.

"How are feeling now, Marie?"

"I can't breathe very well, Mummy. Will that stuff make me better?"

"That's what Dr Roberts says. No time like the present."

She collected a teaspoon from the kitchen draw and carefully filled it with the medicine.

"Open up, Marie."

I didn't like the look of the medicine so I kept my mouth closed. Mother wasn't going to let me get away with this one though.

"Oscailte suas, Marie" she snapped.

I did as I was told. She smiled and placed the tea spoon in my mouth and I dutifully swallowed every drop as Mother had commanded.

"Err that's horrible!"

"Your grandmother used to say the more horrible the medicine tasted the better it was for you." She paused for a moment: "How would you like to live in Ireland, Marie? You know where Ireland is don't you?"

"Is it near Wales, Mummy?"

"Kind of, but much closer to where the sun slowly sets and where the summer days are long and nights are short."

I hadn't a clue what she was talking about but I was excited to learn Uncle Michael had a farm not far from Dublin. I hadn't met Uncle Michael at that point or if I did I don't remember. Mother had previously mentioned him a few times but as a young child I hadn't taken much notice but the farm got my attention. Mother had, on one occasion, taken me to a farm where I saw cows and sheep for the first time. I thought they were wonderful; it began my lifelong love of animals which hasn't diminished to this day. I wanted to know if Dublin was near Ireland and Mother patiently explained Dublin was in Ireland but I was still a little confused but I didn't dwell on it; Uncle had a farm and this was good news to me.

"I'll write and ask him if we can come and stay with him until we find a place of our own. You'll love it there, Marie. Uncle Michael has cows and sheep and you'll get a belly full of fresh air. Would you like that, Marie?"

I nodded even though I had no concept of how far away Ireland was from London but I sensed Ireland was something good. Mother promised Dolly could come as well and I'll never forget, Mother's face was something to behold, her smiling lips almost touched her eyes which shone bright with happiness. Her golden hair as bright as her smile. I remember this day so clearly because I'd never seen Mother so happy and excited before and it'd be a long time before I witnessed such euphoria in her again.

Looking back, Mother was giving up a lot in the interests of my health and the financial implications she'd either dismissed or not considered. The NHS hadn't long come into being and Mother was turning her back on free health care so the timing was somewhat questionable. She hadn't really considered she wasn't paying for Dr Roberts' visits but Mother was like that, she made decisions quickly without thinking them through. Yes, but it was a doctor in Dublin who diagnosed your breathing symptoms as asthma, a conclusion

Dr Roberts should've reached. I won't hear a thing said against Dr Roberts. Fair enough, have it your way.

Chapter 2

It was December 1949, I was eight years old and Mother and I left our London flat for Ireland. Mother had packed, what seemed to me at the time, two huge suitcases which were stuffed full of all our worldly possessions. How she managed to carry these suitcases I don't know but she was always a very strong woman. I was excited by this life change but little did I realise the consequences of returning to her native Ireland would bring upon me. The journey over to Ireland I remember little of as I somehow managed to sleep through most of it. I do remember though boarding a number of trains and travelling on a bus at some point but it seemed in no time at all we were sailing across the Irish Sea to Dublin. The journey over was rough and my stomach couldn't cope with it and all I can remember is me being constantly sick and longing for the journey to end. Not even cuddling up to Dolly could ease my misery; she though seemed to take the journey in her stride. She wasn't going to let a rough ride on a ferry get her down and she was looking forward to new surroundings and making new friends. You and that Dolly! Get a grip, Marie. Dolly was only a toy. Excuse me, Dolly wasn't just a toy, she was Dolly. You live in Cloud Cuckoo Land a lot of the time, Marie and remember it wasn't until we docked in Dublin did your stomach settle.

Uncle Michael was waiting for us, sitting on his great big tractor, his beaming smile greeted us warmly. He was a tall, strong looking man, his face harshly weathered from working outside for many long hours on his farm. He'd attached a trailer to his tractor and Mother and I travelled to his farm in it. The proper constructed roads soon made way to bumpy dirt tracks but compared to the sea journey it felt as smooth as silk. Our journey to the farm must have taken about an hour and along the way Mother encouraged me to breath in the fresh air. I was enchanted by all the wild animals I saw along the way. Hares and rabbits hopping happily across the fields, squirrels scampering up the trees when they spied us and not to mention to the array of different birds landing in the fields looking for food.

Uncle's farm house wasn't what I'd imagined. He wasn't married and he never craved much space which was just as well as the farm house was merely a tiny two up two down. Uncle occupied the larger bedroom which left the smaller one for Mother and I. Having to share with Mother once again took the shine off for me as I'd gotten used to having my own room. For a while I was beginning to wish I was back in London but my grievances soon melted away when Uncle showed me around his farm. I fell in love with the cows, the sheep and the pigs were just adorable but I was too young to understand their fate at the time. Night time comes quickly in Ireland at that time of year and when it got dark it got really dark. There always seemed to be light in London but on Uncle's farm there were no street lights and Uncle's house was lit by a mixture of gas lamps and candles. In London the noise of traffic was never far away but on Uncle's farm the silence was deafening but interspersed by the farm and wild animals who made quite a din.

We stayed at Uncle's farm for a couple of months before moving to a cottage close by. The cottage was even more basic than Uncle's dwelling which was like Buckingham Palace in comparison to the dingy two up two down Mother and I lived in. The kitchen facilities were lacking to say the least. A grubby sink, which, however hard it was scrubbed, it was never clean and just a few pots and pans and little cutlery. The lounge, if you can call it that, housed our only source of heat. An open fire for heating for which we were mainly reliant on bits of wood salvaged from the nearby woods to keep us warm. We'd Mother's cousin Patrick to thank for the wood. Fortunately for us he was a lumberjack and every Friday he'd bring us the wood on his way home from work. Occasionally we'd the luxury of coal which Patrick also provided; who or where he got the coal from he never said and Mother never asked. The bedrooms were too horrible to talk about. No electricity, we had to rely on candles at night but to a young girl candle light was exciting if a little scary. Carefully walking up the stairs, holding a candle balanced on a saucer, I had to have my wits about me. It wasn't so bad in the summer as the days were long but in winter it was a hardship and the darkness seemed to make the cottage feel even more colder than it was. No running water either, if you remember? How could I forget? We relied on a well at the bottom of the garden from which Mother carried buckets of water to the house several times a day. I dread to think how contaminated the water was. To say it wouldn't pass today's standards is an understatement.

For all that, a move from a smog ridden London had been good for your health, hadn't it? In the main, yes, but sadly my life in Ireland wasn't a happy one for long. I didn't miss London though and it was fun spending time on Uncle Michael's farm. I was too young to appreciate the beautiful countryside but Uncle let me help feed the chickens which I loved. The way they used to come running towards me when they saw the bucket was always a thrill for me. They knew there was food for them and they'd cluck with delight. Remember your favourite hen? Oh yes, it was undoubtably Hilda. She'd an endearing little face, beautifully coloured feathers and a cheeky personality. I like to think she'd a fondness for me too beyond someone who fed her. Uncle didn't share my sentiment for the animals but he did say Hilda was a fine producer of eggs. Uncle also let me watch him milk the cows and attend to the feisty bulls in the field. I thought the farm animals had a wonderful happy life but this was before I understood the harsh reality of farming. I was thirteen when I made the connection between these animals and the dinner plate and from then on I became a vegetarian. This didn't go down too well with Mother but I stuck to my guns and she reluctantly had to accept it. Being a vegetarian back then was different from it is today as I never knew anyone else who shared my views and most people thought I was weird. Today I'm proud to say I'm a vegan.

My troubles began when Mother decided to send me to a convent school in Dublin when I was just eleven. Mother said I was very lucky and it was a privilege for me to be going to this school. The likes of me normally didn't get this opportunity but she'd pulled a few strings and got me in. I was supposed to have been grateful but frankly I wish she hadn't of bothered. Up until then I'd been schooled very close to where we were living and this was fine but the convent was a different kettle of fish. It was a grim and uninviting Gothic building and I learnt from the nuns it was built in the 16th Century and was once frequented by Monks practicing their Monastic ideals. For as long as I live I'll never forget this place. It was so depressing and even when I think about it today it sends a shiver up my spine. I could never put my finger on it but I sensed evil things had taken place and there were rumours human sacrifices had once taken place but the nuns were always quick to dismiss this. They said it was nonsense and as far as they were concerned, there was no such thing as ghosts and no such thing as an evil presence. I was ready to accept it was just my imagination but I soon learned there were other children in the school who held the same fears. No child, but no child, felt comfortable walking the corridors alone. Just school children easily influenced by unfounded gossip? Perhaps but, years later, after I'd left the convent I learned there were many local people who believed the place was haunted and I don't just mean the uneducated. Bank managers, solicitors and shop keepers believed evil existed there and many said they'd swear to it.

On a lighter note there were other rumours the school was haunted by a ghost with a sense of humour. I have to say little evidence was ever offered save the hysterical rantings from one or two incredulous pupils. They've claimed a ghost had been seen running up and down the corridors with just a slim towel to hide his modesty and shouting out: "Where's my clothes? Someone's stolen my clothes". Of course the nuns suggested anyone in their right mind should surely dismiss this claim as ridiculous nonsense but there were those who insisted it was true. Despite the nun's scepticism it was enough to make us all feel uneasy which offered another reason for us children not wanting to be wondering the corridors on our own especially at night. So was it all nonsense? Probably. Ah, there's doubt in your mind? Anyway, Mother Superior stated whoever started this rumour in the first place must have been under the influence of the demon drink. Either that or they were possessed by the Devil himself for surely no one could be so mischievous knowing what distress it would cause.

You're the sort of person who quickly makes their mind up about a place and when you first saw the building you decided you hated it. I did at that.

Even the grounds which surrounded the building offered no encouragement to enter the school and I'd have cheerfully gone home on my first day had Mother not insisted I stayed. If you remember rightly, evergreen untrimmed trees grew each side of the steep winding path which led to the main entrance. Yes, I remember, now I think about it. They were so tall to a child they appeared to touch the clouds; what I could see of the clouds that is. The trees provided an everlasting cover of darkness even on a bright sunny day. When the wind blew down the winding path it left me with an eerie feeling someone or something was watching. Again I wasn't the only one who felt this. One half of the pupils confessed at one time or another to being scared out their wits whilst the other half were either too stupid or too proud to admit it.

As I reached the entrance for the first time I tried to dismiss my first impressions from my mind and I told myself the building would look better from the inside. It didn't. The building was cold and drafty and the corridors were dark and creepy. There were large paintings hung on the walls and these served only to make the place look more gloomy. Most of these paintings were of the monks and the nuns who'd once occupied the building and, in my opinion, none of them had been painted in a sympathetic or attractive way. Dark and dingy colours dominated the paintings which made the building feel more creepy, grim and uninviting. The walls were dark and dirty and the floorboards creaked which echoed along the corridors. The classrooms were no better but I wish I could say the dormitories were more pleasant but frankly I can't. Some of the places in London we'd stayed in had been uninviting but in comparison to what the convent had to offer they were the height of luxury. I was used to sharing a bedroom with Mother but it was a shock to the system to share with a bunch of young strangers. The dormitory I slept in was particularly dirty and any child who walked bare foot risked infection. Cockroaches were in abundance whilst rats ran riot and many a child leapt on their beds terrified of these creatures. As well as being filthy the dormitory stank to High Heaven. For starters there was the unmistakable smell of damp and body odour wafted around the room. The worst smell of all came from Emily Gascoigne who broke wind at will and especially at night. Everyone called her Gassy which was appropriate given she could've farted for Ireland. I frequently asked God what I'd done to deserve having Gassy in the next bed to me. Some say boys have a reputation for performing their ablutions inappropriately but surely to God there could be nobody to compare with Gassy. The smells and gasses that came out of her behind must've contributed to global warming? Surely to goodness they must've done? You're being silly now. Oh, do stop giggling you foolish woman.

At least I can look back on this and laugh about it. Most of what I experienced at the convent was no laughing matter and I was so unhappy during my first few months. It wasn't so much the building and the accommodation, although these were bad enough, nor was the constant taunting by my fellow classmates. I could handle this. I was bullied and suffered racist remarks back in London but after a while the local kids got used to me and accepted me for what I was. I felt sure these Irish children would in time do the same. Mother had warned me I'd have to be thick skinned and, as young as I was, I'd developed a strong resolve. No, it was my teacher, Sister O'Brien, who made me so unhappy and frankly I was terrified of her. She'd taken an instant dislike to me and this evil excuse for a human being blamed me for any classroom disruption no matter how unjust. She was known to every pupil as the Evil Witch. I shudder even now when I think of this ugly despicable Cruella De Vil like creature dressed in black with her gruff voice, long crooked nose, fearsome brown eyes and teeth to rival a crocodile's. Come to think of it, sounds like Mrs Brown next door. Don't be cruel, poor Mrs Brown, she can't help it bless her. Be serious now.

From day one she had in for me. She did her best to belittle me in front of the class and she actively encouraged them to be unkind to me. She'd do this by calling me stupid and goading the class to agree with her. As far she was concerned it was also perfectly fine for other kids to say racist things to me and I'd no doubts she too was a racist. From a young age Mother's advice was not to let anyone grind me down and I never forgot this, so I'd ignored the verbal abuse which had been going on for months. One morning though the Evil Witch's verbal abuse turned physical which was a lot harder for me to endure. She'd left the classroom to speak to another nun about something and one of the girls in class, Rita O'Leary, was somewhat of a bully and she was in the mood to taunt me about my colour. It'd been obvious from the start the rest of the class did what she told them to do without questioning why they were doing it. They were probably afraid of her and no one, it seemed, had the gumption to stand up to her. So once she'd stood from her desk chanting terrible and unrepeatable words at me the rest of the class joined in. I wasn't even sure of what some of the words meant back then. You're still not! Amongst other things I was called a freak and some despicable names but as unpleasant as it was I reminded myself I was made of sterner stuff. I certainly wasn't going to let the likes of O'Leary win, even if she did have the support of a spineless class.

The Evil Witch then burst in, her face on fire with rage. She put the fear of God into the rest of the class, including O'Leary, who was the first to sit down and cowardly bury her head in her school work. The Evil Witch's complexion was so red I feared being burned if I got too close to her face. Peter and Sally should be in no doubt the title of Evil Witch was warranted and in no way overstated. She was, as far as I was concerned, evil. Although they'd never say, I suspect her fellow nuns didn't like her either and they may well have drawn on the Bible for a fitting name or description for her.

45

Having returned to the classroom the Evil Witch blamed me for all the noisy chanting. I'd provoked the class according to her and when I protested my innocence she dragged me by my hair across her desk. I'd quite long hair then so it was easy for her to grab hold. I heard the whooshing sound of her cane and I prepared myself to be hit across the backside. Whether or not this was her intention, I don't know, or if she changed her mind at the last second but the next thing I heard was a cracking noise as I was hit on the knuckles of my right hand. Tears ran down my face but I damn well wasn't going to let her see me cry so I buried my face into the desk. It took all my will power not to cry out but Hell was it painful. She then grabbed my hair again and turned my head so she could see my face. I think she was hoping to see me in floods of tears but she had to settle for watery eyes as the rest of the tears had quickly dried from my face. This clearly annoyed her. So she whacked me again and this time she was witness to the tears running down my face but again I denied her the satisfaction of crying out aloud. The tears though were enough for her to reprimand me for crying.

"Stop that crying immediately girl or I'll give you something to cry about. You're a wicked, wicked girl," she shouted as she waved her cane menacingly in my direction. "Ever since you've been here you've been a disruptive influence on this class. This kind of behaviour might be tolerated in London but you'll learn obedience here or suffer the consequences. God is watching you, Benjamin and

He'll ultimately judge you. God punishes evil and if you don't mend your ways you'll pay for your sins for eternity in Hell. Is that what you want?" she barked.

Her rage would've been damming enough for any adult to endure let alone a young frightened girl such as you. Even when I managed to control my sobbing she wasn't finished with me just yet. I was reprimanded for not addressing her as Sister O'Brien and she insisted I apologise. A moment's hesitation lead to another hard whack across the knuckles.

"What's the matter with you girl? Didn't they teach you English back in England?"

"Yes, Sister O'Brien."

"Well then, don't keep me waiting. I don't like being kept waiting."

"I'm sorry, Sister O'Brien."

This wasn't enough for her, she wanted blood. I was forced to say sorry for the trouble I'd caused and I was ordered to kneel down and pray for God's forgiveness.

"Lord forgive me..."

"In silence girl. God will hear your prayers."

I remained on my knees, my hands clasped together, eyes closed, my body shaking with fear. Suddenly she grabbed me by my hair and she pulled me to my feet before letting go.

"That is enough, Benjamin. God has better things to do than to listen to a miserable wretch like you all day. Now you must apologies to the class.

"I'm sorry for all the trouble I've caused," I said addressing the class.

Once more she grabbed me by the hair and pulled me across the floor to my desk. She didn't let go of your hair until she'd forced you into your chair, did she? No, she didn't. Witch!

"Now then, Benjamin. You're arithmetic leaves a lot to be desired. You're the worse pupil I've ever had to teach. We'll start with the seven times table today."

She then instructed the rest of the class to remain silent and no one was to help me. I nearly laughed at that. There wasn't one pupil who had any sympathy for me and in any case none of the class was foolish enough to disobey her instruction. They feared her as much as you did. Perhaps even more so. They knew even the slightest sound from any of them would mean severe punishment. I began the task but rather slowly.

"One times seven is seven, two sevens are fourteen..."

"Faster, Benjamin."

I then got another whack on the knuckles for being so slow so I desperately tried to speed up the pace.

"Three sevens are twenty one, four sevens are twenty eight, five sevens are thirty five, six sevens are forty one..."

"Forty two," shouted O'Brien, "six sevens are forty two. Stupid girl."

I continued: " Six sevens are forty two."

I then hesitated monetarily but came up with the next answer just in time.

"Seven sevens are forty nine, eight sevens are fifty?"

Further hesitation and she was ready to pounce and my next answer was a hurried and a wrong one.

"Eight sevens are fifty five.."

No doubt she'd been waiting and hoping I'd get it wrong and once more I was grabbed by the hair and pulled, this time, across my desk. I looked up to see her raising her cane in readiness to beat my hand again. I felt sure she'd break a bone or something and this time the pain would be unbearable. Fortunately Mother Superior had just arrived in the classroom.

"Sister O'Brien," Mother Superior called out, "I need you to rescue Sister Mary from the Nature Studies class."

On hearing Mother Superior's voice she released me from her grip and rested the cane by her side. I took the opportunity to stand by my desk as did the rest of the class the moment Mother Superior had entered the classroom.

The Evil Witch pleaded: "But Mother Superior, I..."

Mother Superior continued with a diplomatic tone: "Sister Mary tries very hard and her heart's in the right place but she simply doesn't have your teaching skills or experience."

"Thank you Mother Superior. I was just..."

"Yes thank you, Sister O'Brien. I think in future Benjamin would find it easier if she was sitting in

49

her chair rather than slouched over her desk. Don't you think?"

"But I was.."

"That will be all, Sister O'Brien."

"Of course."

Embarrassed and outranked she made a hasty retreat. Mother Superior placed a comforting hand on my shoulder.

"Are you all right, Marie?"

"Yes thank you, Mother Superior."

Mother Superior addressed the rest of the class: "As for the rest of you, I am appalled by your behaviour. I could hear your disgraceful chanting on the other side of the school. No doubt they could hear it in the village! Even Mr Turnball, who runs the post office and who is, poor man, as deaf as a post would probably have heard it." She raised her voice to underline her point. "Even with his hearing aid switched off." I was laughing inside when she said that. Well don't start laughing now. You usually end up in fits of laughter when you relay this moment to anyone. Concentrate on what she said next. Oh, I remember this vividly.

She lowered her voice: "Now I don't want a repeat of this behaviour. Is that understood?"

"Yes, Mother Superior," the class replied.

They knew better than to disobey her and the whole school respected her authority. Yet she was nothing like the Evil Witch, the complete opposite in fact. She was a petite, gentle woman with a face of an angel despite having lived more years than she cared to admit to. She'd been Mother Superior at the school for umpteen years and had seen many pupils come and go. She'd devoted her life to the school and to God. The Evil Witch was no doubt itching to take her place but she wasn't going to retire just yet. She was no soft touch either, if you remember, she expected and commanded discipline from all of the pupils and sisters alike but she was always very fair to everyone. She certainly was but she wasn't going to tolerate bullying of any kind and she made it clear to the class their cruel treatment of me was to stop.

"Now I want you all to say you are sorry to Marie."

There was a moments silence. Mother Superior raised her voice with her authoritative air.

"I'm waiting."

"Sorry, Marie," the class murmured.

"Speak up, you were all in full voice earlier," she demanded.

"Sorry Marie," the class had to keep repeating until the volume of their apology met with Mother Superior's approval.

As punishment she charged the class to read and digest Matthew Chapter 26 – The Betrayal and Trial. Each and every one was to tell her from which verses she was quoting. They were in particular to think about this whilst she attended to me.

"Verily I say unto you, that one of you shall betray me. And they were exceedingly sorrowful

and began every one of them to say unto him. Lord, is it I?"

She took me aside. She was aware my arithmetic wasn't as good as it should be but she also recognised I needed encouragement and support. To master my tables would be a good start and to this end I was transferred to Sister Flanagan's class. I was thrilled, it felt like I'd won the Jackpot as I liked Sister Flanagan, she was very sweet. A bubbly character, Sister Flanagan was kind to everyone, I was no exception. She was very understanding and she did all she could to help me make up for the lack of education I'd in London.

I was also very glad not to be in the same class as O'Leary anymore and I made it my mission to keep out her way as much as possible. The next day though she sort me out and called out to me.

"Benjamin!" she shouted and ran over to me and greeted me like a long lost friend.

Despite her more friendly attitude towards me she couldn't bring herself to call me Marie. Not that I was bothered. She wasn't my friend and I didn't want her to be.

"Respect, Benjamin, respect. I mean fair play to you. The Evil Witch was hoping you would bawl like a baby when she canned you but you didn't. She didn't like that. You were brilliant. She shouldn't have beat you like that, not on the knuckles. I mean, ouch! That must have hurt? I've never seen her hit anyone on the knuckles before, only the backside. She must have it in for you, Benjamin. I hate her.

Everyone hates her. If she hits you again just let me know and I'll arrange for her to get a good kicking."

I was horrified at such a suggestion even though I knew she was all talk. As much as I hated the Evil Witch I'd be no party to violence.

"She's never dared to hit me though." O'Leary continued. "She knows if she did my Dad would come and sort her out. He'd beat her to a pulp, he would. You're all right, Benjamin. You're all right. My sister is a senior pupil here so if any kid here bothers you, you just let me know. My sister will sort them out."

With this she walked away and I breathed a sigh of relief. It was good to know she wasn't going to taunt me anymore but if anybody else did I'd no intention of telling her. By the sound of things I'd no desire to become equated with her older sister and I could only guess her Dad was nothing but a thug. Throughout the rest of my days at the convent I maybe crossed her path a handful of times but I kept my distance. The last I heard she was doing time for theft.

Officially, my transfer to Sister Flanagan's class was seen as demotion. The intention was Sister Flanagan got all the no hopers who weren't expected to make anything of themselves. As we went up a year we were passed onto other Nun's, who had little teaching experience, to practice on us. For a bunch of no hopers it didn't matter if they made a mess of things but as it happens they turned out to be good teachers. The Evil Witch, on the other hand, had those who supposedly showed promise.

God only knows how anyone could have thought O'Leary showed promise? There were rumours her Dad had made threats if his daughter wasn't put in the top class. If he did, he didn't do his daughter any favours. The Evil Witch was tasked with giving her pupils a good grounding before they moved on to be taught by nuns with considerable teaching experience. From things I heard, these other nuns were as ruthless as the Evil Witch and as far as I'm aware nobody in that class went on to be particularly successful in anything. Whereas Betty Crean, taught by Sister Flanagan and others, went on to be very successful in the hairdressing business and progressed to owning a chain of salons. What about you? You didn't do too bad, did you? Well, in the end no, but I'd a bumpy ride along the way.

I'd spent six months in the Evil Witch's class before I was transferred to Sister Flanagan but it had seemed like an eternity. From then on my education improved considerably. The reason for this is obvious, isn't it? Is it? The class were a good bunch, weren't they? Yes, whether or not Mother Superior had any influence on how they treated me I don't know but I felt part of the class straight away. It helped I was in good health by then, the fresh air of Ireland had certainly made a big difference to me. I was invited to take part in their games after school and during the meal breaks. They took an interest in me and they wanted to know what London was like. I told them I was only eight when I left so I didn't remember much about it. They persisted though so I did my best to answer their questions. "Was London a big city? Was it busy with people?" I answered yes to both questions. I told them what I remembered about the Underground. The noise of the tube train and how it would echo in the tunnels before suddenly emerging and coming to a stop in the station. Waiting on the platform, passengers clambered aboard before the electric doors closed behind them. Off they'd go, everybody squeezed together like a tin of sardines and minutes later they'd be another train and more people would squeeze on board. Mother used to take me to the market stalls which were bustling with shoppers and traders doing their best to tempt them to part with their money. There was a number of fruit and veg stalls but I remember one man in particular as he'd most of his front teeth missing. At first I thought he was a vampire but Mother put me right on that score. He used to shout out with regularity things like: "Ten pound for a pound or three dozen a pound" in his strong Cockney accent. I was confused by what he was saying. How could he sell more than one pound for just one? He was losing money? Mother explained things to me. I'd memories of pubs packed to the rafters and young kids waiting outside whilst their dad was inside having a few pints with his mates. If they were lucky, their dad brought them out a glass of lemonade. We'd trolley buses and I remember being fascinated by the metal bar which hooked up to the electric cables as we rode along. During the war the trolley buses were the target of Hitler's bombers and a lot were destroyed. Not long after moving to

Ireland they were replaced with the now iconic Route Master bus and when I returned to London as an adult this public transport system was an established part of London life. I described Big Ben the best I could to the class and yes its dong was loud. Oxford Street? All I could say was Mother used to enjoy window shopping; she'd little money so she rarely bought anything. At least that's what Mother told me so that's what I told them. On Sundays Mother used to take me for a walk by the Thames but according to Mother, although I was really too old for one, I spent most of the time in a push chair. For some reason Craven Cottage the home of Fulham Football Club stood out in my memory although this sport has never interested me. To this day it still sits proudly on the riverbank and Peter might be interested to learn it's the oldest football club in London. That's if he doesn't know already as his father was a Fulham fan. As a young man, Peter played football in Australia as an amateur but to a good standard. It wasn't the most popular sport in Australia especially back then but I suppose his father had encouraged him. Peter intends to go to a couple games whilst he's over here but I can't say I share his enthusiasm. The thought of being crammed into the stadium full of thousands of people isn't my idea of a good time but that's fine, whilst he's "soaking up the atmosphere" at Craven Cottage Sally and I can have some quality time together. So anyway I told the kids in my class the odd things I remembered but really my memory of London wasn't up to much. You still don't know much about London, do you? Well, a bit, a lot more than I did then. The good thing was I was treated like one of them and they were just the opposite to the nasty lot in the Evil Witch's class. Being more at ease in my new class I felt able to concentrate more readily and my times tables didn't seem to be such a daunting task. I also welcomed the change of dormitory which meant there was no more of Gassy's unpleasant smells for me. I still hated the building but schooling became more tolerable. I also started to do better in other subjects and I came to enjoy some lessons especially History which I began to excel at.

As I was accepted by my new class mates I even made a few friends. There was one girl in particular I got on very well with. Her name was Mary Maguire and she'd a very strong Irish accent. Her very pale complexion and blonde straight hair was in contrast to my skin and dark curly barnet. We were nicknamed the Black and White Minstrels but we didn't mind. We soon discovered we'd a lot in common despite a different up bringing. Mary had a middle class lifestyle whereas my life experiences were just above, if not on, the poverty line. She'd always lived in quite posh houses in Irish rural areas in contrast to my city life in London before I'd moved to Ireland. Like me though she didn't have brothers or sisters and like me she'd had an imaginary friend when she was younger. We were on the same wave length when it came to a sense of humour and often the rest of the glass were left wondering what we were laughing about. We seemed to be good at the same subjects and we'd help each other with homework.

We did however differ on some things. Although Mary brought out the Tom Boy in me, unlike her, I never wished I'd been born a boy. I didn't share her enthusiasm for wood and metal work and she loved it when her father let her help him in his workshop. She never showed much interest when her mother tried to teach her to cook and to sew but I was always keen to improve on my basic cooking and sowing skills.

I got to know her parents quite well and they were always friendly towards me when they came to visit her. They were, or they seemed to me, very posh and Mary told me they ran their own business dealing in antiques. Mary and I were the closest of friends for a couple of years but then her parents decided to set up in business in Liverpool and Mary moved to Merseyside with them. She said she'd write but a letter never arrived and I've often wondered why? Once in Liverpool did she quickly forget me? Did she meet another friend to take my place? Or did she write but did the letter get lost in the post? Was it as simple as that? Was the letter simply mislaid? So when I didn't write back did she think I wasn't interested in keeping contact? I shall never know. It was a great shame. I'm sure we'd been the best of friends as adults but it wasn't to be. I often wonder if she's still around and, if so, where is she now? I do hope she'd a happy life.

Life in Sister Flanagan's class was so much better but there were still times when my path crossed with the Evil Witch. On these occasions she normally snarled at me or ventured to clip my ear but she stopped short of giving me a beating. It may be Mother Superior had instructed her not to beat me again? Except there was one occasion when Mother Superior was away from the convent and unfortunately for me my path crossed with the Evil Witch. Sister Flanagan had sent me out of the class on an errand and as I walked down the corridor the Evil Witch was talking to one of the nuns. My path was blocked in as much as there wasn't room for me to walk round either of them. The only way through was to walk between them and the Evil Witch took exception to this. She grabbed hold of my hair with one hand and caned me with the other. The other nun I think was too scared of the Evil Witch to intervene and I was struck a second time across my shoulder. She avoided the knuckles this time but she bruised my shoulder badly and I could hardly move it for several days afterwards. I was saved from a further beating when, fortunately for me, Sister Flanagan had heard the commotion and she came out of her classroom. I have to say Sister Flanagan was magnificent. She grabbed hold of the Evil Witch's cane and threw it down the corridor. She faced up to the Evil Witch, daring her to make another move. The Evil Witch backed off and in defeat she retrieved her cane and carried on down the corridor. The other nun stood there smiling, no doubt impressed with Sister Flanagan's bravado. That was the last time the Evil Witch ever hit me although she continued to snarl whenever she saw me. I have to admit they'd been times when I'd murderous thoughts towards the Evil Witch and I swear to God, had the opportunity arisen, I'd surely have committed murder and only my age would've saved me from the hangman's noose.

Chapter 3

Thinking back now Mother Superior was the best friend I ever had. She offered me encouragement and showed an interest in me and if I ever had a problem or was feeling down her door was always open. Just talking to her made me feel better about myself. After I'd left the convent aged fifteen we kept in touch mostly by letter but occasionally we'd meet up in Dublin if her time permitted. She was always willing to give me advice but she never judged me. When my relationship with Mother began to turn sour she offered me support but she never took sides and after I'd returned to England we continued to correspond with one another. I'd often write and ask her to pass on my regards to Sister Flanagan and Mother Superior was always full of praise for the fine work she did. She was also full of praise for some of the other nuns who had joined the convent but the Evil Witch was never mentioned. Although Mother Superior preached forgiveness I think she accepted my hatred for the Evil Witch and there was nothing that could change this. There were some dark periods in my life and for a time I was too ashamed of my failings to write to her. When I eventually renewed our correspondence and confessed some of my woes she immediately wrote back offering me support and encouragement. She was saddened I hadn't confided in her sooner and I realise now I should've sought her advice sooner.

My pride hadn't done me any favours but it took a long time for me to admit it. It'd be some thirty years before I set foot on Irish soil again but this time only for a visit. Mother Superior by this time was living out her days in a nursing home but our reunion was an emotional and a joyous one. She lived a few more years after my visit and she'd turned 98 before her passing. In my eyes she richly deserved her longevity; I think of her often and I've never failed to pay tribute to her when the opportunity has presented itself. I've gladly told others the World would be a much better place if more people were like Mother Superior. She had her critics and some say she should've done something about the Evil Witch and had her moved on elsewhere. That wasn't her way. Had she moved the Evil Witch on the problem would merely have been passed on to someone else. She saw the best in everyone and I'm aware she regarded the Evil Witch as a good teacher. I respected this but to me the Evil Witch was quite simply evil and if there's any justice, she'll be burning in hell for eternity. "I ifreann le haghaidh eternity" Mother was fond of saying.

Sister Flanagan was a good person and even though she was a nun she was fun to be with. She enjoyed a good joke and tolerated to some extent any practical jokes the children played. They were mindful of not crossing the line but if they did, Sister Flanagan put a stop to it without fuss. She was a tiny woman, only standing at four feet eleven inches tall, she'd very small feet and required only child sized footwear.

I've only good memories of Sister Flanagan and I regretted loosing contact with her after leaving the convent. Cookery lessons were always a joy, weren't they? Oh yes, such fun, I used to particularly like rolling out the pastry. Except that pastry was never your strong point and it was always lumpy when you were let loose with the rolling pin. Peter and Sally should know your pastry comes with a public health warning. No, I've got the hang of it now. Nonsense! Whenever you've attempted pastry it's been as thick as cement and you could use it to make a path or something. That's a gross exaggeration. No, it isn't. Remember the day when you was rolling out some pastry which was especially tough and, as hard you rolled it, you was making little progress. Then with an almighty push, it flew off the pastry board and landed on the floor. At this moment Sister Flanagan stepped into its path which caused her to slip and land on her backside, her habit in disarray. Now look, you always end up in a fit of giggles when you tell this story so stop it. Just say everyone gasped as Sister Flanagan sat on floor, not saying a word. Fortunately Sister Flanagan wasn't hurt and in her typical no fuss style she simply adjusted her clothing and picked up the pastry to examine it.

"One of yours Marie, I presume. Makes a change from a banana skin?"

Sister Flanagan burst into laughter and the rest of us laughed with her. Lucky for you Sister

Flanagan saw the funny side but she could've been badly injured so you can wipe that grin off your face. Got to admit though, the incident wouldn't have been out of place in a slapstick film.

For some weekends and during holidays I got to go home to Mother but I was at the mercy of Uncle Michael's time and whether or not he could come and pick me up in his tractor. Mother rarely came to visit me at the convent but she always seemed pleased to see me whenever I did get home. It was during this period when Mother started taking some interest in politics and she'd opinion about everything and anything. If Uncle Michael was present he'd often disagree with her and then an argument often erupted between the two of them. They were alike in so many ways but in others they were completely different. I was too young to fully understand the political situation but I grasped some of the points Mother made. She was one for a cause was Mother especially if a relative or a friend was involved. For example she was very supportive of the people who descended on Dublin to protest at the employment situation in 1953. Her cousin Eamonn was amongst them and Mother sang his praises even though, as Uncle Michael pointed out, she normally couldn't stand him. Then there was Daoiri, a friend of the family's, who in that year marched down O'Connell Street along with 10,000 Civil Servants to demand a just wage. Mother said it was an outrage the little wages they got but Uncle Michael retorted they should be thankful they'd a job. Dillan, yet another cousin, along with 500 unemployed men marched on Kildare Street demanding employment not dole. There was also Mother's friend Eileen who was amongst the 1000 people who stayed a 15 minute sit-down protest on O'Connell Street. Mother voiced her full support for them all but Uncle Michael said they should get off their backsides and go find work and not expect someone to just hand them a job. The row got heated but Mother never swore at him not even in Irish. For one, Uncle Michael could speak Irish and for two, Mother knew he wouldn't tolerate it.

I left them to it when they started arguing and if I was at Uncle's farm I'd take the opportunity to go and say a hello to my animal friends. Mable The Cow and Henry The Horse were usually the first to come trotting to greet me. Mabel loved it when I stroked her face and Henry enjoyed me stroking his back. A right character he was and if I wasn't looking he'd gently push me over with his head. I've heard it said animals can't laugh but I'd swear Henry and Mabel were laughing at me. Not to be outdone, the hens, led by Doris came clucking with delight when they saw me. Hilda, by this time had departed this World and Uncle told me she died of natural causes. I accepted this explanation at the time but I've since come to the conclusion he'd sent her for slaughter once she stopped producing the eggs he wanted. Bertie The Cockerel did his merry dance and Donald The Pig popped his head out of his sty and grunted a greeting when I called his name. The wild ducks used to scramble ashore anticipating they'd be a little treat in store for them. The sheep used to keep their distance, that is, except for David. He'd no such reservations and I believe he thought he was a sheep dog judging by the way he used to chase the other sheep. These moments meant a lot to me but they were few and far between during the years I was at the convent.

Chapter 4

Mainly due to the convent school's strict rules I'd lived a very sheltered life and I'd no contact with boys to speak of. Unless of course you count Spotty McClery the son of the convent's volunteer part time gardener. Oh yes, nearly forgotten about him. He used to help his dad with the gardening whenever he wasn't at school which seemed to be often. At the time Spotty was an annoying fourteen year old who used to pester us girls for a kiss, or as he so romantically put it, "a quick snog". He never, as far as I know, had any success with this quest; not even a peck on the cheek as nobody was that desperate. He was regarded as a bit of a joke but, I for one pitied him, as all the girls found him repulsive. I always felt embarrassed for him when his advances, in most cases, were harshly rejected especially when Cara McCleland told him she'd rather kiss a pig's bottom. She could be so cruel could Cara. He only ever asked me once so he probably didn't find me attractive, which was just as well, as I blushed and came over all hot and bothered. It wasn't until later in life when I went through the menopause did I have such an uncomfortable feeling again. So I was content he accepted my rejection immediately and he didn't seem to be bothered about it. There were a few girls he fancied and one of them was my friend Mary because he asked her several times. We'd a good giggle about it afterwards but to be fair to Mary she always let him down gently. There was never any nastiness from Mary and she was a good sort. It seemed surprising to me Mother Superior didn't put a stop to his antics for she surely must've known what he was up to. Maybe she turned a blind eye because he was basically harmless and his father was providing his garden services for free? Could be? By all accounts his father made his money gardening for the rich land owners in the area. There was, however, generally a tradeoff for anyone outside the Order who volunteered their labour. Farmer McBride provided free manure and compost for the vegetable plot whilst his daughter Jo, who attended the convent, seemed to get special privileges although this was always denied. Whether she did or not I don't know but not even the Evil Witch dared to cane her. Then there was Mrs Bell who put a lot of her own time and energy into fund raising for the convent and she got her rewards in other ways. I for one was okay with this as Mother Superior had to balance the books somehow so that was just the way things were. As they say: there's no such thing as a free lunch. In any event, all the pupils were expected to help with fund raising in one shape of form or the other. I was chosen to help Sister Flanagan to bake some cakes to sell at the Village Fete as unlike my pastry skills, or lack of, I was and still am good at baking cakes. Today my cakes are egg and dairy free but back then we used lots of eggs and cream and lots of unhealthy white sugar. The convent kept chickens so there was always a good supply of eggs and there were several local farmers who kindly donated some milk taken from their herds. There was half a dozen of us in all selected to bake cakes but Mary wasn't one of them. I can't remember what task she was given.

Other than Spotty, boys were only allowed in the convent if they were accompanied by a parent and provided the purpose of the visit was to see their daughter residing at the school. Even then the parent was under strict instructions not to let their son out of their sight. If the parents could avoid bringing their sons they were encouraged to do so.

My shyness and self-consciousness have always been evident; these two traits have never left me. That's very true. Do you remember the day you started work after you'd left the convent? How could I ever forget? The convent had arranged for me to start as a servant girl in this big posh house called the Glebe which was owned by one of the richest men in Ireland at the time. You should acknowledge you'd Mother Superior to thank for this job as she'd gone to a lot of trouble to get you this position. Yes, I've never forgotten what she did for me but at the time I wasn't as appreciative and I was dreading my first day. I remember looking at my reflection in a mirror that morning and feeling embarrassed by my looks and what my work colleagues would think of me. My basic grey uniform was helping none and was I going to be laughed at? Mother tried to convince me I looked smart but no matter what she said I wasn't convinced. I was told they'd be men working there too and I'd very little experience in engaging with the male sex. I felt terrified. I was that bad. I was out of my comfort zone and the thought of speaking to a boy made me physically sick that morning. Fortunately I managed to stick my head in the toilet just before the avalanche had channelled its way out of my mouth. Oh really, Marie. There's no need to go into graphic detail; it's suffice to say you were sick and leave it at that. Oh, all right, but this wasn't a good start. I'd reached aged fifteen and I'd barely spoken to a boy let alone had a boyfriend. Mother was aware I'd been sick and I confessed to her my anxiety regarding the opposite sex. Mother sat me down.

"Now is a good time to explain the birds and the bees to you, Marie" she offered.

"A bit late for that, Mother," I replied, "thanks all the same."

"Oh!' she said, looking relieved. "You just let me know if any boy behaves in proper towards you".

I took Mother's comment as much as an instruction to me to keep my chastity intact as she was warning me about boys. I assured her I intended to keep my distance from any boy hoping to take liberties.

For all that, I was glad my school days were behind me. As much as I liked and respected Mother Superior and Sister Flanagan I didn't care for the level of Catholicism they preached. I wasn't sure about God then and if I'm honest I'm still not.

70

So despite my nervousness and reservations I was looking forward to starting my working life. I was a bit disappointed I'd have to live at the Glebe rather than living with Mother but I'd have my own room which was far better than the convent's dormitories. I'd also have more freedom to spend time at home when I'd a day off so this didn't sound quite so bad. Mother accompanied me for my first day and she was given permission to help me unpack. I wanted to take Dolly with me but Mother persuaded me to leave her at the cottage. She convinced me the staff would tease me for having a doll in my room and anyway Dolly would be waiting for me when I did go home. I also came to realise it was in my best interests to get used to not always having Dolly with me.

It was good Mother was with you, wasn't it? She certainly helped and it was a bit of a treat spending some time with her. Mother said it'd paid off for me attending the convent because it led to a job. She made it clear though she expected a slice of my earnings to help pay the bills now I was earning. Since returning to Ireland Mother had scraped a living working on Uncle's farm as well as neighbouring farms. She did everything from potato or fruit picking, gathering in the hay or mucking out the cow sheds. If there wasn't work for her on the farms, she'd head into Dublin and tout for a job and she'd do anything to earn a crust even it was for only a few hours. In her time she'd had a bash at waitressing, shop assistant, cleaner, usherette in a cinema, delivered milk, postwoman, you name it,

71

she'd probably done it. I had to hand it to Mother, she was forever resourceful.

Chapter 5

The Glebe was a very grand building full of light and character; a far cry from the depressing convent I'd come from. Much to my delight the building was full of history and I made it my mission to find out as much as I could about the place. You were, dear Marie, obsessed. For a long time you've been obsessed with History. I was never obsessed, just very interested. Have it your way but I suppose you'll describe the Glebe in detail to Peter and Sally? As much as I can remember, I will. Let's hope you don't bore them to death! I shall soon shut up if they're not interested. Good, let's hope so.

On my first day I entered the building through the servants quarters but when I was shown around I observed the high ceiling hallway which greeted those entering the building. The skillfully crafted ceiling was breathtaking; so much intricate design work of various shapes and sizes. I'd look at them and see different things on different days. One day I'd see people's faces and on other it might be an animal such as a cat or a dog. The wooden flooring was spectacularly polished and the smell of the polish was prominent but pleasant. Indeed, hand crafted woodwork and polished floors were evident in every room. Formality was evident everywhere. From the beautifully upholstered sofas complimented with the highest quality curtains, which must have cost a fortune, to the beautifully crafted oak dining table and chairs. The Glebe had it all. It housed valuable, sort after paintings by famous artists which were on display in the living quarters. It appeared to me the paintings were greeting me and the sun seemed to shine more brightly through the windows of every room. Amongst their collection there were paintings by Irish artists such as Thomas Hickey and Nathaniel Hill. I wanted to know all about these artists and I was always pestering some of the more experienced staff for information. They didn't seem to mind and they told me what they knew. Over the years I've developed a growing interest in art and I often indulge myself in an art gallery in London. The Glebe had spacious bedrooms and the owner and his family enjoyed all the mod cons available at the time. For us staff who lived in, far more modest accommodation was provided. As much as I was in awe of the building, what I liked best about the Glebe was the gardens which were a privilege to enjoy. They were bright, colourful and immaculate; the fruit and vegetable plots always plentiful. My favourite spot was down by the pond at the far end of the garden. There I could sit by myself on a log close to the water's edge, save the company of the wildlife in and around the pond. There were frogs galore bathing in the pond with their eyes popping out of the water hoping, no doubt, to feast on some slugs for their lunch. They'd croak a hello whilst the ducks greeted me with a quack in the hope I'd some food to give them. An array of birds always put in an appearance and I loved to sit there quietly

74

watching them go about their business. It was truly blissful.

My job at the Glebe unfortunately wasn't blissful. I worked all hours under the sun for a mere pittance as a general dogsbody including scrubbing the kitchen floor. Whatever you did though it was never good enough for O'Neil, the resident cook. No, it was clear she'd taken an instant dislike to me and the feeling was mutual. No matter how hard I scrubbed the kitchen floor it was never clean enough. When I washed the dishes she'd claim they were still dirty and make me wash them again. If I peeled the potatoes I didn't do them right either. She was such a horrible woman, had it been allowed she would've beaten me like the Evil Witch did. She was quite a plump woman and the pinny she wore in the kitchen did nothing to flatter her. Her cook's hat sat precariously on her head; her hair had undergone an extreme perm at the hairdressers. She couldn't tolerate a hair out of place. I'd say she'd an unkind sort of face; she always looked as if she was ready to do battle. Her shoes were always spotless and polished and it struck me she must have spent hours cleaning them. Whilst I'd initially compared her to the Evil Witch as I got to know her I realised they were different people. O'Neil could be quite nasty sometimes but underneath it all, I could detect some humility. I'm sure it was sadness which made her like she was; she was probably a very nice person once. I never grew to like her but I didn't hate her as much as the Evil Witch but her sharp tongue made things very unpleasant for me.

"Put some elbow grease into it girl, or you'll be here all day." O'Neil would say, "you wouldn't have lasted five minutes in this house a year ago."

She ranted on about the past when Mr Doherty was in charge and how things were so much better then. Nobody dared to step out line, Mr Doherty saw to it they didn't. The staff lacked discipline now that Jennings was in charge; he was far too soft with them. The footman and a chamber maid were sinners and should be sacked immediately.

"All that carrying on," she said, "'tis a disgrace if you ask me. All that kissing and canoodling, 'tisn't right. Not that a young girl like you should know anything about that," she said to me. "If you see them together just close your eyes and come and tell me, you understand?"

"Can I open my eyes when I come and see you?" I asked with a hint of sarcasm.

"What! Oh I see, trying to be funny are we?" she barked. "Don't try and be funny with me girl. I won't have it. Do you understand?"

"Yes, Mrs O'Neil." I replied. I wasn't going to push my luck.

You surprised yourself, didn't you? It wasn't like you to be sarcastic towards your elders back then. Your rebellious streak wouldn't emerge for a few years yet.

"Just don't look at them. Come straight to me" clarifying her instructions.

I nodded and stated Mr Jennings said they were getting engaged soon and wedding bells would follow shortly after.

"Well, I can well imagine why they might want to get married in a hurry. She's a disgrace to her mother the way she flaunts herself. Don't you go disgracing your mother, do you hear, Benjamin?"

"I'd never do that," I quickly replied.

"Good, just see you don't" she said gathering together some cooking utensils.

I was somewhat offended by her suggestion I might disgrace my mother. At that age I wouldn't have dreamed of doing anything Mother might of disapproved of, I was the obedient daughter back then.

Having scrubbed the kitchen floor more than once, washed the dishes several times and spent a long time peeling the potatoes, she reluctantly conceded my efforts were the best she was going to get from me. My request to help with the pudding was immediately dismissed. General chores were all I was fit for and she told me, in no uncertain terms, I'd be packing my bags if it was up to her. On this particular day Mr Jennings had entered the kitchen and had caught the tail end of O'Neil's rant.

"Packing your bags, Mrs O'Neil," he said flippantly, "Not leaving us are you?"

"No Mr Jennings, I was just saying to Benjamin."

"Marie's not leaving us. You're not leaving us are you, Marie? Didn't think so," Mr Jennings said without waiting for my answer. He turned to O'Neil. "It's my responsibility to decide who stays and who goes. Is that understood?" he said forcibly.

O'Neil nodded in submission. As much as she resented it, Mr Jennings was in charge and that was that. If the truth be known she probably resented him because he was an Englishman and because he was well educated. This probably made her feel inferior to him. He'd been to a grammar school and, if it hadn't been for the war and if his parents could've afforded it, he would've gone to University. You'll need to own up to Peter and Sally and confess you used to listen in on people's conversations and you heard the Master and Mr Jennings talking. I was doing no harm. It was, Marie, a private conversation and Mr Jennings was explaining his regrets for not going to University. The conversation wasn't meant for your ears and you'd no business being where you were, standing outside the Master's room. What you were doing there I can't remember but you'd have had some explaining to do if you'd been caught. Well, I wasn't caught so that's that. Hmm, at least you didn't go blabbing to anyone else about what you'd heard. Oh no, I wouldn't have done that. Not to Mr Jennings.

O'Neil reasoned the Butler's position should be filled by an Irishman as it had always been before Mr Jennings arrival. She believed Irish jobs were for Irish people and it was her opinion English people should stay where they belonged in England. Words she repeated over and over again like a stuck gramophone record. This was probably why she didn't like me, I was just another from England occupying an Irish job. Although my mother was Irish this held no sway with her and she dismissed my claim to being half Irish. I suggested she was guilty of racism but I used the Irish word ciníochas because I knew she couldn't speak Irish and knowing I must have annoyed her immensely. Well, I hoped so. I don't know if she ever looked up ciníochas in an Irish dictionary but I'd often say other Irish words just to witness the vacant look on her face.

I'd the impression Mr Jennings for his part treated O'Neil with contempt and it was obvious there was no love lost between them. Naturally I was on his side and, in my eyes, he could do no wrong. He was a man who carried his authority so well and although, in some respects, the years hadn't been kind to him I could tell he'd been a bit of a catch in his younger and fitter days. His face told a story and his wrinkles were like chapters in a book. They told a story of a man who had suffered pain and sadness in his life and undoubtedly the war years had affected him. He was though ever reluctant to speak of his experiences and he'd clam up before the conversation got too deep. He'd never allow anyone to get too close to him; what he endured during the war was his business.

I did, however, discover a few facts about his military life. He'd served in the army as a sergeant during the war and was wounded in battle following the D-Day landings. This was not the first time he'd been wounded in battle but this was the worst injury. He'd had a narrow escape when he was boarding a fishing boat at Dunkirk. On this occasions he'd escaped serious injury when a bullet brushed his shoulder although the wound never fully healed. This time though things were much more serious. Shrapnel had severely damaged his left leg and it was touch and go as to whether his limb would be amputated. Thankfully he kept his leg but he spent six months in hospital before being discharged from the army on medical grounds. He'd have to walk with a limp for the rest of his life but this didn't prevent him from taking up employment in a top London hotel in 1945. He moved to Ireland and to the Glebe in 1947 and took on the responsibility as Footman. Over the years he gained experience and took on more responsibility, before his appointment as Butler just a few months before my arrival. On retirement his predecessor Mr Doherty had recommended him for the post. A fact O'Neil steadfastly refused to acknowledge or accept. He was appointed the position of Butler on merit and he wasn't going to allow the prejudices of a bitter aging woman to prevent him from doing his job the way he saw fit.

As far as I was concerned he was still a tall, dark and handsome man although his hair was then mainly grey. I was particularly struck by his blue eyes and pleasant smile. To me he looked to me so dapper in his dark black suit and neat matching tie and his shoes were so meticulously polishes you could see your face in them. You could say I liked Mr Jennings. Actually you were in love with him. There's no use in you denying it. What if I was? He was so kind to me but I also found him sexy.

That's as maybe but if you intend on telling Peter and Sally all about Mr Jennings you'd better confess how you know all this. Do I? Yes, you know you do. Shamefully you read his file, didn't you? I merely took advantage of a situation, that's all. No, you took advantage of Mr Moore who was a heavy smoker and the Master's rule of no smoking in the building. The Master didn't care for cigarette smoke and he was ahead of his time in this respect. You'd seen Mr Moore, who was responsible for the staff's personnel records, making a habit of sneaking out to the gardens for a fag or two when he should've been in the office working. A good piece of detective work if I say so myself. I timed how long he took and so I hatched myself a plan to sneak into the office when Mr Moore was having a fag break. I gambled on the filling cabinet being left unlocked and sure enough it was. In my defence I'd not intended on reading of all of Mr Jennings file; I only meant to discover his age but I sort of got interested in the detail. That's no excuse, it was a despicable thing to do. Had you been caught you'd have been dismissed and poor Mr Moore would've probably been sacked as well. I don't believe Mr Moore would've got the sack. I'd learned from other staff Mr Moore and the Master were old friends and apparently they were at boarding school together. I think the Master knew about Mr Moore's fag breaks but he turned a blind eye for his old friend. You keep telling yourself this if it makes you feel better. Look, I hold my hands up, I shouldn't have done it. I've done some things in my time I'm not proud of

81

and this was one of them. Satisfied? It was none of your business was it?

I remember on one particular day Mr Jennings wanted a quiet word with O'Neil and so he engineered an errand for me. He asked me to go and find Sean the Footman and tell him Mr Jennings wanted to speak with him in his quarters. Dismissing my kitchen duties as not important didn't go down too well with O'Neil but he'd pulled rank. I left the kitchen but I didn't seek out Sean, I wasn't going to miss this. Instead I stood on the other side of the door and listened intently to their conversation. I was keen to hear what Mr Jennings had to say to her and whether it would lead to another row. Oh I hoped so. I just loved it when she was on the end of a telling off and Mr Jennings was the man to do it.

"Now, Mrs O'Neil," Mr Jennings said presently, "You may have heard young Sean and Katherine are to be married soon. I'm organising a small collection amongst the staff. I trust I can count on you for a contribution?"

I held my breath, Mr Jennings had surely lit the touch paper and I put my hands over my ears in anticipation of O'Neil's deafening squeal. When they thought no one else could hear they often shouted at each other over anything and everything. The noise was always deafening, it was like a crowd in a boxing ring when the contest had hotted up. So you could've knocked me down with a feather when, to my surprise, on this occasion she offered nothing in a way of an objection. Maybe she was too taken aback.

"I'll speak to Mr O'Neil this evening and see what can be spared," she answered calmly.

"Please do," Mr Jennings said firmly, "I'm sure they'd much appreciate it."

"If you would excuse me, Mr Jennings, the Mistress wants to discuss the menus with me for next week's banquet."

"I have informed the Master I would be only too happy to be of assistance with the catering," he countered.

"No need," she replied in triumph as she headed towards the kitchen door, "the Mistress and I have everything under control."

I darted into hiding as she left the kitchen; I watched her walk down the corridor then round the corner and out of sight. I peered again into the kitchen to see Mr Jennings examine his pocket watch, with a wryly smile, before moving towards the door. Quickly retreating back to my hiding place I watched him until he was out of view before hearing footsteps coming from the other direction. Moments later Sean popped his head round the kitchen door and once he had ensured the coast was clear, he scurried in leading Katherine by the hand. I stayed and watched by the doorway.

"Are you sure it will be all right, Sean?" Katherine asked worriedly, " I mean, we don't want that old witch to catch us."

"Don't worry, looks like she's gone to see the Mistress," Sean said noisily.

"Keep your voice down, she might hear you. All she needs is an excuse and I'll be kicked out."

"Never mind about her, she's tried to get others sacked before. As long as you don't upset Mr Jennings you'll be all right. Now if Old Doherty was still here, you'd have something to worry about. Now give us a kiss."

I watched as Sean wrapped his arms around Katherine and kissed her passionately. Mother's kisses were nothing like that. No more than a peck on the cheek which never felt like genuine affection. I'd not seen anyone kiss like this before and I longed for some good looking man to kiss me in such a way. Let's be honest here. You longed for Mr Jennings to kiss you, didn't you? What if I did? You were quite envious of Sean and Katherine. I suppose I was. They were obviously enjoying it very much and, to my surprise, I enjoyed watching them. It was all new to me and it seemed very exciting. I certainly would've enjoyed being kissed like that but not from Sean. No, I wouldn't have liked that. He wasn't ugly by any means, in fact he was very good looking, at least the other girls thought so. They said Katherine was a lucky girl and they begrudgingly admitted she was very pretty. Good legs they said and a suitable bust to attract the boys. Sean had nice body they said, he'd make a good athlete. The girls all agreed Sean and Katherine were well suited and they all said they were envious of her. For my part I felt no envy but then again I never felt attracted to boys his age. As inexperienced of boys as I was at that age, I knew even then I preferred older men. A fact I'd later regret. Mr Jennings on the other hand was a much better prospect although his wife, damn her, would've had something to say about that. In any event I needed to deliver the message to Sean. Mr Jennings would've expected nothing less. Couldn't have disappointed Mr Jennings, could you? All right, I've already admitted it. I was in love with Mr Jennings but I never tried to do anything about it. I couldn't help feel the way I did. I'm sure Peter and Sally won't judge me for being in love with him. There are other issues which happened in my life which I'm nervous about telling them but tell them I must. So end of lecture, all right?

"Mr Jennings would like to see you in his quarters, Sean," I said after knocking on the kitchen door, waiting a few seconds, before entering.

"Mr Jennings?" Sean repeated. "I wonder what he wants?" he said flummoxed.

"You'd better go and find out," said Katherine anxiously.

"I'll go right away."

Taking a coin from his pocket, he placed it in my hand. He pointing his finger at me and commanded.

"We haven't been here, understand?"

I nodded and Sean left leaving Katherine standing there looking awkward and embarrassed. Her face was so bright red it would've out shone the sun. With a nervous giggle she left the kitchen.

I did very well out of Sean, the additional pocket money was welcomed but I didn't really understand at the time why he kept giving me money. Looking back, I can see why he thought he needed to bribe me but the truth is he wasted his money.

Chapter 6

Life at the Glebe would've been lovely if it hadn't been for O'Neil. I remember vividly on one particular day she was telling me to forget cleaning the floor and to get on with peeling the potatoes.

"Are your hands clean?' she asked.

"Yes, Mrs. O'Neil. I've just washed my hands and I haven't picked up the scrubbing brush yet."

"That's all right then. The Mistress doesn't want your dirty hands all over her food. I suppose you picked up your bad habits in London. Pity you didn't spend more time at the Convent school. You should've learnt cleanliness there. Can't think why you didn't. Who took your lessons?"

When she learned I'd been, for most part, in Sister Flanagan's class she ranted on some more.

"Sister Flanagan! No wonder! From what I hear she's far too soft. Not like Sister O'Brien. She taught my daughter and I don't mind admitting it Bernadette was a disobedient child before Sister O'Brien took her in hand. She beat her into submission and taught her discipline and she'd beaten you to a pulp as well. You're like the rest of the staff here. No discipline. Sister O'Brien would've been your saviour. She should've been appointed Mother Superior by now. 'tis her rightful position. No doubt about it. I can't imagine Sister Flanagan ever caning you? Sister O'Brien would've done and you would've deserved it."

When I learnt her own daughter had been disciplined by the Evil Witch it explained so much. She was clearly happy, proud even, the Evil Witch had beaten her daughter. I felt for Bernadette and I'd nothing but contempt for O'Neil but then, in a moment, my heart was breaking for her. For the first time I witnessed tears in her eyes when she went on to say her daughter had moved to Cork as soon as she was twenty-one despite pleading with her to stay. I remember thinking at the time this was a heartless thing for Bernadette to do even taking into account she'd O'Neil for a mother. The irony was I was to do the same thing to my mother when I reached that age but at the time I'd sympathy for her. O'Neil said all lines of communication had ceased, not even a Christmas card, she wasn't even aware of her address in Cork. Why she told me this I don't know, perhaps it all came out by accident? Then of course she tried to play it down. She reasoned Bernadette was just very busy but in no time soon she'd hear from her. Other staff members told me afterwards Bernadette had left three years previous and nobody it seemed knew where she was living in Cork or if indeed she was still there. Bernadette had left just to get away from her mother and they'd no sympathy but I sensed the pain she must've been going through. It must be terrible, I thought, to lose contact with your own child. Little did I know then, the same fate would be bestowed on me many years later.

Despite my sympathy I've always called her O'Neil. To use her married title would somehow soften my resentment of her. Same as it's always the Evil Witch and not Sister O'Brien and I get some satisfaction from this. Petty! Petty maybe but this is just one of my many faults. Some people claim they don't hold a grudge but I'm not like this, I'm not this good. I will always hold a grudge against those two although in O'Neil's case I believe she was once a good person. She lost her way at some point, which is more than I can say for the Evil Witch.

Like a fool I admitted I'd been caned by the Evil Witch and O'Neil was very pleased to hear it. She scowled though when she learned Mother Superior had transferred me out of her class into Sister Flanagan's. I should have kept my mouth shut.

"'tis a pity she wasn't given more time to sort you out." O'Neil declared.

"I wasn't aware that Marie needed sorting out," exclaimed Mr Jennings entering the kitchen.

"I was just saying what a wonderful teacher Sister O'Brien is," replied O'Neil.

"From what I hear they call her the Evil Witch," he countered.

"May the Lord strike you down for saying such things. How dare you bring Sister O'Brien's name in vain like that" she said displaying the sign of the cross.

"Why? It's true, isn't it! A number of former pupils have told me so. They can't all be wrong, can they?"

"I'll not stay and listen to this a moment longer," O'Neil shouted as she left the kitchen."

Clearly enjoying the conflict: "Did I say something wrong?" Mr Jennings chuckled.

Throughout my time at the Glebe they bickered continuously and if the truth be known they probably enjoyed it as much as one another. It was quite entertaining at times but sometimes it was very embarrassing particularly when I was the subject of their argument. Like the day she decided to have a go at me for the way I wore my hair.

"Can't you do something about your hair? It looks like you've used a scrubbing brush on it," she charged.

"Marie's hair looks very nice," he said in my defence. "It's certainly much nicer than yours."

"And what's wrong with my hair?" she demanded.

"What's right with it would be more appropriate. It looks like a pile of shredded cabbage dished out haphazardly by a clueless cook. Of course you'd know all about clueless cooks, wouldn't you?"

They proceeded to trade insults and both of them determined to have the final say. Usually, as on this occasion, one of his insults would render her speechless and he'd leave the room in triumph. This was the way things were. The more she put me down the more he came to my defence. I knew he probably did it just to spite her but I kidded myself he loved me. I'm sure he liked you but he was a married man, remember? He may have only liked me because I was English and the English should stick together, no matter what? More likely it was because he was a nice man and he didn't like her picking on you or anybody else. Yes, that's probably it and let's face it he was a nice man and she was certainly a horrible woman.

The day came when O'Neil got her way and I got the sack. I'd been at the Glebe a year by then and she went to the Mistress telling tales I'd been stealing things from the kitchen. A little bit of food, a few kitchen utensils, a few loose coins from her purse. She told the Mistress she'd had her suspicions for some time but wanted to be sure before reporting me. It was all a pack of lies of course but the Mistress had better things to do and I was simply summoned and dismissed on the spot. She could've asked O'Neill to prove it but, from what I gathered, her personal hairdresser was calling that day and she needed to look her best for the important ball that evening when anyone who was anyone would be there. I didn't know the Mistress well but I knew enough about her to realise I was on a hiding to nothing and I was a nobody in her eyes. As I turned in defeat she was wading through her many dresses and complaining she'd nothing to wear for the evening. Oh how terrible it must've been for her and travelling into town would've been such a bore. Now you're just being sarcastic. Well, I can imagine it. She was too busy to treat me fairly, her vanity was far too important. I don't think I've ever met anyone quite so shallow as she was. I wish now I'd told her there and then no matter what she wore she'd look like a dog's dinner and there couldn't be a hairdresser in the World capable of doing anything about the mop on her head posing as a head of hair. I didn't, I kept quiet. Besides I didn't want to make things more difficult for Mr Jennings.

He kindly told me he was sorry I was leaving and he'd done what he could but the Master made it clear he wouldn't reconsider letting me stay. He wouldn't go against his wife's wishes and after all I was nobody important. Mr Jennings though made sure I left the Glebe with a first class reference which he wrote and signed personally and the Mistress was happy to go along with this. I can only surmise she would've wanted to avoid the Glebe's reputation from being even slightly tainted and any hint of a scandal was to be avoided. After all, the Mistress had standards to maintain and she didn't want anyone to know they'd employed a petty thief. That simply wouldn't do. To hell with justice as long as the Glebe's and her standing remained intact. You're being sarcastic again. Yes, well, she was that sort of woman. I've no doubt her standing in society was of the utmost importance to her and she wanted everyone to admire and respect her. Anyway I weighed things up and decided it was in my best interests to leave without any further fuss with my first class reference thanks to Mr Jennings. When I reflected on it later, I realised O'Neil had played her cards brilliantly and against my better judgement, I admired her strategy. She'd wanted me sacked from day one but she bided her time and waited for the right moment to present itself. She would've known the Mistress was in a flap that day, worrying about the evening ball, so this was the perfect time for her to stick the knife in. So I thought, well played O'Neil, you bitch! I even afforded her a round of applause although my clapping lacked sincerity. It was the kind of applause one offers at some tedious awards ceremony or having sat through a dull play where applauding is purely out of courtesy.

Having left the Glebe it meant returning home to live with Mother but I wasn't looking forward to breaking the news to her I'd been sacked. I thought she'd be furious with me but she was upset for me and she was genuinely angry with O'Neil. Mother said she was partly to blame because I'd made her aware of O'Neil's treatment of me on more than one occasion and she hadn't acted on it.

"That bitseach" she said, falling into her Irish, "I should've gone into that kitchen and shoved a cooking utensil up her asal."

"Mother!" I responded laughing. "If you're going to use rude words you may as well say it in English. You know I know what those Irish words mean."

"And so will she if I ever get my hands on her. How dare she get my daughter the sack. Rotten, buggering, sodding, bloody, fat, shitty cow! Is that rude enough for you in English?" she replied trying not to laugh.

I smiled, grateful for her support: "Yes, Mother".

I wished Mother had been as supportive when the Evil Witch was giving me a hard time but it was good to have Mother on my side for a change. So when I told her I'd a job lined up at Mulligan's Bakery she was positively pleased and declared my leaving the Glebe would be a blessing in disguise. She automatically assumed I'd get to bring home free bread and cakes, as a perk for being in the job, although I hadn't received such an undertaking from my new employers. I wasn't though going to say anything to shatter Mother's optimism; I was just relieved she wasn't ranting at me for my dismissal at the Glebe. Mother was also quick to recruit me for helping out with household chores and of course, as I was now going to live at home, I would be paying an increased contribution to the household income.

Chapter 7

Shortly after I'd had left the Glebe I happened to meet Katherine in Dublin's town centre. I was on my lunch break and I was just coming out of a chemist shop when I saw Katherine approaching. She didn't recognise me at first, too busy dreaming about her wedding day no doubt. We both stopped outside the chemist shop and chatted. Katherine was out on errand for the Glebe and she told me Mr Jennings was furious with O'Neil for the lies she'd told so an almighty row between them ensued. Katherine claimed she happened to be walking past the kitchen when she heard O'Neil's and Mr Jennings' voices. I suspect Katherine engineered it so she'd overhear their conversation as she was more an eavesdrop than I was. Their conversation had started calmly enough but their voices quickly lifted to a point when the kitchen window was beginning to shudder.

"Oh Mr Jennings, I thought you were attending to the Master?"

"Yes, I was, Mrs O'Neil. Be assured, Marie has taken an excellent reference with her and has found employment at Mulligan's Bakery. Our loss, their gain. Wouldn't you say, Mrs O'Neil?"

"I don't know, I'm sure".

"I think you know very well, Mrs O'Neil," his voice rising countless decibels.

"Don't you take that tone with me," she shouted back.

Losing all control: "I'll take whatever tone I like, you nasty, vindictive, evil woman!"

"How dare you?"

"How dare I? How dare you? Marie didn't steal from your purse, take any food, not even a teaspoon did she pinch and you know it. What has she ever done to you?"

"I'm not staying here to be insulted. Just wait 'til the Mistress hears about this."

"Fine, go and tell tales to the Mistress, you're good at that. Bear in mind though whatever you tell her she'll tell to the Master so I'd keep out of his way if I were you. Having to replace staff never puts him in a good mood."

He stormed out of the kitchen and slammed the door as he left. Katherine was of the opinion O'Neil said no more on the subject. She'd got rid of me which is what she'd wanted. To be honest, apart from the indignity of getting the sack, I wasn't bothered. Thanks to Mr Jennings, I got a job at the bakery and no O'Neil to make my life a misery. Though I missed Mr Jennings. Lovely man.

With O'Neil out of my life I settled into my new job which offered me more freedom. A lot less do's and don'ts and the bakery had a much more relaxed atmosphere and everyone seemed happy in their work. Mother was quite satisfied with my new job and as I was living at home once again we got to spend more time together. I'd like to think this pleased her even though she never said.

I enjoyed working at the bakery and I loved the smell of freshly baked delicious bread wafting under my nose. I got to take home the reject bread or sometimes a loaf they hadn't sold. There wasn't much wrong with the reject bread but it fell below the bakery's high standards. It was perfectly edible even if the loaf wasn't quite right. Sometimes it came out of the oven with a few splits in it or maybe a few overcooked bits which Mother cut out and fed to the birds. She always looked forward to the fresh bread and she soon forgot all about my dismissal at the Glebe. Which was a pity in some respects as I'd loved to have seen Mother confront O'Neil. It wouldn't have surprised me had she carried out her threat to shove a kitchen utensil up O'Neil's backside. You were in her good books then and your relationship was probably as good as it had ever been? That's true but sadly it didn't last long.

I got to learn about the different types of bread such as white, brown, wholemeal or granary and there were some breads with added seeds in them. I was enthusiastic to learn and the head baker, Jack Finch, recognised this. We discovered we both loved History and Jack shared with me his knowledge of bread making. Oh Hell, Marie! You're not going to dish out a History lesson on bread, surely to God? I'm just going to say with shear enthusiasm he informed me twenty-three thousand years ago, in the Upper Paleolithic Period, humans began to process and consume wild cereal grain. From the Neolithic Period, 9500BC, simple mechanisms were used for smashing and grinding various cereals to remove the inedible outer husks. We evolved to mix cracked and ground grains with water to create such foods as a stiffer porridge and by leaving the paste out in the sun a bread like crust was formed. Oh dear God, you'll bore the pants off them. Spare them the History lesson, for goodness sake. You love History and fair enough but forget the Neolithic and Paleolithic Periods or they'll be on the next plane back to Australia! All right, then.

Anyway the bakery had opened my eyes to what was on offer and then there was all those lovely fancy cakes. It was a real treat to taste some of these but I was also quite partial to an Irish Tea Cake which I'd always share with Mother. Although we'd an early start each day to get the bread baked on time I never exactly got a lie in at the Glebe either. Sisters, Dianne and Dorothy, were my work colleagues but their surname escapes me. Dianne, I seem to recall, was a year older than Dorothy but they looked very much like twins. Their dark hair were always neatly tied up in a bun and their rosy cheeks were in contrast to their otherwise pale skin. They also dressed alike and often they'd come to work wearing the same outfits which was either a pink or pale blue skirt and always a white blouse. Their practical black polished shoes completed their formal dress code. In a locker they kept their white coats which they donned before beginning the process of baking the bread. They'd a collection of these coats which were rotated on a daily basis and thoroughly cleaned before wearing again. Although

I was only allowed to assist them I too was given a collection of white coats and it was my responsibility to ensure mine were kept clean.

Prior to arriving at the bakery I'd never experienced a social life but Dianne and Dorothy were determined to change that but they'd have to convince Mother first. They were good enough to come to our home to meet Mother and she was soon satisfied they were suitable chaperons. They lived in the village near our home and as they promised to always call for me for any social event, I wouldn't be travelling anywhere on my own. Aged seventeen, my first social engagement was a dance in Dublin and we three travelled from the village by bus. Whilst I was excited by the prospect of a social life I was still very shy particularly of boys and I spent hours in the bathroom desperately trying to look my best. You were so nervous you changed your mind four times which dress you'd wear even though you'd only two which were suitable. It was a dilemma. Part of me wanted to look attractive to boys but I wasn't sure if I was ready to converse with them. As I walked into the dance hall I immediately convinced myself everyone was staring at me. More likely everybody was too busy enjoying themselves to notice me. The band played traditional Irish music and although the evening was still young many were already on the dance floor. I hadn't a clue how to dance least of all traditional Irish music. I stood surveying the hall, looking for a suitable table where I could go and hide but then Dianne and Dorothy took control and led me to a table in the corner. Dianne went off to the bar and returned with fizzy drinks for us all.

They were regular visitors to this venue and everybody seemed to know them and I noticed they were constantly waving to those dancing and others as they arrived. The hall itself was fairly nondescript but it served its purpose yet for me I was just hoping the ground would open up and swallow me. Dianne and Dorothy sat chatting to me but I sensed they were soon regretting inviting me along. I suppose they thought I should've made an effort to mingle but the practice of mingling was alien to me. I didn't think there was much chance of them inviting me again and even if they did I'd already decided I'd make an excuse not to go. They'd mentioned previously about going to the pictures one evening and this was more appealing to me. Mother had taken me on a couple of occasions and I'd enjoyed sitting in the cinema as it was nice and dark and I could be invisible in there. The dance wasn't any fun for me and they were very pretty girls so it wasn't long before men were asking them to dance. As the evening progressed they spent more and more time dancing whilst I sat there twiddling my thumbs. Occasionally one of them would return to the table and ask me if I was all right but before I could answer they were back on the dance floor.

Whilst I wasn't too pleased being left on my tod it was preferable to having to play gooseberry. I can't deny though I was feeling uncomfortable sitting on my own but then I thought I might as well make the best of it. I began playing my observing game and I watched with a mixture of interest and amusement the various couples dancing on the floor. I couldn't help but notice a very tall man dancing with a very short woman. He must have been at least six feet six inches tall and she was no more than five feet and he looked very smart in his dinner jacket, bow tie and pristine pressed trousers whilst she looked lovely in her pink dress. I couldn't help thinking they'd come to the wrong dance though. I was no expert but surely their dress was more suitable for ballroom dancing? Certainly no one else was dressed formally and for all that they looked awkward as dancing partners but they seemed happy enough. What made me laugh was an overweight man who seemed to think he was Ireland's answer to Fred Astaire. Not that Fred Astaire was known for Irish Folk dancing but no doubt he'd been brilliant at it. He was brilliant in the film Mother took me to see when he danced with Ginger Rogers. Can't remember what the film was called now but I loved it. Unlike Fred Astaire this overweight man's big bottom stuck out a mile, bumping into several couples, as he pulled his partner around the floor. She looked as if she was desperate for someone to take her place but he was never going to let that happen. There was another couple who not only looked the part but they danced together like they were born to be dancing partners. Majestically they glided effortlessly around the dance floor and they even avoided the overweight man who looked as much out of place as they

101

looked born to dance. After a while I began to lose interest in people watching and I started to wish I was at home with Mother. Dianne and Dorothy by now had abandoned me altogether and they both seemed to be very happy with their dancing partners. There didn't seem to be much prospect of any man asking me to dance and even if anybody did I doubted if I'd have the courage to accept. I thought about sneaking out and catching the next bus to the village but Mother would've been furious had I done so. I just had to sit it out and I looked at my watch and I sighed at the prospect of sitting there for another couple of hours. Next thing I knew a scruffy youth out for trouble had come to my table.

"Do yer wanna dance, darlin'?" he asked.

His speech was slurred and I'd difficulty understanding him as he mumbled some other words. His broad accent didn't help but had he been sober I might've understood him more. So my memory of what he said is determined by what he I think he said or what he was trying to say. He didn't appear to be at the dance with any friends so he didn't even have the excuse of showing off to his mates. Is showing off to your mates an excuse? Probably not but at least I could've understood his behaviour.

"No thank you," I replied, too embarrassed to even looking at him.

"Come on darlin', let's 'ave a dance," he persisted. "You'll not get another offer."

That got my goat. What was he suggesting? Did he think no other man would want to ask me? To be fair, it didn't look like anybody was going to ask you, there wasn't exactly a queue for you. True but how dare he imply he was doing me a favour? Was that what he was implying? I think it was, so I parted with my inhibitions right there: "I'm not your darling," I said forcibly, spitting daggers at him.

He mocked my English accent: "I'm not your darling". Reverting to his broad Irish accent: "What 'ave we 'ere? A stuck up, English girl!"

"Go back to where you came from," I demanded as I turned my chair round so that I'd my back to him.

I was facing the wall but I could see his reflection in a mirror and I was shaking and regretting my bravado. He wasn't taking no for an answer and he walked round and stood in front of me, his face inches from mine.

"Darlin', I live 'ere".

"So do I," I retorted.

"What yer doing 'ere? Got an English boyfriend 'avyer then?"

I didn't answer his question. I turned my back on him once more by turning the chair back to face the dance floor.

"What's up, English girl? Us Irish folk not good enough for yer, is that it? Go back to England if we're not good enough for yer."

Regrettably I had risen to the bait: "If they were all like you I'd be on the next boat."

He laughed: "How about you and me going outside for a bit of fun, eh?" he said resting his hand on my shoulder.

"Leave me alone," I cried.

He grabbed my arm and pulled me out of the chair. I tried to pull away from him but he was too strong. I had to put my hand to my face to stop him from kissing me. His breath stank of drink and I nearly threw up it was so disgusting.

I decided to use my Mother's tactic and be rude to him in Irish: "Fód amach" I said forcibly. He could have knocked me down with a feather when he replied in Irish.

"Agus tá tú soith" he said grinning.

"Would you credit it," I answered, "an Irish moron who speaks Gaelic".

"Listen, darlin', my mammy taught me. I've a right to. How come you can speak it?"

"My mother taught me too. Now please, leave me alone," I cried.

"Is this man bothering you, miss?" I heard a friendly voice ask.

"Clear off and find your own girl." the Irish youth retorted.

"Are you with this man?" asked the friendly voice, ignoring the youth.

"No, I've never seen him before," I replied.

Addressing the youth: "This lady says she doesn't know you and from what I can see, she doesn't want to."

"Look feller," the youth said defiantly, "two's company, three's a crowd. You English never heard of that expression? Well clear off then," he shouted not waiting for an answer.

The youth took a swing at him which he easily dodged. He retaliated by landing a punch to the youth's stomach who fell to the floor crying like a baby. The youth's dangly and skinny frame had been no match for a man who'd been three times boxing champion whilst in the army. Today an incident like this would've probably led to him being arrested for assault but things were different back then. Besides, he hadn't hit the youth all that hard who I think was looking for sympathy which he wasn't going to get.

Dianne and Dorothy hadn't been in the hall when the incident happened; I learned later they were both outside kissing and cuddling their respective dancing partners. So a fat lot of good they were but I thought it best not to tell Mother because I wouldn't have been allowed out again. Clearly they weren't as reliable or mature as we thought they were.

The manager of the dance hall had contacted the police station which was only across the street so the local Garda arrived in minutes. It didn't take them long to establish my saviour had acted in self defence and was defending my honour. I'd given my account of the incident and I was backed up by the group of people on the next table. Everyone agreed the youth got what he deserved and besides only his pride had suffered any lasting damage. With the Garda gone and the youth having skulked off home my Knight in Shining Armour took my hand and introduced himself.

"Frank Brown," he said, "nice to meet you."

"Marie Benjamin," my face lit up, "nice to meet you too."

Let's face it, your face more than lit up. It was love at first sight and don't try denying it. You thought you'd met your Mr Perfect. Well, I was young and naïve and a man had never paid any attention to me before and Frank was so charming. So exciting. So wonderful. My shyness left me right there and then. Frank spoke so confidently and seemed very interested in what I had to say. Everybody else in the dance hall had suddenly become invisible and we were the only ones there. At least it seemed like it to me.

Frank suggested we retreat to a quiet pub just round the corner from the dance hall. It didn't occur to me I was being very naive and this was a risky thing to do to go off with a stranger. On my way out of the dance hall we came across Dianne and Dorothy with their chosen boyfriends for the night. Their jaws dropped when I introduced them to handsome Frank and I told them where we were going. Frank assured them they needn't worry about me, he'd drive me home and I'd be back long before midnight. He was true to his word, I was at home just before eleven. I could see that Dianne and Dorothy were impressed Frank had a car and I suspect they were rather jealous. At the pub we talked for what must have been a couple of hours but I was enjoying myself so much it seemed like

106

five minutes. Frank was an Englishman living in England but he spent a lot of time in Ireland on business. By coincidence his home in Hammersmith was but a short walk away from where I'd once lived with Mother. He spoke about places in Hammersmith but I explained I could remember very little of it. He regarded himself as an entrepreneur and he was well respected in the business community. He was proud to tell me he dealt with everything and anything. One month he might be dealing in property, another time it could be electronics or even fizzy drinks. He was on business in Dublin trying to close some important deal but he couldn't talk about it. That impressed you, didn't it. It all sounded so exciting. You'd fallen for his charm, good looks and as he was ten years older made him the more appealing. You couldn't have Mr Jennings but you could have Frank if you played your cards right. Mother of course wasn't enthusiastic about Frank. That's an understatement. Mother likened your relationship with Frank to a lousy hand in a game of cards which you should've chucked it in when you'd the chance. Mother wasn't going to be happy with anyone I chose. Not even a member of the Royal Family would've satisfied her. The first meeting between Mother and Frank predictably didn't go well. Frank was Christened a Protestant although, as far as he was concerned, he was an Atheist. I begged him not to tell Mother but it kind of slipped out. He came round one Sunday afternoon for tea and Mother went out of her way to provoke Frank. Criticism of the Protestant faith failed to break Frank's temper, he wasn't interested in religion. It didn't even provoke him when she called him the Devil's son when she learned of his Atheist views. The breaking point came when she questioned his work.

"So Frank, what exactly is it that you do?" Mother asked ready to criticise.

I could see the fire in her eyes. I knew what was coming but I could do nothing to prevent it.

"I'm a businessman," Frank replied.

"Yes but what is your trade?"

"Everything and anything. If I see a business opportunity, a chance to make money, I'll pursue it."

Mother screwed her face. I knew she'd a low opinion of anyone whose prime concern was to make money.

"But you'll need to get a proper job at some point, won't you? I mean, a man needs to have a proper wage. Especially when he has responsibilities. Messing around dealing with this and that will just lead to rack and ruin."

"I shan't repeat what Frank said but suffice to say Mother's jaw dropped. I didn't know whether to laugh or cry. Frank left. Mother's opinion of him had been set in stone before she ever met him. As difficult a task as it was I had to keep them apart as much as possible. I ignored Mother's constant suggestions I should attend more social events to meet a more suitable man.

Chapter 8

My life changed from the moment I met Frank. He was like no other man I'd ever known. Not that I'd known many. When we started seeing each other he showered me with expensive gifts, took me dancing and frequently treated me to dinner in some expensive restaurant. Whenever I tell this to anyone, women in particular, think it most romantic. A Knight In Shining Armour had rescued a Damsel In Distress and how lucky I was. Thinking back, my friends and work colleagues at the time made the same comment. They wouldn't have thought that if they knew how my life was to pan out. During this time though most of them were envious of the life I was leading with Frank around. I must admit I was enjoying being spoilt by Frank and if I ever wanted a new frock or a pair of shoes he'd buy them for me and it didn't matter to him what things cost. If I wanted it, he'd buy it for me. I'm ashamed to say I took full advantage of his generosity and I took him for granted in this respect. Mother wasn't impressed with my new wardrobe and in her view I wasn't appreciating the value of money. I didn't agree with her back then and we'd often argue about this but now I have to admit she was right.

I've often wondered what would've happened if I'd danced with that youth. My life could've turned out totally different and who knows he may have become a loving husband and a good provider. His immaturity may well have given way to a level headed, sensible adult. I could've had a husband with a good, steady job who came home every night and who helped with the household chores. Someone who was kind and considerate. Perhaps a modest holiday once a year? Spending time on the beach with the kids building sand castles. He may well have been perfect. Who knows? Perhaps though he became an alcoholic and a good for nothing. Someone, when not in the pub, spent his time in the bookies being relieved of his week's wages after he'd foolishly gambled on a horse which fell at the first fence. Yes, that's a more likely scenario. It's best I believe this. The thought I could've had a better life with someone else, anyone else, is best not dwelled upon. No point in taunting myself with what might have been.

There's no escaping the fact I should've listened to Mother. She did her best stop me from marrying Frank although all for the wrong reasons. He wasn't a Catholic and therefore I shouldn't marry him was the way she saw it. From the day I met Frank my relationship with Mother started to deteriorate. Up until then we generally got on well together and I let her have her own way most of the time. After I met Frank I was no longer the obedient daughter and the odd occasional row now became a common occurrence. Looking back I realise how much of this was down to Frank. He manipulated me in a subtle way and little things he said encouraged me to stand up to Mother. Like giving something up for Lent. She took this task and the religious implications very seriously and I was expected to do

110

the same. Before I met Frank I'd find something to give up which wasn't really inconvenient but I'd pretend to Mother it was and she'd be happy. Frank though actively encouraged me to defy Mother and to refuse to give anything up. This in turn upset Mother terribly which resulted in a big row and we didn't speak to each other for days.

I could go on for hours describing the many rows Mother and I had but I can no longer remember who started most of them. One disagreement though is fixed in my mind and I remember it clearly as if it was yesterday. I hadn't seen Frank for a couple of months but he was due another business trip to Dublin. He'd usually send me a telegram to confirm when he was coming and we'd a pre-arranged place where we'd meet. Frank had telegrammed to meet me on a particular Sunday afternoon but Mother had other ideas. She wanted me to attend some distant cousin's, who I didn't even know, daughter's Christening and she expected me to drop everything.

"Your cousin Jennifer has invited us to the Christening," she casually announced.

"Cousin who?" I asked.

"Jennifer."

"Who's Jennifer when she's at home?"

"You know, Eileen's daughter. She was at Brian and Bernice's Wedding recently. You must remember Jennifer?"

"Oh yes, I vaguely remember. I've got so many distant relations who keep crawling out of the woodwork it's hard to keep up."

"Don't exaggerate. There's not that many."

"Seems like millions to me."

"Don't be silly. Anyway the Christening's next Sunday at two o'clock."

"I won't be able to go then. I'm meeting Frank next Sunday."

"You'll have to tell him you're not available."

"Mother, I haven't seen Frank for two months. I need to see him. I could always ask him to come to the Christening."

"You'll do no such thing. I'll not have that man making a mockery of such a special occasion."

"He'll behave. He won't disturb anyone. In fact he'll probably fall asleep during the service through sheer boredom and I probably will too."

Mother flew into a rage and I retaliated and then some. I must confess I'm not proud of some of the foul language I hurtled at Mother. You certainly shocked and upset her. She must've said more Hail Mary's than she'd done in her entire life. The only thing in my defence was I learnt most of these horrible words from Frank. This was no defence and it won't wash you blaming him. It was you who said these things to Mother so you've no excuse. Just assure Peter and Sally you don't swear like that anymore and leave it at that. At least you attempted a compromise after your disgraceful behaviour by attending the service. I did but as soon as it was over I left the church to meet Frank at the pre-arranged time and place. Mother wasn't best pleased I'd skipped the afternoon tea and my absence was noticed. Mother never spoke to me for weeks and living in the same house became unbearable for both of us. I think we were both very unhappy in each other's company at that time. I certainly was.

I was only seventeen so I had to have Mother's permission to marry Frank and there was no way she was going to give it. I was determined though not to be beaten and I resolved to wait patiently until I was twenty-one and then she could do nothing about it. Frank didn't mind us waiting although he did offer to elope with me to Gretna Green but I said no. I appreciated the romantic gesture but I can't say his marriage proposal was in any way romantic. He just said to me one day: "Shall we get married, then?" and I said: "Okay!" That was it. We really didn't discuss it any further. I suppose in Frank's mind's eye the deal had been done, a verbal agreement was all that was needed. For Mother's part she was banking on me seeing it her way and breaking up with Frank long before I was twenty-one. She'd even eyed up a couple of suitors for me and kept dropping hints.

"Tim Docherty is a fine lad," she'd say. "He stands to take over from his father and run the farm. Fine business they have and he'll be needing a wife. Or there's Ralph Blanchflower. Another fine lad. He's a skilled carpenter, you know. There'll always be work for him. I'm sure it won't be long before some lucky girl marries him."

Mother could drop all the hints she wanted but I was never going to take any notice. They were just boys to me even though they were four to five years older. I thought Frank was the man for me and no matter how many times she questioned his integrity I wasn't prepared to listen. Nor would I listen when she frequently warned me Frank was up to no good even though she did admit she knew nothing about business.

When Frank was in town Mother did her best to make things as difficult as she could to stop me from meeting him. There were a few occasions when she succeeded but usually I got my way and each time Mother and I ended up having an almighty row.

I realise now I never got to know him as well as I should've and at the time I quite liked having a part time romance. When Frank was in town we'd a good time together but then he'd be gone and I'd go back to being single and care free.

I'd continued to work at the bakery and I lived with Mother during my four year courtship with Frank. On Frank's business trips I only got to know the good side of him; he kept his dark side well hidden. I never questioned what he did in his spare time when he was back in London. Yes, what a fool you were. Oh, thanks for that. I know I was bloody fool and I don't need to be reminded. Deep down I probably knew if I probed him more I'd learn something I didn't like. He probably had a hatful of girlfriends and probably never had a second thought for me when we were apart. I was so naive and I remained faithful to Frank throughout those four years. I felt guilty if I as much as had an innocent conversation with another young man and I'd blow things out of proportion and reprimand myself. I know I was an idiot but hindsight is a wonderful thing. I mean, how could I've known what was going to happen? After all, he'd treated me like a Queen before we were married. Yet the point is you did know. You just wouldn't admit to yourself you weren't right for each other and foolishly you married Frank just to spite Mother. Yes, I've only myself to blame. One thing I've never got to grips with. What was Frank's motive for marrying me? Why was he was content to wait four years? He certainly didn't marry me for money and I don't believe he ever loved me. These questions I've asked myself a million times and I don't have any answers.

On my twenty-first birthday Mother came home from work with an excited look on her face. I wasn't expecting her home so early.

"I've booked Patrick's restaurant for this evening at eight." Mother announced proudly. "You like it there, don't you? Oh and they've made a cake especially for you."

I looked at Mother with trepidation. This wasn't supposed to happen. I intended to be long gone.

"Why are you standing there with your hat and coat on?" she asked with a worried look on her face. "What's going on? What's that suitcase doing there?"

I'd been caught red handed. There was no other way other than to just blurt it out.

"I'm moving to London, Mother, to be with Frank. I'm booked on the ferry from Rosslare tonight."

Mother stood there in a state of shock. I don't think she ever expected me to go through with it.

"But it's your twenty-first birthday. Surely you're not going tonight. What's the hurry?"

"Mother, I've been waiting four years until I was old enough not to need your permission to marry Frank. I don't want to waste another day."

"But surely one more day won't make any difference. I've been so looking forward to tonight. Spending some time with you." she pleaded.

"Goodbye, Mother."

"What's happened to us, Marie? Has it really come to this?"

"There's nothing more to say, Mother."

"Don't go."

Tears were rolling down Mother's face. I could see how distraught she was but my mind was made up and I didn't consider her feelings. You were very cruel. It wouldn't have hurt you to have gone out with her that evening. You cut your nose off to despite your face by choosing buses, a train and a ferry over spending your birthday with Mother. I'm eternally ashamed. Poor Mother, she didn't deserve to be treated like this. I've no defence.

In desperation she grabbed hold of my suitcase and she tried to wrestle it from me. I hadn't properly closed the suitcase and my clothes ended up on the floor. I knelt down and hurriedly repacked.

Mother was frantic. She cried out: "I'm not going to allow my daughter to marry a man like that."

"A man like what?"

"He's a liar and a thief."

"I'd be careful what you say, if I were you, Mother. Frank could sue you for slander if you repeated that accusation. I for one, would encourage him to."

"Oh you'd do that, wouldn't you? You'd do that to your own mother. Shame on you."

"I'm not wasting my time arguing with you. I've a boat to catch."

"Don't marry him," Mother pleaded, tears continuing to roll down her cheeks.

"Give me one good reason?" I challenged.

"He's not even a Catholic, he's not anything, he's an Atheist." Mother replied desperately.

"Here we go," I said mockingly, "that's all that matters to you, isn't it? So he's an Atheist. So what? Not sure if I don't agree with him."

Mother gasped. She was clearly horrified. Her own daughter an Atheist wasn't something she could entertain. I wasn't willing to debate my faith or lack of it but in truth I only said it to annoy her. Pathetic as it may sound, I would've said anything just to annoy her, I was in that frame of mind. At the same time I think Mother realised challenging Frank's views on religion held no sway with me and I believe Mother regretted it as soon as she said it. No doubt looking for a change of tack, Mother noticed a garment on the floor. I'd failed to spot it under the hallway table.

"I've wondered what happened to this. This is mine."

I laughed but more in anger: "Mother, you gave it to me," snatching the garment from her.

"I did no such thing. Give it back," she screamed.

"What do want it for, you've never worn it?"

"Give me it back," Mother demanded in a rage.

I laughed again but this time more out of pity. I threw the garment into her face.

"Do what you like with it," I shouted, "Frank prefers me to wear something more sexy anyway. He likes me to wear revealing clothes, he adores my figure."

"Lord forgive you, 'tis disgusting the way you talk." Mother cried displaying the sign of the cross. "You've learned that filth from that man. Let me tell you, he has no morals. That's what you get from a man with no faith."

"Don't start that again, I've told you I don't care he doesn't believe in God" I replied, shrugging my shoulders. "He's a good man and he loves me."

Mother's eyes were now red with tears. She knew she was losing her daughter.

"I love you," she said softly.

"Then don't try and stand in my way. I love Frank, can't you see that?"

"Yes I know you do, my dear, but the only thing he loves is money. That's his religion."

"Oh, Mother, you're impossible."

"I can't allow you to ruin your life."

"I'm twenty-one and old enough to decide my own future. Now if you will excuse me, I've got a life to live."

I barged passed Mother with my suitcase in hand and I could hear her shouting as I marched down the street. Mother's hysterics must've been heard a mile away.

"Don't come crawling back to me when he runs out on you. You won't get a penny from me."

Peter and Sally are going to be disgusted with me when I tell them this. Yet tell them you must. The fact that you regret what you did is in your favour. They'll respect your candor. I hope so. Oh how could I have been such a selfish cow for treating Mother the way I did? I can offer no excuse save to say our relationship had broken down to such an extent I was prepared to do such an unforgivable thing. If there was one day, apart from my wedding, where I could go back in time and change things it'd be then. I should've gone out with Mother on my birthday and left home a few days later. Broken it to her gently before I left. She might have least got used to the idea of me leaving but I was too stubborn. Let's face it, you inherited your stubbornness from Mother.

At the time I wasn't feeling any guilt, I just felt free and elated. Some of this elation diminished once the realities of what I was embarking on started to hit home. There was no turning back I told myself, this was what I wanted and I'd waiting long enough for. The first part of my journey was by bus to Rosslare to catch the late night crossing. It was late arriving at my stop which made me anxious waiting for it to turn up. I remember thinking dear God don't let it not come as it was the last one out of town. The thought of going back to Mother after the row we'd just had would've been unthinkable and unbearable. The bus stop had a concrete constructed shelter but to my eyes it didn't look very safe so I chose not to stand under it despite the pouring rain. Fortunately the bus arrived after a few minutes and I was relieved to get on it and out of the rain. I looked for a seat but at first it seemed full. Thankfully I spied an empty seat at the back so I parked myself down with my suitcase in between my feet. In front of me were two middle aged women who, between them, never stopped talking the whole journey. I tried not to listen to their gossip but I found myself listening all the same. I don't remember a thing they said; it was just unimportant drivel and more fool me for listening. Apart from these two women I can remember endless miles of countryside and I frequently kept checking my watch; worried I might miss the night ferry to Fishguard. I knew in reality I'd no need to worry as the bus was going to get me to Rosslare with plenty of time to spare but I couldn't help feeling anxious. So I was feeling more relaxed when I boarded the ferry. I showed an official my pre-purchased ticket which Frank had bought for me which I'd managed to keep well hidden from Mother. Frank had also given me a train ticket from Swansea to London and a generous amount of cash to cover bus fares and refreshments. I settled myself into a comfortable seat for the journey having decided to keep hold of my suitcase as I didn't want to trust anyone with it. It was only a small one, as Frank had already taken most of my clothes to London. Mother never twigged, or if she did, she never said. The ferry crossing that evening though was particularly rough and unfortunately my sea legs deserted me. Once we were out on the open sea I began to feel queasy. I tried sipping water but that feeling in my stomach persisted. I made my way to the open deck hoping the fresh air would do me good but if anything I felt worse. The high and ferocious waves were tossing the ferry about and I was unable to walk on deck in a straight line. Anybody who saw me must have thought I was as drunk as a skunk. I sat in my seat again and I sipped some more water but I knew there was no way I was going to last the journey without vomiting. My resistance lasted about an hour and I hastily made my way to the ladies; fingers crossed they wouldn't all be occupied. At least I was in luck there, a lady had just come out of one and I was in there like a shot before someone else could get to it. I bolted the door, knelt down on my knees and vomited into the toilet basin. Initially this made me feel better although by this time I was feeling very dizzy. I flushed the toilet and unbolted the door and was greeted with stares from other women. By the look on their faces they must've thought I'd too much to drink and it served me right. I felt grieved by the injustice of it all as I hadn't touched a drop. I suddenly remembered I'd left my suitcase on my seat and I hurried back but fortunately it was still there. There were a half a dozen more trips to the ladies, this time with suitcase, before calmer waters were reached and before I began to feel better. Stomach more settled I ventured to the duty free shop and I bought a bottle of Frank's favourite brandy for him with a bit of spare money I'd stored in my purse. Although I was feeling better I was glad when the ferry docked at Fishguard and I was able to alight. By the time I'd got off the ferry and gathered my thoughts it was 5am and on checking the bus times Frank had given me I'd an hour to spare. I sat in the waiting room and tried to read but I couldn't concentrate and I spent more time looking at my watch than I did reading the book.

Before I knew it was 5.30am and I decided I'd best establish which bus stop I needed for there'd sure to be many different ones for other destinations. On leaving the terminal I spied a gentleman whose uniform suggested he was a bus company official and he kindly showed me to the right bus stop. He asked if it was my first trip to the UK and I replied it was my first for a long time. I was pleased to see nighttime was giving way to daylight and I sat patiently waiting for the 6am bus which thankfully was on time.

Two long bus journeys lay ahead of me before I'd reach Swansea's rail station. First I'd a two hour journey to Carmarthen where I'd have to wait until 9am for a bus to Swansea. Thankfully this time there were no annoying women to distract me. The bus was near empty save a handful servicemen who sat quietly at the back. I think one of them was their commanding officer, judging by his uniform and his air of authority, so they were on their best behaviour. The roads to Carmarthen were very bumpy and before long I fell off my seat much to the servicemen's amusement. One of them though was kind enough to help me up and I sat back on my seat, my pride slightly wounded. Later, the bus driver was driving too fast when he came to a sharp corner and swerved to avoid driving into a ditch. This almost threw me out of my seat and before I could regain my balance the bus went over another bump and, the next thing I knew, I was being helped back to my seat once again. Even after the Commanding Officer had asked the driver to slow down he continued to drive too fast for my liking.

I arrived in Carmarthen just after 8am and I immediately sort out the bus stop I'd need for Swansea which I located without any difficulties. I noticed a cafe across the road and I was thankful for a strong cup of coffee and some beans on toast. Despite taking my time with my refreshments it was still only 8.30am when I'd finished but the proprietor was happy for me sit there reading my book. I kept close eye on the time and I was looking forward to seeing Frank. Excited about what the future would bring.

I left the cafe with time to spare and I boarded the 9am bus to Swansea Station. I was feeling exhausted from my journey and no sooner had I sat down when I fell asleep. Two hours later I awoke as the bus pulled into Swansea Station and I made my way to the cafe for coffee and a sandwich. I boarded the train to London at midday which turned out to be a four hour trip. The clatter of the railway track was somehow soothing, its rhythm served to make me feel relaxed, again I managed to drop off to sleep for a while. Refreshments were a few carriages down but it gave me an opportunity to stretch my legs and as I'd a reserved seat I didn't need to fear losing it. Frank was waiting at Paddington station to pick me up in some posh car he'd borrowed from some client or other. Frank didn't own a car of his own but he was never without one. His wheeling and dealings enabled him to borrow all sorts of cars and usually ones top of the range. It could be said this was a shrewd bit of business of Frank's but, if the truth be known, his motives were more due to meanness than anything else.

I was thrilled to see Frank and he seemed pleased to see me and he presented me with a large bunch of roses. I mentioned the bottle of brandy, which was now in my suitcase, which pleased him somewhat. As he drove us back to his home in Hammersmith I was running on adrenalin and chatted away describing my epic journey but I didn't share with him the row I'd had with Mother. Yes, you always tried not mention Mother to him because of the hate they'd for each other. He listened whilst I babbled away and he didn't add much to the conversation but his smile suggested he was content with this. By the time we'd arrived at

124

his flat I'd been travelling for close on 24 hours. Today, I can fly from London to Dublin and, even taking into account checking in time, I could comfortably do the journey in three hours. Back then flights weren't an option, at least not to me, so when I got to Frank's I just flung off my clothes and went straight to bed. The next thing I knew Frank was waking me at 8am the following morning. He gave me a quick peck on the cheek before leaving for work and although he said he'd be back about six it was closer to eight before he finally came home. Until the wedding I lived in sin with Frank and Mother wouldn't have approved even it had been with someone she liked.

Chapter 9

I quickly settled into London life and it's faster pace. I busied myself mainly window shopping in Oxford Street and I got by on the small allowance Frank had given me. Eventually Frank and I married at Hammersmith Registrars Office when it was meant to happen a few days after I'd arrived in London. Frank told me he couldn't get a photographer for the original date and he was all for going ahead with the wedding without one. For me though it was important to have some photos to record the day so our wedding was delayed. I found out later Frank could've got a photographer for the original date but, typical of Frank, he'd done a deal with someone he knew and Frank changed it to fit in with him. I was furious when I found out but as far as Frank was concerned he'd saved some money so that was all that mattered. Even in the early days of our marriage I realised everything revolved around him doing deals. Like when I asked him for a vacuum cleaner he wouldn't just buy the one I saw in a shop. No, he had to get one from some bloke he knew who worked in a factory where they were made. He said it was much cheaper than the one I'd wanted but it was probably nicked if the truth be known. Then there was the time he agreed, under protest, to get a television set. In those days people tended to rent one but Frank couldn't just go to the shop around the corner. It had to be from someone he knew who knew someone who provided a television for half the normal rental price. Damn thing never worked properly.

Naturally Mother didn't attend the wedding. I wrote to her with the details but I knew she'd never set foot in a Registrar's Office for a wedding not even her daughter's. Frank even agreed to pay her travelling expenses, which I indicated in the invitation, knowing she wasn't going to come. The reality was she would've declined the invitation even if we'd married in a Catholic Church and even if Frank had converted to Catholicism.

So the wedding took place without her which saddened me but that was how things were so I had to accept it. Frank's mother was there, more's the pity, interfering with everything but this was the way she was and I didn't let her spoil the day. Until I'd arrived back in London I didn't realise Frank had a mother. Well, obviously I knew he must've had a mother but as he never mentioned her in Ireland I assumed she was no longer around. Frank's father wasn't. Apparently, in her words, he'd buggered off when Frank was only a toddler and I can't say I could blame him. Horrible woman! Frank appeared to be unfazed with not having a dad. He said he was too young to remember him so what you've never had you don't miss was his reasoning. I can't help thinking though it affected him more than he'd ever admit. Perhaps his father abandoning him sowed the seed for Frank growing up to be the rotten shit he turned out to be?

Other than Frank's mother there were only a handful of guests, all Frank's friends or associates, including his best man Bill Baxter. Frank had known Bill from school days and he travelled up from Brighton for the occasion. Bill was a quiet, unassuming man, not like Frank at all so it's a wonder they were such good friends. You know what they say, opposites attract. I took to Bill straight away. He was very polite and attentive towards me and I think he recognised is was very awkward for me not knowing anyone. After the wedding I got to know Bill quite well and he'd always bring me a bunch of flowers when he was in London on a visit. Apart from Bill, I hardly spoke to the other guests at the reception afterwards in the Kings Arms. In fact, if you recall, you never saw any of these people again after the wedding. That's true, I didn't. From what I could gather, apart from Bill and Frank's mother, all the other guests were his business associates so none of them were real friends. From which gutter the two witnesses crawled out from I'll never know but they came across to me as the shiftiest couple of rogues I'd ever met in my life.

Our marriage was doomed from the start but I didn't want to admit it and even our honeymoon was a disaster. He'd driven us down to Bognor in an old Vauxhall he'd managed to wangle a loan off from some car dealer he knew. Three nights in a second rate hotel wasn't the best of starts. Frank said it was all the time he could spare but the crummy hotel was another example of his meanness. The carpets in the hotel were worn and threadbare with horrible dark wallpaper throughout. Our room was quite a good size but the bed had seen better days and the mattress was rock hard. The luxury of en suite in those days was hard to find and the only bathroom was at the other end of the corridor. Invariably there was someone in there when I needed to use these facilities. I think I'd preferred it if he'd taken me to the Butlins holiday camp there. It's fair to say their chalets at that time didn't have a favourable reputation but anything had to be better than the hotel.

Our days were mainly spent wondering around Bognor's town centre and sometimes Frank left me sitting in a cafe whilst he conducted a business deal nearby. His excuse was either it was a bit of business that couldn't wait or it was the only opportunity he had. Being left alone a lot of the time I appreciated the company of some of the local people. They were very friendly but it seemed to me many were far from well off. For instance I learnt that from 1960 a slum clearance had begun as many homes were without bathrooms. I could empathise with them having lived in far from salubrious accommodation back in Ireland.

Whilst I was rationed on the time I spent with Frank I was happy or at least I'd convinced myself I was. The time we did spend together, which was mainly in the evenings, we'd go out to dinner and Frank then was good company. When it came to eating out, no expense was spared, I suspect Frank put it down to business expenses. Any means of denying the Taxman and Frank was up for it.

I'd settled into Frank's home in Hammersmith and I added my feminine touch to it. I say Frank's home for he often made the point it was his home and not mine and I felt more like his lodger than his wife. He continued to go away on business a lot and all the kindness and romance had gone once we were married. It was just little things but all together they added up to a lot. Before we were married he regularly bought me flowers but this all ceased once I became Mrs Brown. He stopped taking me out dinner except when my presence was required when he was entertaining a client and his wife or girlfriend. Compliments were few and far between and were replaced with criticisms of either my appearance or the way I kept the flat clean. It was as if Frank had gone away and someone who looked exactly like him had taken his place. To make things worse Frank had given over the spare room to his mother whilst she waited to move back into her flat. A ferocious fire had broken out in her home due a faulty appliance and it meant the whole place had to be gutted. Luckily for her the fire started when she was out of the flat as she probably wouldn't have made it out alive.

She didn't like me, I was clearly not good enough for her son. I'm sure there are thousands of mothers who don't think their son's wife is good enough but she never minced her words. Whenever I tackled Frank about this he just shrugged his shoulders and said she didn't mean it. She meant it all right. She'd no regard for me at all. Frank would never admit it but I don't think he liked his mother very much. I think he was appreciative she'd brought him up as a single parent and for this reason he tolerated her. He turned a deaf ear to her insults and not just the ones aimed at me but at him as well. Besides, he kept out of her way as much as possible and this was easier for him as he spent little time at home. For me though, I was much more in the firing line. She'd no sympathy when I bemoaned my three night honeymoon. As far as she was concerned I was lucky to have got that; she only got the one night in a boarding house in Southend. She was a short petite woman but she could certainly bark out her displeasure when she wanted to. When she lived with us she'd constantly tut at me if I didn't do something to her liking but this I could just about tolerate. What I couldn't bear was her leaving her false teeth in a glass in the bathroom overnight so I was thankful for small mercies when she eventually moved back into her flat.

Chapter 10

Almost a year had passed and I was trying my best to be a happy and contented wife. I even managed to find myself a part time job working as a cleaner in a nearby newsagents which Frank wasn't keen on me doing. Then it was back to the flat to do more cleaning. Frank expected me to keep everything spotless; scrubbing floors daily and all the washing I did by hand. When he wasn't away on business he expected his meals on the table and on time. I'd no social life not that I'd had time to make any friends apart from Bill and Mrs Houseman, a neighbour. I was just Frank's skivvy. Yes, what a mug you were! Thanks for that, I know I was a mug but I didn't want to face the facts at the time. Friends have since asked why I didn't just cut my losses and get a divorce from Frank. Why did I stay and have two children with him? It sounds barmy I know but I didn't want to admit to myself I'd made a terrible mistake and I didn't want Mother to have the satisfaction of telling me she'd told me so. Not that she was around at this time. She was in Ireland and this was where I thought she'd stay. She'd not answered any of my letters and although I thought about her often I honestly never expected to see her again. Then, out of blue, she turned up on my doorstep one lunchtime.

"Mother! What are you doing here?"

"Is that all you have to say to your mother? Aren't you going to invite me in?"

"Of course, you've taken me by surprise that's all, come on in".

The customary hug followed but I didn't feel any affection from her. Let's be fair, when you last saw her you hadn't parted on the best of terms so what did you expect? All the same I was disappointed with myself because my hug also lacked sincerity. She followed me into the sitting room where she sat whilst I made us both a cup of tea. I confess I tipped a little drop of whisky in mine, I felt I was going to need it but I didn't tell Mother what I'd done. She'd been furious if I she knew I'd used Scottish and not Irish and just as furious to know I'd adopted the Scottish spelling. She explained she'd moved back to London and had taken residence, a few days ago, in a one bedroom flat in Chancellor's Road, a short walk away.

"Why didn't you write and say you were coming?"

"I didn't want to bother you, I'm sure you're very busy." Mother replied with a hint of sarcasm.

"It's wonderful to see you, Mother," I said hoping this sounded sincere, "but what made you decide to come back?"

"Oh I've grown tired of Dublin, it's not like it was when I was growing up".

"Things change, places change, London's not the same as it was when you were last here." I pointed out.

"Are you disappointed I've come back?" Mother countered looking rather hurt.

133

"No of course not. I'm thrilled to see you, really I am." I replied trying to convince myself as much as her.

She did admit the attraction of the NHS influenced her decision now she was getting older. She also reasoned if she'd stayed in Dublin the only communication open to her was to write to me. Neither of us at the time had a telephone; Frank somehow managed to conduct his business dealings by using public phone boxes when meeting a client face to face wasn't possible. Mother omitted to explain why she hadn't written to me in a year and she offered no excuse for not coming to the wedding. A subject I chose not to raise anyway. Let's be honest here. You were worried she'd do her best to cause a rift between you and Frank. Yes, I believe it was her mission to cause a break up between Frank and I which in itself was a dilemma for her. As a devout Catholic she couldn't condone a divorce and she believed marriage was for better or for worse.

Mother and I talked some more but we both skated around the last time we saw each other when I should've bitten the bullet and tried to clear the air. You wanted to, didn't you? You just couldn't find the right words and Frank wasn't mentioned until she finally asked.

"So where's that husband of yours?'

"Frank won't be home 'til late. He's got a business meeting with somebody or other."

"Tomorrow's your birthday, isn't it? I haven't forgotten. I assume he'll be taking out to dinner somewhere nice?" she enquired with added sarcasm.

"Yes," I said fearing we were sailing close to the wind as far as the unspeakable subject of my twenty-first was concerned.

"In which case, get your coat on, I'll treat you to lunch at the Bull just round the corner from here. And I'm not taking no for an answer!"

So I dutifully did as I was told and we left for the Bull and I must admit I was glad to get Mother on neutral ground. She was less likely to kick off if the wrong thing was said or if the right thing wasn't. Be honest, this applied to you as well. Yes, that's true. At the Bull we chatted amicably but the tension was ever present. I sensed she was seething over my twenty-first and I think her timing, a day before my birthday, was her way of making a point. She never said but clearly she'd not forgiven me and from her point of view I could understand why. We chatted a little about her move back to London and she'd used an agency to arrange her accommodation whilst she was still living in Dublin. She was proud to inform me she'd managed to find herself a part time job working in a launderette. One thing I can say about Mother was she was always resourceful.

To say Frank was not best pleased when I told him Mother had moved back to London was understatement. He made it quite clear he didn't want any contact with her and fortunately Mother was only too pleased to come round to the flat when

135

Frank was out. Frank's Mother was the opposite. She'd come round when she thought he'd be in. Neither Mother or Mother-in-Law could resist poking their nose in and both of them criticised me for the state the place was in. The carpets hadn't been vacuumed, there was dust on the mantel piece, the dishes hadn't been washed properly. It was like being back at the Glebe and being scolded by O'Neil again. They made it their mission to find anything else that hadn't been cleaned or tidied to their standard. They were like two peas in a pod as far as this was concerned. It was worse when his mother was dishing out the criticism as Frank usually joined in and I'd have the two of them having a go at me. At least with Mother I only had to put up with her criticism and if ever she timed it wrong and Frank was at home he'd leap to my defence. The two of them would start yelling at each other and eventually he'd clear off down the pub with the echoes of Mother's screaming ringing in his ears. I often wished I'd cleared off to the pub with him and left the Old Bat, as Frank called her, to it. There was one occasion, I can recall, when Frank, his mother, my mother and I were all in the flat at the same time. I think, as far as I can recall, it was the only time did my mother and his mother meet. Which was just as well as I knew this would be a recipe for disaster. It started off with Mother going on at me, then his Mother joined in so Mother shouted at her so then Frank started yelling at Mother and there was me yelling at them all.

Chapter 11

I'd not long turned twenty-three when Peter was born. When the doctor had told me I was pregnant it was mixture of surprise, fear and happiness. Getting pregnant wasn't planned and whilst I'd always wanted to have children I thought Frank would go stark raving mad. The thought of breaking the news to him made me feel physically sick but instead, when I told him, he hugged and kissed me and he was overjoyed. However both mothers were united in their negative reactions. Most women would be overjoyed at the prospect of becoming grandmothers but not Mother and, not surprisingly, not Frank's mother. All they had to say on the subject was it was too soon to have a child and I'd regret it. Frank said I wasn't to mind what they said and I have to say he seemed happy during my pregnancy. He continually expressed how much he was looking forward to the birth. He even showed me a lot of consideration and insisted I took frequent rests and not to lift anything heavy. More surprisingly he did some of the household chores, that is, when he was at home. He continued to work long hours but I was content with this; I could see he was doing his best to provide for me and our child to be. During this pregnancy I felt the happiest I'd ever felt in our married life and nothing could get me down.

I'd reason then to feel optimistic about the future and I thought perhaps this would be the making of Frank. I thought or at least I hoped he'd sort out what his priorities were but if I expected him to put his family first I was to be sorely disappointed. Days before I was due he was off on another business trip but he assured me he'd be back in time for the birth. Needless to say this didn't happen and he returned a week after Peter was born. On the day the contractions started I was alone in the flat and I was desperate for some help. As luck would have it Bill knocked the door hoping to see Frank. I opened the door and let Bill in but realising the urgency he helped me to his car and he kindly drove me to the hospital. God bless Bill because he wanted to remain in the hospital waiting room. The nurses thought he was the father but I laughed and put them straight on that score. I asked one of the nurses if they'd ask Bill to fetch my mother and mother-in-law. With their addresses scribbled on a piece of paper he dutifully went off to collect them. He returned an hour or so later looking embarrassed as they both refused to come to the hospital. It was me who should've been embarrassed but I think he felt embarrassed for me. He remained at the hospital until Peter was born and he returned days later to take us back to my flat. When Frank came home he showed little interest in me or Peter and all he could talk about was the lucrative deal he made in Paris. He made it very clear to me he wasn't going to do anything to help me take care of Peter. Feeding, washing, dressing, those were my jobs and not his responsibility.

You shouldn't have been surprised. Frank had never shown a liking for children from the day you met him. Whenever you were in the company of any relatives' or friends' children the look on his face was one of horror. That's so true. If any of them came to him he'd just ignore the child or he'd even get up and walk away. The thought of holding a baby in his arms horrified him. So I needn't have been surprised he'd returned to type after coming home from his trip to Paris.

I convinced myself I didn't care or at least I didn't mind Frank taking little interest. Peter was my world and I doted on him. Whether it was feeding him, changing his nappy, washing and dressing him, I loved every minute being a mother. I took pride in pushing him down the street in his pram and there were lots of women, strangers most of them, who came up to me for a chat and smile kindly at Peter. Peter though didn't seem interested in them, he was content having his toy pig by his side. There were a couple of other women with whom I met regularly in the street and who had babies like me. Karen had a girl and lived only a few doors down and I seem to recall her husband was an electrician. Then there was Amanda who had a boy and she lived in the next street and her husband was a brick layer. I must confess I can't remember their babies names but I'd some nice chats with Karen and Amanda. Unfortunately around the time I became pregnant with Sally both of them had moved away which was a shame because we'd developed a nice friendship.

When Sally came into the World six months after my twenty-fourth birthday Frank was again conspicuous by his absence. He'd found an excuse to go away on business in Spain days before I was due, leaving me to deal with the birth without him. I'd half expected him to do this which influenced my decision to give birth at home. Seven weeks after Sally was born Frank finally came home but he was at a loss, it seems, to understand why I was angry. He just shrugged his shoulders when I told him I could've done with his support. His mother stayed away, as she did when Peter was born but I wouldn't have wanted her around anyway. I was though disappointed Mother made no effort to be there for either Peter or Sally's birth. She'd shown very little interest in Peter and whenever she did look after him to give me a break, which wasn't often, it was done under protest. I can't remember her ever buying him a little toy or something or even a few sweets. To give him his due, whenever Frank came home from a trip he'd bring home a Dinky toy for Peter. Always a Dinky toy. Peter must've had one of the finest collections of Dinky toys in the country. Mother and I had many rows over her lack of generosity and as a feeble excuse she'd plead poverty. When that argument wouldn't wash she'd point out she never asked to be a grandmother as if I needed her permission to have a child. This didn't stop her though from lecturing me because I hadn't had Peter baptised. Frank and I agreed we wouldn't play that game and Sally wasn't baptised either. It was our view it would mean more if our children chose to be baptised once they were old enough to decide for themselves. Mother said we were wicked and refused to try and see our point of view. She of course blamed Frank and said it was all his doing. According to her, Frank had only agreed to the name Peter in an attempt to get into her good books. For one thing he couldn't have cared less about getting into her good books and for another it was he who chose the name Peter. The fact that it's a Bible name wouldn't have occurred to him. She wouldn't listen, she was having none of it, I was lying according to her. When Sally was born she dismissed the name adding Mary was far more suitable. She claimed Sally was obviously Frank's choice when in fact I'd chosen her name but she wouldn't believe me.

You were angry Frank and Mother had deserted you on each occasion you gave birth. Yes, I was more upset the second time. My second pregnancy had been plain sailing up to the day I gave birth to Sally but during labour God did she make up for it? Peter, it seemed, couldn't be born soon enough but Sally was in no hurry and I was in agony for hours on end. She'd be born when she was ready thank you very much! The birth really took it out of me and I was poorly for several days afterwards.

"Deep breaths, Mrs Brown, deep breaths," advised the Midwife calmly.

I yelled as I breathed as instructed and I cursed Frank for not being with me. The Midwife said my yelling had been so loud it was a wonder Frank didn't hear me in the depths of Europe.

"Frank, Frank, you rotten swine," I cried. "You pig, you're never here when I need you."

"Men are all the same, dear," said the Midwife dismissively. "It's us women who runs the home, brings up the children, sees to it everyone is fed. You'd better get used to the idea. Now push, Mrs Brown, push. I can see the baby's head, almost there. Push, push, push."

The Midwife expressed a very dim view of men but all the same she wore a wedding ring. Her mature face suggested she'd brought many babies into this World but she'd only say she'd been a Midwife for more years than she cared to remember. On one level she was very firm with me but at the same time her voice was very reassuring and encouraging. I was glad she was there for the delivery for I couldn't have managed without her. It never ceases to amaze me when I read about women who have given birth all on their own. How did they manage it?

I screamed. I was begging for the pain to stop.

"That's it, that's it," the Midwife encouraged. "You're doing very well, very well indeed.

"I can't do this, I can't take it anymore."

"Yes, you can. You can't give up, come on now. Young Peter is depending on you. He's looking forward to having a brother or sister. Now push – PUSH!"

The Midwife had hit the right note. My darling little boy meant the World to me and I was thankful,

Mrs Houseman, a kindly neighbour, was looking after him and he couldn't hear my screams. It would've upset him so. He was at a too young an age to really understand what was happening. I tried to explain to him, as simply as I could, he was going to have a baby brother or sister. He kind of accepted this baby was in my tummy but understandably he was puzzled by it all. He was excited though and I think he liked the idea of having someone to play games with and to share his toys with someone.

As weak as I felt I found the strength. I screamed, the Midwife gently gave assistance and young Sally was born. She wrapped Sally in a clean blanket and placed her in my arms. I lay there exhausted but thrilled and elated all at the same time.

"Congratulations, Mrs Brown. Young Peter's got a baby sister. He'll be so pleased and he'll always protect her, I'm sure. She's beautiful. Beautiful."

As young infants, Peter did just that. Always ready to defend Sally whenever she needed him.

I stared at my new born. All that pain was no longer relevant.

"Oh, she's so lovely," I cried.

"She's a fine young lady, Mrs Brown, She's got your eyes. I'm sure your husband will be thrilled.

"When he bothers coming back home, that is," I snapped defiantly. "He's been away six weeks this time. He knew the baby was due. He promised me he wouldn't be away long. It was the same when Peter was born. He missed his birth as well."

"In my experience it's best the husband keeps well out of the way otherwise they hang around making a nuisance of themselves. Take my word for it. You should be glad your husband isn't here. After conception, men are of no practical use whatsoever when it comes to child birth. No actually they are of no practical use at all."

She giggled at this point and I raised a smile. I realised then she wasn't so anti men as she made out but she continued with her pretence.

"Men are a waste of space. I always send them packing down the pub when their wives go into labour."

I couldn't take any comfort from her ramblings although she did make me laugh. I wasn't going to forgive Frank that easily. He'd promised he'd be home in plenty of time for the birth but he'd let me down again. Why oh why I believed him, I just don't know. I suppose the answer to this was I didn't believe him but it was easier to kid myself. It wasn't as if Sally had been born early, in fact she was a day late. The Midwife told me not to worry and I should get some rest. She said she'd call round at Mrs Houseman's and ask her to come and stay with me.

I couldn't have that: "Mrs Houseman is very kind but she's enough to do. Would you be so kind as to call on my mother on your way home and ask her to come."

"I'll do that with pleasure. I'm sure she'll be thrilled to see her new grandchild."

"Huh," I said. "She's hardly shown her face recently, been too busy she says."

144

"Is there anyone else who could come? What about your husband's mother?"

"You must be joking. She's made a point of keeping away and good job to. At least Mother had shown some interest in Peter on her occasional visits. His mother completely ignored him. No, it'll have to be Mother, for all her faults, there's no one else I can turn to."

Begrudgingly Mother dutifully looked after me and the children until Frank finally arrived home a week later. As he walked in the door, Mother took one look at him, said nothing and walked out of the door. I could've done with her support but I was too furious with Frank to think of asking her to stay. I demanded to know why he'd been away so long but he insisted it couldn't be helped. He had to close an important deal and it had taken longer than he'd anticipated. We rowed for days on end but we eventually called a truce. I'd two children who needed my attention and all those arguments were getting us nowhere. I could also see all the shouting was affecting Peter, he clearly could sense bad things were happening so the rows had to stop for his sake. Frank and I agreed on one thing. We wouldn't have any more children.

"At least we agree on this," I said to Mrs Houseman on one of her frequent visits when Frank was out.

Mrs Houseman smiled. As was her habit, her glasses rested on the edge of her nose as she peered over them. It was only when she needed to read something she pushed them nearer to her eyes. As much as anything that's what I remember about her from a visual perspective. I also remember she was a short, petite woman, a few years older than Mother but, most importantly, she'd a heart of gold and for me she was a Godsend. She didn't regard my marriage troubles as any of her business so she never judged me or made comment unless I asked for it. She'd listen quietly and patiently and she seemed to know instinctively when the time was right to speak. Frank had no time for her and, if the truth be known, I'm sure she didn't think much of him. She was always there for me when I needed her and she helped me so much in getting things off my chest when I was burdened with troubles. Then and, only when, I'd said what I needed to say she changed the subject matter around to her family.

"I remember when I was in labour with Raymond," Mrs Houseman said referring to her first born. "I screamed the place down." She giggled. "Raymond was in no hurry to pop out and he's never changed. Never hurries to do anything does Raymond. He'll say he'll do it in a minute but he never does. A half an hour will go by and still nothing would've been done. He'd be hopeless working in his father's restaurant. The diners would die of starvation before he got round to serving them but that's Raymond for you. Still, he's a good lad."

Mrs Houseman continued her affectionate rant about her son but I didn't mind. In fact I was glad of it. Anything that relieved me from the misery of a failing marriage was welcome and Mrs Houseman made me laugh. I smiled and nodded at the appropriate time and Mrs Houseman talked for what seemed hours but she'd say nothing of consequence. Mrs Houseman's husband often joked that his wife could talk for hours and say nothing.

Peter and Sally were well behaved children even at a young age. Thank God they were with Frank away most of the time, I wouldn't have coped otherwise. I always knew Peter would mature into a fine, responsible young man and I just hoped neither of them had inherited their father's selfish traits. The image of Peter and Sally have remained firmly in my mind; facially Sally looked more like her father whereas Peter was very much like me. They both had dark hair but a little lighter than mine and much straighter. These things I've never forgotten. The colour of their skins wasn't as dark as mine and most people thought they were white children so they were surprised I was their mother.

Two years after Sally was born and not long after I turned twenty-six my troubles stepped up a gear. Just when I didn't think things could get any worse I came home one day with the children but no Frank. On the kitchen table was a note from him saying he'd had to go away unexpectedly but he promised he'd be back from his trip within the week. I took this promise with a pinch of salt as his concept of a week was in reality more like three or four. His timing was annoyingly inconvenient as Mother was in one her stay away moods and Mrs Houseman wasn't able to help out as much as

147

normal due to other demands from family. I'd had to give up work when Peter was born so at least I'd no employer to concern myself with. Though when it came to shopping I had to take the children with me if Mrs Houseman wasn't available and I knew I couldn't rely on Mother. Having to attend to my children's needs whilst also carrying home bags of food made things a lot more difficult and typically of me, in my haste, I'd come home without something essential. In a sense I was relieved when I read his note; the thought had crossed my mind he might have left me. We'd be arguing quite a lot so in one way his absence was a blessing and I'd get some peace from all the bickering.

It wasn't all bad though, was it? How do you mean? You had some quality time with the children, didn't you? What about those days you took them to the park? You had fun with them. In the summer you took them out for picnics and the children loved sitting on the grass eating an ice cream or a sugary bun. You'd play football with them. Remember that little ball a neighbour had given you? Peter could kick it a little way but it was much more difficult for Sally but it didn't stop her trying. Some days you walked with them and pointed out the animals who shared the park. They were overjoyed to watch the squirrels run up the trees and flip from branch to branch. They loved the birds and Mr Robin was their favourite. They used to laugh when he hopped about pecking the ground and he flung any leaves that got in the way. They never passed up the opportunity to stroke a friendly dog if one came by with their owner. So, there were good times as well and you should tell them this. I wonder if they remember those times? You'll be able to ask them later, won't you?

When Frank hadn't come home after four weeks I wasn't too concerned but when the weeks away grew into months I started to get worried. The larder was beginning to empty and the money I managed to get from Frank before he went away had nearly run out. Before I knew it six months had passed and there was still no sign of Frank. I was unable to pay the electric bill and they were threatening to cut me off. The rent was in arrears and the Rent Man was running out of patience. One morning there was a knock at the door and when I answered it the Rent Man came barging in, not waiting for an invitation to enter.

"Pardon the intrusion, Mrs Brown," he said without actually meaning it. "Your three months behind on your rent," he said as a matter of fact. "I'm instructed to have the arrears paid today."

"But I can't right now. Just give me a bit more time, please," I pleaded.

"You've had plenty of time, Mrs Brown," he replied unmoved by my plea. "I must consider the other tenants. It's not fair on them. If they can pay their rent then so should you."

"I'm not trying to avoid paying, really I'm not," I said trying to reassure him. "My husband has been away these past six months but he'll be home soon," I said more in hope than anything else.

"So you keep saying. Can't you write to your husband and ask him to send you some money?"

"I've already told you, I don't know where he is. He's overseas somewhere. That's all I know. There must be a problem with the mail."

"As far as I'm aware there's no problem with the postal service. I know for a fact the mail as far away as America and even Australia arrives in this country on a regular basis."

Yes, I'm sure that's true but my husband might be in an undeveloped country somewhere, trying desperately to get money to me."

"I think that's hardly unlikely, Mrs Brown," he said dismissively. "Even if it was, he should have the good sense to come home."

"Maybe he can't get home. He might be in trouble, unable to communicate."

"Aren't you being somewhat melodramatic, Mrs Brown? I sympathise with your predicament but I can't allow these arrears to remain unpaid any longer. I'm afraid you either pay me now or I shall be forced to evict you."

I was horrified at the thought of being evicted. The sheer shame of it all would be bad enough but most of all I feared for my children's welfare. The Rent Man though was in no mood to compromise and he'd probably heard all the excuses a thousand times before. From his point of view he'd a job to do and he was only doing what his employer had instructed. No doubt he endured verbal abuse but there was nothing to suggest he'd been physically abused. A short and tiny man such as himself would surely succumb to physical violence? Perhaps that was his best defence? Perhaps nobody had that heart to hit such an insignificant helpless looking man not that I was in any way a violent person. I knew I needed to keep calm and somehow appeal to his better nature.

"You can't evict me, you simply can't. I've got two children to consider. You can't turn us out onto the street," I pleaded and without intending to I'd gently placed my hand on his arm.

He calmly pulled his arm away from me: "You can't stay here. If you report to my office they will find you more modest accommodation to stay in."

I was aghast. I decided to go on the attack: "This is hardly the Ritz. We've only this room, a kitchen, lavatory and two bedrooms. My children's bedroom is very tiny even for them. The plumbing doesn't work properly, there's damp everywhere and we can barely keep warm in winter."

"You won't mind leaving then, will you?" he curtly replied.

I changed tactics and in desperation I fell to my knees and I found myself clasping my hands together as if I was praying to God. My mind was cast back to those early days at the convent school in Dublin. I remembered how the class sneered at me and just for a moment it was as if the Evil Witch was looking down on me. The image of her cleared in an instant and I looked up to see the Rent Man staring at me in disbelief. I don't suppose he was used to people getting down on their hands and

151

knees and I think he was rather uncomfortable with the situation.

"Please don't turn us out, please. I'll pay you as soon as I can, I promise."

"I can't give you any longer," he replied shaking his head. "I have my orders."

Remaining on my knees, I grabbed hold of his arm once again. I had to win him over.

"But surely you can use your discretion?" I pleaded.

"I've already used my discretion, Mrs Brown, in allowing you three months," again removing my hand from his arm. "I simply can't give you more time. My superiors will not tolerate it. It's either pay up or leave. It's as simple as that. I'm sorry," he said shrugging his shoulders, "but that's it."

"At least give me until tomorrow," I asked rising to my feet.

"Is there really any point?" he sighed.

"My mother. I can ask my mother for help. She only lives round the corner in Chancellor's Road. You probably know her. Mrs Benjamin?"

"Yes, I believe I'm familiar with the lady," he replied nodding his head. "You think she can help, do you?"

"She's my mother. Wouldn't your mother help you?"

"Hardly. She's six feet under," he replied flippantly.

"I'm sorry, I didn't know that. But if she was alive and you needed help?"

"Very well. You have until twelve noon tomorrow. Be sure to be in when I call. If necessary, we can force entry. Do you understand, Mrs Brown?"

"Yes, I understand and thank you."

He nodded. He turned to the door and left.

Fortunately on this day Mrs Houseman didn't have any family commitments and I was able to leave the children with her. I made my way to Mother's flat with a heavy heart knowing the chances of her helping me were slim. No matter how humiliating it would be, I had to try, I'd have to grim and bear the "I told You So" lecture which was sure to follow. I'd no doubt Mother would relish telling me she was right and I was wrong. I knocked at Mother's door and presently it was opened.

"Oh it's you," Mother said sounding almost disappointed as she returned to the kitchen leaving me standing on the doorstep.

"Can I come in Mother?" I called out.

"Now that you here you may as well," Mother shouted back from the kitchen sink.

"What can I do for you?"

"Mother, I'm your daughter, not some door to door salesman," I responded having entered the kitchen. "Please don't treat me like one."

"You're obviously here for a reason. Never come here unless there's a reason. It's weeks since I've seen you. You never bother with me much now, do you?"

"Now Mother that's not fair, I do have two children to look after, you know. Talking of which, you haven't called round lately, have you? The children do like to see you."

"It's that what you've come here for? To lecture me on not seeing my grandchildren lately?"

"No, that's not it, I'm just saying that's all."

"So out with it, why are you here?" Mother demanded whilst continuing to wash the dishes.

"Very well," I replied taking a deep breath, "I need to borrow some money."

"You've come to the wrong place," Mother replied flippantly, "the bank's further down the street."

"You know very well the bank won't lend me any money."

"So why do you think I should?"

"Because I'm your daughter and because I need your help."

Mother took off her kitchen gloves and placed them on the sink drainer. She turned to face me, rested her back on the sink and her arms folded, ready for the battle to commence. The look on Mother's face suggested to me she was going to enjoy this conversation.

"What do you want it for?"

"I'm three months behind on my rent."

"And you expect me to have that kind of money," Mother gasped. "Where's that lazy husband of yours? Doesn't he give you any money?"

Mother already knew the answer to these two questions but she just wanted to rub it in. The way Mother saw it, Frank had left me but there was nothing she could do to help. She'd warned me not to marry him but I wouldn't listen so I'd brought it on myself.

"I know you told me not to marry him but I need your help. If I don't pay the arrears by twelve tomorrow they'll evict me."

Mother was unmoved: "You made your own bed, now you must lie in it."

"But you don't understand," I cried more desperately, "I'll be homeless."

"They'll not see you on the street," Mother replied dismissively, "they'll find you something."

"But they'll put me in a slum. If you won't do it for me, do it for Peter and Sally."

Mother's stern exterior softened and for a moment I thought I had her. I could sense she was visualising Peter and Sally being turned out of their home and not understanding why. They were after all her only grandchildren and although she would never admit it, I was sure she loved them. I observed her bottom lip quiver but only for a moment and any hope of Mother giving in was quickly dashed when her stern look returned with vengeance.

"'Tis your husband's duty to pay not mine," Mother said, clearly not giving a tinker's damn.

"Please don't keep rubbing my nose in it. You were right, I was wrong. I should never have married Frank but that's done now. When he turns

155

up, if he turns up, I'm going to ask him for a divorce."

"You'll do not such thing," Mother replied looking shocked and horrified. "You married him for better or for worse. Death do us part."

"But you hate him, you always have. Why should you want me to stay married to him?"

"You know how the Church feels about divorce."

"It's not the Church who's married to him is it? It's nothing to do with the Church."

"How do you expect me to hold my head up high when I attend mass? What would Father Kelly say?"

"To Hell with Father Kelly," I shouted, "It's me and the kids that matter here."

"How dare you speak of Father Kelly in that manner," Mother replied as she made the sign of the cross. "Have you no shame?"

I could tolerate Mother's indifference no longer and I just lost it. In the vain hope of holding sway with her I'd purposely worn my St Christopher's chain which she'd given to me for my sixteenth birthday. Clearly this wasn't going to work. I ripped the chain from my neck and threw it at Mother's feet. Mother immediately went down on her hands and knees, picked up the cross, then caressed it in her hands.

"All right. Keep your rotten money," I screamed. "I wouldn't take it now if you begged me. From this day onward, Mother, you're dead!"

I turned and ran to the door and flung it open. Fighting back the tears I again screamed at Mother.

"Do you hear me, Mother? You're dead!"

I slammed the door behind me as I exited the flat and I vowed there and then never to return. As one last act of anger and defiance, with the sole of my shoe I kicked her door which caused it to crack. It was always going to end badly, Mother wasn't going to help but you had to try. Kicking the door wasn't one of your smartest moves though. I was expecting to be in trouble with the Rent Man once he'd found out but it was never mentioned. Mother probably thought it would cause her less hassle if the Rent Office didn't know you'd done it. No doubt she blamed on hoodlums and the Rent Office would've been obliged to fix it.

My adrenalin had been running so high as I'd hurried home I wasn't aware I'd damaged my foot. It was only when I got home and I'd calmed down did I realise what I'd done. When I removed my shoe I could see it was swollen and it was throbbing like mad. Just the slightest touch and I'd yell out in pain and I noticed it'd turned purple. I headed immediately to the doctor's surgery hobbling on the other foot as much as possible. People must have thought Hop A Long Cassidy was in town. Hop A Long Cassidy, eh? You'll need to explain that one to Peter and Sally. Fortunately I was able to see the doctor straight away. Of course I didn't tell him the real reason why my foot was hurting instead I claimed I'd tripped on an uneven curb outside my front door. I don't think he believed me but he didn't press me for a further explanation. He heavily bandaged my foot and he told me to avoid walking on it as much as possible. I collected the children from Mrs Houseman before returning home. Peter in particular was curious about my foot. Why was it bandaged? How did I hurt it? Was that why I was crying? Every answer I gave was a lie and I avoided telling them they wouldn't be seeing their Nanny again at least for a while. In fact it was many years before Mother and I were reunited but sadly she never got to see her grandchildren again.

It was three weeks before I could walk without pain. In the meantime I was evicted and given a studio flat, as they called it, which I can only describe as a dump and it should've been condemned as unfit for human inhabitance. I argued successfully I wasn't liable to repay the rent arrears as the tenancy was in Frank's name and not mine. I think they realised I couldn't pay them anyway and it'd be pointless taking me to court. They said they would pursue Frank for the arrears once he'd returned but whether he ever did pay up I don't know. The children of course were full of questions such as why we'd moved to another flat. "Why wasn't the new flat as big as the last one. Was Mrs Houseman coming to see us? Would that man be coming there?" They meant the Rent Man. They didn't like him. "Would we be going back to the other flat as soon as Daddy came home? When was Daddy coming home?" It was heartbreaking having to deal with these questions and I could see they missed being in the last place and the move had unsettled them. I tried my best to explain things to them but they were too young to really understand. All in all, though, they seemed to accept their new environment without too much fuss.

For the children's sake I had to make the most of our accommodation, as hellish as it was, it was so heartbreaking for me because they deserved so much better. I thought about going to see Mother but I talked myself out of it each time and as the weeks went by Peter and Sally spoke less about their grandmother and the questions eventually stopped. What went through their minds I don't know but I expect they were missing their dad more than their gran. They continued asking when Daddy was coming back and I would say it would be soon. In truth I'd no idea when he was coming back, if at all. The other granny called in on one or two occasions but never to offer any support only to criticise the more. She voiced her disgust at our new accommodation and was of the opinion it was all my fault we were living in squalor. None of her precious son's doing, you understand. Oh no, he was totally blameless. I regretted giving her our new address but then I felt I needed to tell her in case Frank contacted her. Whenever I asked her if she'd heard from Frank she insisted she'd no contact with him and I had to accept she was telling the truth.

Frank returned to London some two months after my eviction but he'd managed to track me down after visiting the Rent Office. By this time I'd lost my self-respect as the children and I were forced to survive on the minimal amount of food. Peter and Sally both needed new shoes and clothing which I couldn't possibly afford and it broke my heart to see them looking like a couple of ragamuffins.

I came home one evening and I was surprised to see Frank waiting for me. I couldn't believe my ears when he said he was angry with me for being evicted. It was even more excruciating to see, whilst I was dressed like a tramp, he was wearing an obviously expensive new suit and sporting a healthy looking sun tan. Clearly he'd been enjoying himself somewhere although he was reluctant to give me any details of his whereabouts these past eight to nine months. He'd brought nothing home for me and not even a stick of rock for the kids.

What made things worse it was the one night Mrs Houseman was unable to baby-sit whilst I went to work. She had flu and had sent word to let me know she couldn't come. Out of desperation I'd recently taken on a job working in a pub three nights a week. It didn't pay much but it was better than nothing and at least I could put some food on the table. Mrs Houseman's husband was restauranteur and he knew the landlord at the Red Lion who was in need of bar staff and he put in a good word for me. I didn't want to let the pub down and besides I needed the money so I reluctantly put the children to bed and went off to the pub. I know it sounds like a terrible thing to do but those were different times and I was afraid of losing my job.

"What the Hell is going on?" Frank demanded when I returned from the pub. "Why have you left the children alone, upstairs in bed?"

"Frank, where have you been?" I asked not answering his question.

"I get back from Europe only to find you've moved without sending me word."

"I didn't know where you were. I haven't heard from you since you left."

"Why have you moved to this Hell hole?"

"I'll agree with you there, it is a Hell hole but I got evicted, Frank. You didn't send me any money. The Rent Man ran out of patience and chucked us out."

"What do you mean? I sent you money."

"When?"

"Regularly. You must have got it."

"I got nothing from you. Not even a postcard."

"So what's the meaning of leaving the children alone? What kind of mother are you?"

"I've been to work," I countered.

"Working? Where? You've been drinking!" he said accusingly, smelling my breath.

"I've been working in a pub," I explained. "Some of the customers buy me a drink."

"Provide some of these customers special favours do you?"

I slapped his face. He then grabbed hold of my hand.

"Do that again and I'll kill you," he said through gritted teeth.

161

I didn't have the courage to slap his face again but he wouldn't have hurt me. Don't be a silly cow, you don't know that. Admit it, you was terrified of him, there was no one who could've come to your aid. You were wise to refrain from demanding an apology for his absence. I didn't because there was no way he was going to offer one so there was no point.

"How did you find me and how did you get in here?" I asked.

"Key under the mat. You must be more careful, it's a bloody obvious place to leave a key. The Rent Office told me where to find you only I couldn't get here any sooner. I had some business to attend to."

"That's typical of you, isn't it? You always put business before your family. You should've been here nine months ago."

Well, I'm here now."

I decided to seize the moment: "Well now that you're back I want a divorce," I demanded.

Frank laughed: "You'll get a divorce all right and as soon as I'm fixed up I'll take the children with me.

I hadn't expected this reaction from Frank. I was sure he wouldn't object to a divorce but I hadn't thought he'd want the children. He was a lousy husband and an even more lousy father. I stared back at him and the look on his face suggested to me he meant it which made my blood run cold. I told him I see him burn in Hell before he took the children. He couldn't have them. They were staying with me.

162

"The children can't stay in this dump," he said.

I then noticed a toy stuffed in his pocket and I knew instantly it belonged to Sally. I demanded he give it back but Frank accused me of not being fit to be a mother.

"Give me that toy," I shouted.

Frank threw the toy on the floor: "Have the toy then, if that's all you care about."

"How dare you! My mother was right about you."

Frank laughed again: "Your mother's a scheming, Evil Witch."

The insult didn't end there. He used some of the most vile words I'd ever heard from him, he held nothing back. I could hear the children calling out for me, the noise we were making must have woken the whole neigbourhood.

"There, see what you've done now. You've woken Peter and Sally up. I need to see to them. Now get out, get out, get out," I screamed.

Frank left, slamming the door behind him, whilst I collapsed on the sofa in floods of tears. A few more springs on the sofa had broken, as I'd sat down, which made me sob the more. There couldn't be many more springs to break and there was no way I'd have the money to buy another. I'd been lucky getting this one; Mrs Houseman knew someone who just wanted rid of their sofa. Frank's threat of taking the children from me was racing round and round in my mind as I sobbed uncontrollably clutching Sally's toy. It began to dawn on me I was in for a battle with Frank over custody of the children but they always ruled in the mother's favour, didn't they?

I could understand why he hated Mother after the way she'd treated him but I couldn't reconcile why exactly things had gone sour between him and I. The question you kept asking yourself was when did he become rotten? The answer is he was probably always rotten but you were too in love to notice. So the next day I took the opportunity of getting things off my chest by talking to Mrs Houseman which was a comfort to me.

"Unfortunately it's the way some people are," she reasoned with impeccable timing. "Take my cousin, Ted." She paused for a moment and then offered a little giggle. "On second thoughts you wouldn't take him but Ted's a classic example. Never done a decent thing in his life has Ted. He'll beg, steal and borrow from anyone and never pays them back. I've never known him lift a finger to help anyone. Not even his own mother. Ted would've a lot in common with Frank. Except that Ted wouldn't want the children. He hates kids."

Mrs Houseman's description of Ted made me smile to think he and Frank would've got along well together as a couple of selfish rats. Perhaps I was doing rats a disfavour but they make an ideal comparison with Frank and, by the sounds of it, Ted. All of them are vermin. I know it sounds weird but I was somehow comforted to know there were other people like Frank and I hadn't picked the only man like him in the whole World.

164

Chapter 12

It took me a long time to admit to myself I'd become an alcoholic. There'd been many times when I told myself I needed to stop drinking but then I'd quickly dismiss it. Each time I convinced myself I didn't have a problem and from the next day I'd stop. When the next day came I vowed to stop the next day and then the next day and so on. I came up with lots of excuses. Frequently I told myself the drinking was because I'd been under a lot of strain and trying to make ends meet seemed to me to be an impossible task. Once I was on a more financial footing I'd be fine but the truth is my road to alcoholism began the day I started working in the pub. Regular customers bought me drinks which at first it was just a couple a night but this soon turned into three or four and then five or six. Long before I admitted it to myself, I was addicted.

I'm convinced Frank only took the children from me out of spite. Up until then, he'd shown little interest in the children so there can be no other explanation. It happened on a night when I was working at the pub and poor Mrs Houseman could do nothing to stop him. She answered a knock at the door and the brute forced his way in and shoved her out of the way. Poor woman must have been terrified. He went upstairs and lifted them from their beds and left with them in tears. When I came home Mrs Houseman was sobbing on the sofa. It was her fault she said and I couldn't convince her otherwise. Frank's aggressive behaviour frightened Peter and Sally and Mrs Houseman said Peter cuddled up to his sister in attempt to protect her. I know Frank never actually hit her but they were very fond of Mrs Houseman so no wonder it was upsetting for them. A few months later Mrs Houseman died. A heart attack they said but I believe it was Frank who was responsible for her death and nobody will convince me otherwise. I still feel guilty to this day I'd involved a kind and innocent lady with my domestics and she'd died as a consequence. Frank never expressed any regret over her death.

Frank had taken the children to his very posh rented flat in Chelsea. He had to have the best money could buy and he was fond of boasting the children had everything they wanted. He'd have a smug looking grin on his face when he said it. I would've liked to have shoved his smugness up his backside so if he'd thought I'd be impressed he was well off the mark. As far as I was concerned, they may have had all the material things they wanted but I don't believe he gave them any love. Frank never saw it that way.

In an attempt to get the children back I had to go to the High Court and several agonising months went by before I was given the opportunity. I felt sick to the stomach as I stood in court to state my case. Frank was there of course, looking very sure of himself having given me an intimidating look

166

when he arrived. The judge was an elderly man who's demeanor suggested he was way beyond retirement. A tall, large and God fearing man he made me feel like I was on trial for murder rather than pleading for my children's custody.

"Now tell me again, Mrs Brown..."

I interrupted him: "Miss Benjamin," I said, "I prefer to be addressed as Miss Benjamin.

I caught a glimpse of Frank with a smug look on his face but damn him. I'd no desire to continue using my married name. The judge rolled his eyes but conceded to my request. It was the only concession he granted me.

"Very well, Miss Benjamin, tell me again why you constantly left your children alone whilst you went out at night."

"I've already explained," I said irritated, "that was an exception. Mrs Houseman normally looked after the children but she had the flu that night."

"Is Mrs Houseman a relative?" the judge asked.

"No she is... Was," I said correcting myself, "a very good friend. A very dear friend."

"But she's not now?" the judge enquired not getting my meaning.

"She's dead now. Poor woman," I replied sadly.

"So why did you go out if you had nobody to look after the children?" the judge demanded.

I fired back my answer: "I had to go to work."

"Couldn't you have contacted them and explained?" the judge countered.

"I didn't want to lose my job." I reasoned.

The judge wasn't convinced. He said my employer would've been sympathetic and understood.

"They were short staffed," I continued trying to explain, "I couldn't let them down at such short notice.

He was unmoved: "You were prepared to let your children down, weren't you? Two young children left all alone whilst you went out to work in an unsuitable establishment."

"It's a perfectly respectable public house," I snapped. "Besides it was the only job I could get."

"But surely not suitable for a mother of two children," the judge suggested. Thank goodness your husband came home or I dread to think what might have happened."

"But he'd been away for nine months," I protested. "Not a word from him and no money either."

I could see by the look on the judge's face he wasn't convinced. He paused to consider before he picked up some letters from his desk.

"I have letters here sent to you from Mr Brown but these were returned to him marked 'gone away'. It seems you'd moved?"

"I did eventually." I admitted. I knew what was coming.

"And why was that? He demanded. "Why did you move?"

"Because I was evicted," I replied.

"And why were you evicted?" He asked eagerly.

"Because he," I replied angrily, pointing at Frank, "didn't send me any money."

The judge shook his head. On the contrary he'd evidence to prove Frank regularly sent me money orders and each time these were cashed at the bank. I was flabbergasted to hear such nonsense, it simply wasn't true. Not once did I receive a money order payment but the judge was in no mood to believe me. The evidence said otherwise.

"The evidence is a lie." I cried.

He dismissed my plea. He declared that in view of the evidence provided to the court he'd decided to award custody of Peter and Sally Brown to their father, Frank Brown. He added that the decision of the court was I may visit the children for two hours per week provided their father was present.

On hearing his verdict my head began to spin and I fainted. A kindly court official helped me to my feet and sat me in a chair. By then I was so devastated I was sobbing uncontrollably. I couldn't believe my ears. I couldn't take it in. Frank, it seemed, had pulled off the almost impossible. How could a lousy husband and father like this, who'd deserted his family for the best part of a year, get custody of two children most precious to me? It wasn't fair and it didn't make sense unless, as I suspected, Frank had bought the judge's verdict. I'd no other explanation for it and I still believe it to this day. When I thought about it, it made perfect sense. Frank knew people and I truly believe he made it his business to find out who the corruptible judges were. He'd have bribed as many people as he needed to ensure he got the right judge to win his case. I realise this may sound a bit far-fetched, something which only happened in films. In make believe. Yet this was real and it happened to me.

Even today I feel nothing but bitterness for the injustice of only being allowed to see my children two hours a week. This was heart breaking enough but with Frank presence this denied me any real intimacy with Peter and Sally. Bloody hell, I mean, bloody hell, what sort of justice was that? Now calm down, Marie, there's no use in crying over spilt milk. Spilt milk? I'd liked to have given him spilt milk. I'd liked to have poured the whole damn lot over his head along with anything else I could've laid my hands on. Now don't start giggling again and let's pass on the milk analogy. Just say you believe the so called evidence must've been rigged but you'll never know how Frank succeeded in this. It was a miscarriage of justice and Peter and Sally should know this.

Over the next three years Frank made it as difficult as possible for me to get to see the children for my two hours a week. His usual excuse was he wasn't available when I wanted to see them so I'd challenge him as to who was looking after the children whilst he was out. He always said his mother saw to them but I suspect it was his lady friend doing the baby sitting. Oh yes, there was a female in his life other than his mother and daughter and it was pointless him denying it. Why he did so I'm not sure. It's not as if he'd have cared if I'd voiced my disapproval. Frankly, I didn't give a toss. Any woman was welcome to him but for some reason he always denied having a girlfriend but I'd witnessed a woman leaving his flat on more than one occasion. When I asked him who this woman was he claimed it was his cleaner but I knew this wasn't true. Mr Bruce, a gentleman I knew casually, told me his cleaner was also Frank's and his description of her was nothing like the woman I'd seen. When I did get to see my children I got the impression they were under strict instructions not to say anything about who was looking after them when Frank was away. If I asked them if they'd enjoyed staying with granny they'd look to their father for guidance before offering an unconvincing nod. It was a ridiculous situation but he kept up the pretence anyway.

My first and last priority was getting to see Peter and Sally and I cherished these moments. I remember, on one occasion, being permitted to see them when it was Peter's birthday but this was about as generous as Frank got. I didn't have much money to buy Peter a present but I'd scrapped up enough to give Peter a toy police car. Much to Frank's annoyance Peter discarded all the other more expensive presents he'd bought him in favour of the police car. It's a funny thing, maybe he was destined to become a policeman?

Frank also got annoyed when Peter and Sally were so pleased to see me when I called. I'd give them each a loving hug and they wouldn't hide their excitement at seeing me. They'd tell me about the

171

things they'd got up to the last time I saw them such as any birthday parties they'd attended. Apparently there were a lot of children living in the same street so these events were quite frequent. When my two hours were up Peter and Sally desperately clung to me like an octopus clinging to its prey and they begged me not to go. Each time Frank pulled them off they'd scream, shout and cry. This was heartbreaking for me and I'd go home and sob afterwards but I don't think he was ever bothered by it. He'd no qualms when it came to him coming between the affection the children and I shared. He didn't seem to care how much this upset Peter and Sally. No doubt it pleased him how much it hurt me.

Frank made a point of making sure he never left me alone with the children. I began to notice, as well as the police car, other toys I gave Peter or Sally were missing the next time I called. I realised they'd a lot of toys and children do tend to discard them in favour of new ones but I was convinced Frank was throwing them away once I'd left. Each time I accused him he denied it and Peter and Sally had been well trained not to say anything. I couldn't afford to have the little I earned wasted and besides I didn't want Frank getting away with it so I stopped buying them toys. Which is exactly what he wanted, he was jealous of what you bought them. You never spent much on them, you couldn't afford to, yet the children were probably happier with these things than anything he bought for them. This must have riled him. I got round it though. I like to think I scored a small victory by buying them a few sweets for each visit. They didn't need any encouragement to eat them all before I left and I could see the resentment on Frank's face.

Frank regularly moved from one flat to another which made it more difficult for me to see the children. He'd never tell me he was moving and many's a time I'd turn up to find him and the children gone. It took me days or even weeks before I'd catch up with them. Every time Frank lied through his teeth and insisted he'd given me the forwarding address. He must have realised I knew he was deliberately trying to give me the slip and his blatant lies were pathetic. I could've had more respect for him if he'd admitted what he was up to but he kept up the ridiculous lies.

I constantly lived with the fear there'd come a day when I wouldn't be able to find out where they'd moved to. Although I must say I'd turned into a very good detective in this respect and it gave me great satisfaction when I tracked them down and witnessed the disappointment on Frank's face. Tracing them was sometimes easy but other times I'd have to do a bit of leg work. The day came though when my worst fears became reality. I turned up one day only to discover he'd moved on yet again, which I'd gotten used to, though this time I'd an uneasy feeling this was going to be different. As usual I went to Frank's landlord's office as up until then his landlord was only too happy to give me the forwarding address. The landlord was away for a couple of days so I had to wait his return as the neighbours didn't know Frank's address or even that he'd moved. On his return the landlord was unable to give me a forwarding address. Frank had paid all his rent up to date and he'd taken residence with another landlord. He must've finally twigged his usual landlord was giving me his forwarding addresses and changing landlords was going to make it more difficult for me. Undeterred at this point I called at the premises of all the other landlord's I was aware of but to no avail. I couldn't be sure though if they didn't genuinely have Frank on their books or if they were just protecting client confidentiality. I went home and sobbed. This time Frank had done a very good job of covering his tracks and I'd icy feeling in my body as I faced the prospect of never seeing my children again.

As the days turned into weeks and the weeks turned into months I got more and more depressed as any lead I got came to nothing. I asked anyone and everyone but they all just shrugged their shoulders and said they couldn't help me. After six months I was well passed tearing my hair out and I'd come to the conclusion I may as well be looking for the Invisible Man. I was sure somebody knew where Frank was but they just weren't saying. I wouldn't have put it passed Frank if he'd paid people off for their silence. In desperation I wrote to Bill Baxter because if anyone knew where Frank was it'd be him. Whilst Bill was Frank's oldest friend I think he'd a soft spot for me and, although he never said, I don't believe he approved of the way Frank had treated me. My hopes were dashed when my letter was returned in the post; Bill himself had moved on and all I could do was hope he'd eventually get in touch.

I was at my lowest ebb. I pondered on my life and wondered how things had gone so wrong. Some people believe in reincarnation and if they're right what on earth had I done wrong in a previous life to deserve this? I must have been a terrible person and I was being punished for it. Except you don't believe in all that stuff, do you? No, I don't and I never have but life was Hell.

I thought of the war years as a very young child and my life in Ireland during the fifties wasn't the happiest most of the time. The swinging sixties in London somehow passed me by whilst the seventies said goodbye to pounds, shillings and pence. It seemed everywhere took advantage of decimalisation by increasing their prices which made it more difficult for me to get by. The Beatles had come and gone and the youth of the day took ownership of Glam Rock. Whilst I liked most of the music I didn't care for the fashion of those times especially those ridiculous platform heeled shoes they were all wearing. Needless to say I never bothered myself with any of this. Be honest. You never bought any of this stuff because you couldn't afford it. You'd little money so you couldn't afford to waste it on fashion and politicians kept promising better times if we joined the European Union. Better times seemed a long way away for me and, although the policy of Europe I never quite grasped, it sounded like a good idea to me. To cap it all there was I, thirty something, barely scraping a living, estranged from my Mother, recently divorced and I was missing my children something chronic.

The pub I'd been working in offered me more hours and as my circumstances had changed I accepted the offer of five nights a week. More time though to be tempted with drink especially when the customers were so generous. Wednesday nights was always a busy night as the customers seemed to be attracted to the live music which was on offer albeit in an understated way. There wasn't a stage as such, just a small platformed area in one corner, so it suited the solo acts who didn't need much space. Most of them were male guitarists who strummed their stuff singing popular songs of the day. Only occasionally a female got the gig and they were always well received. There were no big amplifiers or sophisticated sound systems just a solitary microphone if you were lucky. There was one trio though who played there from time to time. There was one guy on guitar, another played a mixture of wind instruments mainly trumpet and the other was on double bass. It must've been difficult carting that thing about especially as the three of them used to turn up in a small van. Their music was a mixture of jazz and folk but I remember them because they called themselves *Born Again Atheists*, which amused me. It wouldn't have amused Mother. "Aindiachaí! Aindiachaí!" she used to say in her mocking judgmental tone. "Aindiachaí é an diabhal é féin." She hated Atheists more than she did

Protestants so Frank had no chance as an Atheist and being Christened in a Protestant Church. Ironically the guitarist in this band later became a village vicar somewhere in North Devon.

It was on one Wednesday night when I was having a few too many drinks, which had become the norm I'm ashamed to say, when this man came in and approached me at the bar. I'd never seen him before but he struck me as the cocky type and I sensed I needed to be on my guard. His short well-trimmed moustache and trilby hat certainly supported my immediate, if biased, assessment of him as a shifty character. I decided he was probably a used car salesman or a small time crook and as far as I was concerned all used car salesman had a dodgy reputation. I know it's not fair to tarnish them all with the same brush but my suspicions proved to be well founded.

"What can I get you?" I asked innocently.

He ordered a light ale and he laid the exact money down on the bar which I deposited in the till. I poured out his light ale and he remained at the bar sipping his drink and momentarily he spoke again. He lowered his voice so only I could hear him.

"I'm looking for Marie Benjamin, I understand she works here?"

I was on my guard: "What do you want her for?"

"I prefer to discuss that with her," he retorted.

"Are you the police?" I asked directly.

He laughed at my question: "Lady, do I look like a copper?"

"I don't know," I countered. "What does a copper look like?"

"Look, are you Marie Benjamin because I think you are?"

"So why are you asking?" I replied realising I needed to come clean.

He revealed he'd some information concerning the whereabouts of my ex-husband and my children. He wouldn't say how he knew this or how he knew where to find me. I'd made it my business to let my regulars know I was looking for Frank and I can only surmise he'd over heard something from someone. I soon learned he wasn't a good Samaritan eager to do his good deed for the day. He wasn't interested in helping out a woman desperate to see her children again; no this information came at price.

"Fifty pounds and I'll give you the address," he demanded.

"Who are you? How do you know where Frank lives? How can I trust you?" I asked, firing these questions at him.

"Who I am isn't important. For my own protection you'll not learn my name. Let's stick to the matter in hand. Fifty pounds is a small price to pay," he said trying to justify his extortionate demand.

I was starting to get angry: "If you know Frank, you'll know I don't have that sort of money. Why can't you just tell me where he is?" I demanded, although I already knew what his response would be.

178

"The price is fifty pounds," he repeated. "Finding out where your children are must be worth something."

I realised there was every chance this man was trying to con me but I was desperate to find my children. I couldn't let this opportunity to go by so I'd no choice but to trust he was telling the truth. I emptied what money I had from my purse onto the bar but there were just a few coppers and nothing else.

"That's all I've got, take it!"

"Not much there," he said and walked towards the door.

"For pity sake," I pleaded, " please tell me where Frank is. Please, he's got my children. I haven't seen them in months," I cried.

His hand gripped the exit door. I felt a chill as he opened the door. I swear the chill was oozing from his body rather than from the weather outside.

"If that's all you can offer me then I'm afraid we can't do business," he said as he turned to leave.

"Wait!" I cried.

I'd just remembered a very generous regular had given me a ten pound note earlier in the evening as a tip. He was often very generous with his tips; he said he appreciated my smile when I greeted him. He was by all accounts a very rich man but also a very lonely one no doubt. I pulled the ten pound note from my pocket.

"Please, I'm begging you. This is really all I have. I'm just a barmaid, for God's sake."

He returned to the bar. He picked up his light ale and drank what remained in the glass.

"Okay," he said, holding out his hand."

"The address first," I demanded.

"No, money first," he countered.

"Why should I trust you," I challenged.

"Because you want to see your children again," he retorted.

"All right." I paused before picking up a pen and a plain piece of paper which I handed to him. "You write down the address and then we exchange. Okay?"

He agreed. He wrote the address down on the piece of paper and clutching it he cautiously moved his hand towards me. I did likewise with the ten pound note and with my other hand I took hold of the paper and he in turn gripped the money. At the count of three I let go of the money and he took his grip away from the paper. With the paper firmly in my hand and the money in his, he left. I read the address quickly before placing it safely in my purse but it was all I needed to memorise it. I wasn't going to forget it. I was desperate to go straight off to Frank's flat in Fulham but I had to finish my shift first. I was excited, nervous, angry and happy all at the same time. It was only two hours until closing time but it seemed like days before the pub manager was ringing the bell and shouting out last orders. Thankfully there were no hangers on that night and the pub was soon empty of customers. I begged a lift from the pub manager as I knew he lived in the area and he happily agreed. I had a long wait though whilst he completed his chores including balancing the tills. This frustrated me beyond belief, I was becoming increasingly anxious so I offered to help to speed things up. He declined my offer explaining this was something he had to do himself. I considered if it might be quicker to walk but I realised Frank's flat was a fair distance from the pub. I kept looking at my watch, each time I thought it'd stopped, so I kept checking the pub's clock. Whilst I waited I'd a few more drinks for Dutch Courage for when I'd confront Frank. Eventually the manager was ready to leave and I couldn't get in his car quick enough.

At two o'clock in the morning I banged on Frank's door. This was a big mistake, wasn't it? Especially as you'd had too much to drink. When Frank opened the door you fell flat on your face, on his hallway floor, drunk and incapable. I'm ashamed to say I did but when Frank picked me up from the floor, as drunk as I was, I can remember everything we said. It was always the case with me no matter how drunk I got I could remember everything afterwards. You're kidding yourself now, aren't you? Well, on this occasion, I swear I could remember everything that evening. Notwithstanding this, getting drunk was a fool hardy thing to do and you just played into Frank's hands. You should've gone straight home that night and called at Frank's the next day. Sober! So admit it. Okay, Okay, I admit it. I swear though, this is what was said.

"What the hell do you think you're doing?" he demanded in an angry whisper. "Don't you realise what time it is?"

"Way past your bedtime," I laughed, my speech slurred. "Why aren't you in bed?" I giggled.

"I could ask you the same question," he replied clearly not amused. "Now what the Hell do you want?"

"I've come to see Peter and Sally. Why are you whispering?" I giggled once more.

"Because the children are in bed asleep. Now keep your voice down and get out of here," he ordered.

I raised my voice: "I've come to see Peter and Sally. I'm not going 'til I've seen my children."

"Haven't I just told you to keep your voice down?" he retorted.

"Yes sir," I replied with a mocked salute. "You didn't let me know your address. You're always doing that. Why do you keep moving?"

"You're drunk. Now clear off you bitch."

He was beginning to lose his more reasonable demeanor and the old aggressive Frank was starting to emerge.

"And you're ugly," I giggled, "but in the morning I'll be pretty!" I giggled again. "No, that's not right, is it. What was it Atley said?"

"Churchill." Frank retorted, his face a thunderous red.

"What?" I giggled.

"It was Winston Churchill," Frank clarified. "A lady accused him of being drunk and he told her she

182

was ugly and added in the morning he'd be sober. Now clear off, you cow. I won't tell you again," lifting his hand in a threatening manner.

The argument continued and Frank got more and more aggressive. You put yourself in danger, anything could've happened, he might have killed you. No, Frank would never have done that. He was a rotten swine but he was never capable of being a killer. You think? You took a Hell of a chance and you know it. You were pushing your luck and his temper had reached boiling point.

I was just trying to get some answers but all he kept telling me was to come back on Saturday afternoon. I protested, I didn't want to give him the opportunity to disappear again. How much had he paid the judge? Frank repeatedly ignored this question, he denied leaving me penniless, he insisted he'd sent me money orders which had been cashed. He threatened me with a restraining order before I accused him of destroying my relationship with Mother which he refuted. Frank said it was all my mother's doing and she'd taken an instant dislike to him. I couldn't deny this but Frank said my mother was a lousy grandparent and I retaliated by accusing him of not being a good father.

"I take care of the children." Frank replied defensibly. "I see to it they don't go short of anything. I'm paying for them to go to a public school, did you know that?" he announced proudly.

"Aren't they a little young to be going to a public school?'

"Of course not. Peter's seven and Sally's five."

"I know how old they are, Frank, but couldn't a normal school do for now until they're older?"

"I want to give them the best start in life. Public school at an early age is a must."

I wasn't impressed: "Bully for you, Frank. How much love do you give them? That's what I want to know!"

"Love won't pay the bills, Marie," Frank replied turning his back.

"That's the first time you've called me Marie since we got divorced," I said, sensing a trace of humility left in him.

Any chance of some reconciliation soon evaporated when I demanded to see the children again. Frank repeated his demand for me to come back on Saturday afternoon and soon the conversation once again escalated into a slanging match. The sound of children's voices from upstairs restored order.

"Daddy, Daddy!"

I rushed to the bottom of the stairs: "Is that you, Sally?"

"Daddy, Daddy," came a frightened voice. "Who's that lady down there?"

Frank stood in front of me at the foot of the stairs: "It's all right, darling, Daddy's here. Go back to bed and go to sleep." He turned to me: "Are you satisfied now?"

"She didn't recognise me," I cried with a mixture of despair and disbelief.

"It's no wonder," responded Frank. "Just look at yourself, you're a mess."

He'd a point there, you did look a mess. No wonder Sally didn't recognise you. As Frank virtually dragged me to the door the realisation my child hadn't known me had left me weakened and wounded. Before I knew it he'd tossed me out like a discarded rag doll and I landed, with a thump, on the pavement outside. I got up trying to salvage some pride.

"Come back on Saturday afternoon, that's your allocated time with the children. I shouldn't have to remind you of the terms laid out by the court," Frank said slamming the door closed.

"I'll be back Saturday," I cried out. "I'll be at my best. She'll know me then."

I'd woken a neighbour who shouted at me to keep the noise down using, to say the least, colourful language. I thought it best not to engage with this person and I quickly fled the scene. The problem I'd then was getting home; I clearly hadn't thought things through. I didn't have the money to pay for a taxi or a bus for that matter even if one was to come along. There was nothing for it other than to start walking but home was several miles away. I'd started walking briskly but I knew I wouldn't be able to keep up the pace for long. I kept to the main streets but I cursed myself for potentially putting myself in danger at that time of night. Oh, what an idiot I was! I'll second that. Thank you, I don't have to agree with myself. Fortunately for me a police car stopped after I was spotted walking along the pavement. The police officer asked me where I was going and what was I

doing out so late. I told a white lie and said I'd lost
the money for a taxi fare. I don't think he believed
me but I was relieved when he offered me a lift
home which I gratefully accepted.

Chapter 13

I regretted not returning to Frank's flat the next day rather than wait until the Saturday. I'd been through this a million times before and the answer is always the same. There'd have been no point, Frank wouldn't have let you in and you'd have made the situation worse. Except that I'd given him the chance to move on and this is exactly what he'd done when I arrived on the Saturday. I stood outside his door, sober I might add, dressed in my best outfit with my hair neat and tidy with tears rolling down my face. All my efforts to see Peter and Sally again had been dashed and I just didn't know what to do next. The stress of it all had taken its toll and given the opportunity I'd have slit my throat with a knife. You don't mean that, do you? No, I couldn't have given up on Peter and Sally. As I stood there in tears a kindly neighbour came out from his flat and, noticing my distress, he asked me if there was anything he could do.

"I'm at my wits end," I cried, "I've come here to see my children only to discover their father has moved them on again".

"Oh dear," he calmly replied, "who is it you're looking for?"

"Frank Brown," I answered, eager for his response.

"The man who lived there?" he asked, pointing to the door.

I nodded: "Can you help me?" I asked.

The man sighed. He shook his head.

"All I can tell you is he's moved to somewhere in Kingston. He didn't say anything else. They kept themselves to themselves so I didn't know they were leaving until I happened to open my door to witness him and the woman, suitcases in hand, leaving with the two children. In a neighbourly way I asked if they were going on holiday and it was then I learned they were moving to Kingston. You're their mother, you say?"

"Yes," I said, "Frank and I are divorced and he has custody of the children."

"Really? That's unusual," he said surprised.

I explained. I could tell by the look on his face I'd won his sympathy.

"Look, I can't promise anything but I can see you're distressed and as it happens I work for Kingston Council for my sins. I'll see what I can find out. I'm not supposed to do this but a mother shouldn't be parted from her children. If I can find out his address I'll let you know."

I thanked him and it was agreed I should return the following Saturday when hopefully he'd have some news for me. It took three consecutive Saturdays before he was able to hand me an address in Kingston.

"For goodness sake," he stressed to me. "Don't say where you got this from. I'd be in trouble if Kingston Council knew I'd given you this."

"I promise I won't. You've been so kind." I shook his hand. "I don't know how to thank you."

"Think nothing of it," he said modestly. "I hope you get to see your children again soon."

With this he bade me farewell and I caught the next bus to Kingston only to discover they'd moved on again. I could've screamed. I couldn't take much more disappointment but I'd no time to feel sorry for myself. I needed no motivation to start knocking on neighbour's doors and asking if they knew of Frank and the children and if so, did they know where they were? Each flat I knocked on I got the same response; a shake of the head and the door was closed in my face. Eventually though and old lady answered her door and she directed me to a property agents office in the high street. My heart was beating fast as I hurried on down to the high street and I remember thinking if they couldn't help me I'd be back to square one. Finding their office I went inside and I was greeted by a middle aged man with a golden sun tan and wearing far too much after shave. I thought I was going to pass out from the strong aroma.

"Good day to you," he said gleefully. "How may I help?"

"I'm looking for my ex-husband and my children," I said handing the piece of paper with the Kingston address written on it. "It seems they've moved on from there and a neighbour has suggested you might be able to tell me where they're living. So can you help?"

Shaking his head: "It's against regulations. I'm afraid I'm not at liberty to reveal such information."

"Look," I said forcibly, "My ex is messing me about. He keeps moving from place to place trying to prevent me from seeing my children. So I don't give a stuff about your regulations. I assume the black book you're clutching for dear life has your clients records? So please, look in your book and tell me where they're living." I demanded, slamming my fist down on his desk.

He looked at me for a moment, his face told a story. Should he or shouldn't he help me? His compassionate face won the day and he flipped through his records.

"There's nothing I can do for you I'm afraid. I remember the gentleman now. When he handed back his key he was in a buoyant mood. He showed me his sailing tickets. I'm sorry to tell you they sailed to Australia a few days ago."

The shock was too much for me and I fainted. I woke to find myself lying on the floor and I was feeling numb all over. The man got me to my feet and any sympathy for me was secondary to getting me out the office. My distress wasn't good for business but my mind kept asking me the same question. How was I going to see my children again?

I decided to try the Australian Embassy but I got nowhere with them. I got the impression they thought I was some kind of mad woman. Oh they said they could sympathise but even if they'd the man power they couldn't possibly disclose confidential information without some kind of official request. I asked if they didn't have the authority to give me information on Frank's whereabouts what about my children? Surely I was entitled to know where my children were? I was politely told to go the British Embassy and perhaps they could help me. I realised I was just being fobbed off but none-the-less off I trotted but, as expected, I was met with the same bureaucratic attitude. Over the years I've made numerous visits to both Embassies in the vain hope of a more positive response but the answer was always the same. The people at reception were always very nice but they must have rolled their eyes when they saw me coming. I was on first name terms with some of them but this never earned me any brownie points.

Chapter 14

Forward on three years little had changed in my life. I was no further forward in tracing my children and I'd little money to do it with. My earnings from the pub was mainly consumed paying the rent and other bills. I was left with very little to buy food let alone anything else. If it hadn't been for the tips I could never have kept afloat. It wasn't as if I was living in some posh penthouse in Chelsea. Far from it. All I could afford was this one bedroom flat in a not so sort after area of Hammersmith. Putting it bluntly, the flat was a dump and it'd be condemned today. Earning a living in the pub wasn't the best place for me to be working when I'd a serious drink problem. To make things worse customers regularly bought me drinks and, I'm ashamed to say, I sometimes pinched a bottle spirits from the cellar. The more I sought comfort from the bottle the deeper I fell into depression. I knew the escape from my misery was always short lived and my constant drinking was doing nothing but worsen my mental state but I couldn't stop myself. I kept telling myself, I was just going through a rough patch that's all and I'd get through it. I could stop drinking at any time.

My children were growing up on the other side of the World and there was nothing I could do about it. I missed them terribly. Many a time I convinced myself I'd done something horribly wrong at some point in my life and this was my punishment. I must've deserved it. You didn't deserve this, old girl, you really didn't even though you ignored your doctor's advice to stop drinking. I know, I was a stupid cow. Regardless of the amount of times I was told I was damaging my health I kept on drinking despite vowing many times to stop. Of course I was never going to stop.

I'd no contact with my children and how I longed to just hold them and tell them I loved them. I often wondered what they were up to in Australia. I often visualised them playing on a beach in the hot sunshine. Did they make sure they were wearing enough suncream? Did they drink plenty of water to keep themselves hydrated? If they went into the sea did they take care. They'd have to watch out for sharks.

"Take care, my loves."

It was also three years since I last saw Mother but I was too proud and I didn't have the courage to go and knock on her door. I thought she was sure to slam the door in my face and wouldn't want to speak to me again. It was easier than reaching out for help and I realised I didn't have a friend in the World. Life was the pits for me; I just existed and if I'd ended it all nobody would've cared. I was tempted on many occasions to kill myself and there were two instances where I set out to do just that. I left home one morning full of intent to throw myself off Putney Bridge. I trampled along the streets this cold misty morning and I shivered as I felt the wind cut right through me. When I reached my destination I stood on the bridge, waiting for the right moment to jump, I didn't want some good Samaritan coming to my rescue. As I looked around I felt like a naughty school girl trying to make sure I wouldn't be seen doing something I shouldn't. The tension grew as the right moment to jump arrived. Then bizarrely I remembered I hadn't switched the radio off and I worried the noise at night would surely annoy the neighbours. I decided jumping off the bridge would wait for another day. On another occasion I contemplated putting my head in the gas oven where I could just kneel there until I was overcome by the fumes. There'd be no pain, I reasoned, I'd simply go to sleep forever. Searching through my purse I found I'd one shilling left to feed the meter which would give the gas sufficient time to do its work. Then I thought, wait a minute though, who'd find me? I could lay dead for weeks before I was discovered. There'd be an awful smell, I couldn't have that. Another trip to Putney Bridge would be the best bet but of course I never did. Let's be honest you never had any intention of going through with it because despite it all, no matter how low you got, Mother believed suicide was a sin and this belief she'd instilled in you so you'd never go through with it. This was one of life's ironies, wasn't it? Mother's actions had contributed so much to my state of mind and yet the beliefs she'd instilled in me meant I'd never take my own life. Perhaps though it was more simple than that? Perhaps I was hanging on to the vain hope I'd see my children again even though there was no possibility of me affording a trip to Australia? I just had to hope Frank would grow tied being on the other side of the World and he'd bring the children back to London.

My drinking continued unabated and I got more and more depressed. My mood was noticed at the pub and my manager was very concerned about me. He took me aside one day and tactfully suggested I seek professional help for my depression. I tried to make light of it all but he persisted. He suggested or rather insisted I consulted my doctor who perhaps would refer me to a specialist. I wasn't keen but to appease my manager I made an appointment with my doctor. At first he was very good with me and much to my relief he felt he'd be able help without the need to involve a specialist. Initially he prescribed some pills but frankly they didn't really do any good. I was though having weekly appointments with him and I have to say talking about my problems seemed to help. These consultations went on for several months but one day I arrived in his surgery to find another man there with him. My doctor explained this man was a college of his from Harley Street who specialised in mental health and he was here to help me. Why someone from Harley Street was bothering with the likes of me I don't know but I gathered the two doctors had trained together at University. My doctor claimed I'd agreed for this specialist to be present but I didn't recall agreeing to any such thing. Neither do I remember this specialist's name but his diagnosis was somewhat alarming. Things seemed to happen so fast, one minute I was feeling optimistic and the next minute I was pleading for my freedom. According to this specialist I was suffering a mental breakdown and there was no alternative but to refer me to a mental institution. My head was spinning, I couldn't believe what he was saying and I felt my doctor had betrayed me. I pleaded it wasn't that serious a problem and I wasn't mad, I was just feeling a little depressed. I promised to give up the booze but my doctor was quick to point out I'd previously said this many times before. A mental home was for my own good but I protested a mental institution wasn't going to help me trace my children; I just needed the means to find out where they were.

Worse was to come. When I tried to leave the surgery I was met at the door by two burly blokes in white coats who forcibly held me down whilst my doctor stuck this dirty great big needle into me. It was like some horror film. It all seemed so unreal. Surely they couldn't do this? Wasn't there laws against this? They put me into a strait jacket and they dragged me into the back of a van with me kicking and screaming. There were other patients in the surgery waiting room but they just looked the other way when I cried out for help. If only Mother had been there but we weren't on speaking terms. I just couldn't believe this was happening and I must've passed out presumably from the effects of the drug. Next thing I knew the van doors opened and I was dragged from my seat and frog marched into this mental institution. I happened to glance up at the clock which sat proudly above the buildings entrance and I deduced the journey must have taken about forty-five minutes to an hour. So where was this place? I kept telling myself I was just having a nightmare and at any minute I'd wake up to find myself at home in bed. I was taken to this sterile looking room where I was left alone still wearing a strait jacket before I was finally released from it. To say I was terrified was an understatement and I spent these hours sobbing continuously. This was the most terrifying situation I'd ever been in and I was infinitely more terrified than I ever was of the Evil Witch. As I sobbed though, my head began to clear and I became more calm. I reasoned what was happening to me was surely illegal but I'd no means of alerting the Police or contacting anyone who could help me. It even crossed my mind at the time that somehow Frank was behind all this. I tried to dismiss this thought and I told myself Frank was in Australia and therefore couldn't possibly have anything to do with it. Or could he? Had he conspired with these doctors against me? If I was locked away, declared insane even, I'd have no chance of finding out where my children were. People have since reasoned I must've remembered the incident wrong and protocol would've been followed. I think some thought I was lying but nobody said it to my face. All I can I say is a lot of things that went on back then wouldn't happen today. I know it sounds implausible but as God is my witness, I swear this is the truth and I'm not exaggerating. I was alone and scared shitless. I feared for my life and I kept asking myself who were these monsters and what had I done to deserve this?

When finally one of the doctors came into the room and informed me he was tasked with assessing my state of mind, I didn't feel any better about the situation. He soon made his mind up, or he'd probably decided before he'd even met me, I'd suffered a mental breakdown. He told me rather coldly, in his professional opinion, I was a danger to myself and to others. This was getting far too ridiculous I thought. For goodness sake I wasn't a danger? I wasn't mad I told him. I tried to assure him things had just got on top of me lately but I'd be all right now. He was having none of it and he said I needed rest and my alcoholism must be tackled with the utmost urgency. I tried to laugh it off. I wasn't an alcoholic and, even if I was, this was surely not the place for me to be. It was just there were occasions, I'd admit, when I'd have one drink too many. I was asked to hold out my hands which gave me away; it would've been clear even to a blind person my hands were shaking. I reasoned it was just nerves and once I'd a couple of drinks I'd be fine. Stupid cow. Fancy saying this, what a dope! You'd talked yourself into a corner but deep down you knew the doctor was right and he knew you knew it. You were an alcoholic. Then you went and blew it. You were assured you could be cured but you flew into a rage when he said you'd have to stay in the hospital for about six months. I shouldn't have done this, I know, but I tried to explain about my children but he wasn't listening. I stressed the need for me to speak to the British or Australian Embassy and I explained I'd tried several times before but I was always fobbed off. I said I must try again but he just shrugged his shoulders and merely suggested I could write a letter. I could see I wasn't getting through to him and the shrugging of his shoulders suggested to me he didn't care and then I lost it. You lost it all right, you shamefully and violently attached him by forcibly slapping his face several times and simultaneously kicking at his ankles. Don't forget the left hook I landed on his chin. It's not funny. It was a very silly thing to do and this landed you in more trouble. Great left hook though, wasn't it? It's nothing to be proud of. Don't tell Peter and Sally you hit this doctor, for goodness sake. Why shouldn't I tell them? It's best they don't know this. Just say you became so hysterical a male nurse was summoned. I hit him as well, didn't I? So you did but don't admit this either. Just explain you were put back into the straight jacket after the doctor had injected you with a calming drug. The same drug, no doubt, my doctor had given me hours before. I certainly passed out again, that's for sure.

Whilst I was at the hospital I was kept in a ward with a number of other patients. Most of them were sadly old and senile which made me fear what would become of me if I remained at the hospital. Apart from a few of the patients, I couldn't have a chat with these poor people. Even the ones I could

199

talk to it soon became apparent to me there was something amiss with them. For example: there was Liz who was convinced she was the Queen and she demanded everyone should kneel at her feet. In our ward, at least, we were all fitted out with hospital gowns but Liz had gotten hold of this fake crown decorated with obvious fake diamonds which she wore on her head. I overheard a member of staff suggest her son must have given it to her as he worked in the props department for a theatre in London. As this crown looked less than convincing it was surmised he'd given it to his mother as probably no self-respecting actress would want to wear it. Nobody dared to take it off her, though, if they did she'd scream the place down and for a quiet life the nurses let her wear it. Curiously her hair was similarly styled to the Queen's but any resemblance ended there and she certainly didn't possess any of Her Majesty's elegance. I remember one day I was sitting at my bed, reading a book, when it was suddenly snatched out of my hand.

"You there!" Liz said pointing at me. Go and fetch the dogs, I desire to walk them in the grounds. I may even adventure to the riverbank."

"Riverbank? What riverbank would that be?" I asked.

"Your Majesty," she barked. "What riverbank would that be, your Majesty?"

I decided to play along: "What riverbank would that be, your Majesty?"

"The River Thames, of course," she tutted. "Don't you know the Thames runs through Windsor?"

"Oh, we're in Windsor, are we your Majesty?" I replied with a little sarcasm.

"Where did you think we were, girl?" she demanded.

By this time I was finding it hard not to laugh: "Buckingham Palace, your Majesty?"

"Silly girl," she replied, shaking her head. "We don't spend our weekends at Buckingham Palace!"

She then walked off and I started to giggle. On other occasions she'd sentence me to the Tower, which is curious, because she thought she was the current Queen. She seemed oblivious to the fact the Monarchy no longer had this power and the Tower is no longer used as a prison. To keep her sweet though I'd just got up and walked out and came back later when she'd forgotten all about it.

In the bed next to Liz was Doris who was capable of holding a sensible conversation one minute but then be totally crazy the next. She wore glasses which were generally perched on the end of her nose and she'd peer over the top of them. Her hair was long and it was often spiked up just like Ken Dodd used to have his.

"How are you today?" she asked me one day.

"Not so bad, Doris" I replied, not wishing to discuss how I was feeling.

"Don't let them grind you down. If you do, they'd have won," she warned.

"You mean the staff here?" I asked.

201

"Some of them are not so bad but watch out for that Donaldson fellow, he's a nasty piece of work," she said with a mixture of fear and defiance.

"I don't like him either," I nodded. "Ex-military, isn't he?"

"CIA, no less," she countered.

I nodded again. Donaldson was a British as British could be, so why he was once part of the CIA was beyond me but I played along.

"What's a CIA man doing in a place like this?" I asked.

Ignoring my question: "The Martians are coming!" she shouted. Quick, everyone, hide under your beds. They'll take no prisoners."

Doris ran around the ward telling everyone to get under their beds. She got herself worked up and she became hysterical, shouting and screaming at everyone. She picked up anything she could lay her hands on and threw them at other patients. The nurses could do nothing but restrain and sedate her but the next day she behaved as if nothing had happened.

Mary occupied the bed opposite to me and on first impressions she appeared to be completely sane. She wore her hair neatly tied in a bun and she clearly took pride in her appearance but my question as to why she was a patient was soon answered. It became clear to me that Mary, in her mind's eye, was living in Tudor times. With all sincerity she'd talk about King Henry VIII as if he was still ruling England. She even suggested to me she nearly became his wife but she was passed over in favour of her younger sister, Anne Boleyn. It is documented Ann Boleyn did have a sister called Mary but, as far as I know, there's no suggestion the two sisters competed for Henry's affections. Mary firmly believed he'd live to regret marrying Ann and then he'd realise she was a much more suitable wife for him. It was only a matter of time, she believed, when he'd send for her and she'd live out the rest of her life at the Palace. Maggie, one of the patients in our ward, who wasn't in the least bothered about dispelling Mary's fantasy was blunt enough to try and put her straight.

"But Mary," Maggie said bluntly. "Even if you were Ann Boleyn's sister, which clearly you're not, you should consider yourself fortunate you didn't marry Henry as he had Ann Boleyn executed".

"My point exactly," replied Mary, "it just proves Henry picked the wrong sister."

Maggie was persuaded by the nurses not to continue with the debate for it was best to leave Mary to live in her own fantasy world. As for Maggie, I couldn't fathom out what she was doing there as a patient. As far as I was concerned she was as sane as I was.

I didn't feel sorry for the likes of Liz, Doris and Mary. They were at least living albeit in a world of their own. It was the other women who just lay there in a vegetive state I pitied. Drugged up to the eyeballs, as far as I was concerned these people may as well be dead. From what I could gather the official reason for drugging these poor people was due to their violent tendencies. Violent tendencies!

My arse! These people were far too frail to be capable of violence. No, they were drugged because then they'd be less of a problem for the hospital. Their lives didn't matter. It makes angry even now to think about it. It was absolutely horrifying they were treated this way and I knew I had to watch my step. I didn't want those in charge to conclude I'd violent tendencies and I also realised I had to get out or I could easily end my days there. The trouble was getting out wasn't going to be easy. My feeling was it'd be some considerable time, if ever at all, when the doctors would decide it was safe for me to go home. I wasn't allowed outside the grounds so I couldn't just leave and not come back. It was clear those in authority weren't going to give me the opportunity to escape. I wasn't even sure where I was; I only knew I was in a mental hospital which was called Hillbury. Other than that nobody seemed willing to tell me exactly where Hillbury was and it seemed to me its location was a secret. So secretive was everybody I began to think if anybody spoke of Hillbury's location they'd be tried for treason. Not even the groundsman, who was a friendly sort of bloke, was willing to discuss Hillbury's location. I knew I was about forty-five minutes from London but I'd no idea if I was north, south, east or west of the city. Not having any visitors made things even worse for me and I often felt very lonely and isolated. Some of the patients had visitors but if I ever tried to talk to any of these people the nurses immediately intervened. Not that these visitors showed much willingness to have a conversation with me anyway. I came to the conclusion they'd all been briefed on what they were allowed to do and what they were allowed to say and it didn't include talking to the likes of me.

Hillbury was a grim Victorian building with grey corridors and dull yellow walls provided the backdrop for each hospital ward. To some extent it reminded me of my days at the convent and the Evil Witch would've been in her element. I could've just imagined her carrying out her own brand of cruelty and reeling in it. In contrast to the wards the hospital grounds were somewhat pleasant and calming with attractive flower beds and neatly cut lawns each way I looked. For me the exit gate was by far the most appealing part of the grounds if only the security guard wasn't there. Climbing over the wall wasn't an option as this was thoroughly layered with barbed wire. Anyone would've been forgiven for thinking Hillbury was a prison as in all tense and purposes it was. Some of the inmates, if this is the right word, were allowed out during the day and provided they weren't a threat to the public they were free to roam Hillbury Village by themselves.

I often overheard gossip amongst the hospital staff and I learned quite a lot about some of the inmates. One of those who was allowed beyond the gates was known to everyone as Spider Trapman. Admittedly he was only allowed out to visit his mother but my instincts told me to be wary of him. I can't explain why because he never bothered me but his whole demeanor concerned me. I'm probably being unjust but I always felt he was capable of violent acts. He was a big man so I imagined if he'd suddenly gone crazy it would've taken several male nurses to restrain him. What his real name was I never found out but for reasons be-known only to themselves some village children had given him this nickname and it stuck. It wasn't because he'd an interest in spiders, as far as anyone could tell, so it was probably just the wild imagination of some twelve year old. From what I could gather, he didn't take kindly to being called Spider Trapman and I can't blame him for that, it's hardly a flattering nickname.

One day I heard some of the hospital staff talking about Spider Trapman. I was in one of the lavatories and the window was open. I could hear them talking and they were probably outside having a quick fag or something. From what I could gather, before being admitted to the hospital Spider Trapman had lived with his mother in a bungalow in Kings Street. I didn't know where King Street was but I'd gathered it was somewhere in the village. For whatever reason he'd always lived with his mother and when I knew him he was man probably in his fifties and I remember his face was ruddy and blotchy. His hair was short and curly. One of the staff said a pedestrian alleyway, called The Cut, rang alongside the property. Some barbed wire had been tied across the width of The Cut which stretched head height to a telephone poll. One evening an unsuspecting cyclist, who admittedly shouldn't have been cycling on the path, fell off his cycle after the barbed wire cut forehead. Fortunately he only suffered minor cuts and bruises but immediate suspicion lay at Spider Trapman's door. It has to be said there wasn't any evidence to prove he'd been the culprit and no one was ever charged for this incident. There were those who came to his defense and argued just because he lived by The Cut didn't prove he done it. After all, they pointed out, someone also lived on the other side of the alleyway but nobody was accusing them. The most likely culprits, they argued, were the local yobs who probably thought it'd be amusing to cause someone harm.

Some of the children used to wind him up by running down The Cut and chanting "Spider Trapman" and he'd come out of the bungalow swearing and cursing. The children's taunting upset him so much he went to his doctor asking to be admitted to Hillbury as he'd become very depressed. He must've thought a short spell in the hospital would give him a bit of peace but he got more than he bargained for. Not only did his doctor recommend a long stay in the hospital he became a virtual prisoner. So was he a villain or a victim? Had he simply paid the price for being different or was he a danger to himself and to others? Who knows?

I also overheard them talk about another inmate called Kenny who was also privileged to leave the grounds. It was clear for all to see Kenny was harmless and they knew he'd never try to run away and why would he? Where would he go to start with? This sounds unkind but he didn't have all his marbles and I think the hospital was the best place for him. After all, he'd free board and lodgings and the hospital staff afforded him a certain amount of freedom. He was a short, baldheaded, plump man and he was mad in my opinion. Apparently, goaded on by the children, he often wondered down King Street shouting "Vietnam, Vietnam, join the army, Vietnam". The children often joined in and he became more agitated and started swearing at them. One day a firework exploded in a rubbish bin just at the point he walked by and the air turned blue in more ways than one.

It was ironic then that these two men aided me in my escape from Hillbury. How they came to help me escape was purely unintentional but, all the same, I shall always be grateful to them.

Before my escape I'd made up my mind to break into the office to make a telephone call to the British Embassy in Australia. I'd chosen the moment carefully. It was late in the evening and I was confident I wouldn't be discovered in the office especially if I didn't turn the light on. Breaking in had been easy. The lock wasn't a very good one and I'd no trouble in forcing it open. It was also the right moment to make myself scarce in the ward. I'd observed the nurse on night duty always sneaked out for a fag and she'd be gone about fifteen minutes. Whilst she wasn't at her desk I'd taken a small torch from the draw and as long as I put it back where I found it no one would be any the wiser. I located the phone and with the torch shining on the dials I called the operator.

"Operator, can you get me the British Embassy in Australia, please?" I asked kneeling behind the desk."

"Have you the number, please?" enquired the Operator.

"I don't know the number," I replied.

"I need the number caller," the operator advised.

"Yes, I understand that but this is an emergency. Please help me. I desperately need to speak to the British Embassy in Australia. Somebody in your organisation must know the number. Please, I'm begging."

"I'll see what I can do. I'll call you back," the operator replied.

Whilst I waited for the operator I could hear footsteps coming from the corridor so I crouched down on the floor to avoid detection. The door opened and a flashlight shone around the room. I held my breath. After what was only a few moments but seemed like eternity the flashlight was switched off and the door was closed. I breathed a sigh of relief. I hadn't factored in the caretaker doing his rounds before retiring for the night. I don't know why he hadn't registered the lock had been forced open but I thought this was my lucky break. The phone then rang and in my haste I knocked the receiver off the desk. I remember thinking had the caretaker heard the phone ring? Perhaps he hadn't or had he chosen to ignore it? Maybe he was in a hurry to get home and he didn't want to be bothered dealing with a phone call? Whatever my luck was definitely in, I thought. I scrambled along the floor and I picked up the receiver.

"Your call to the British Embassy in Australia," announced the operator. "I'm putting you through."

"I need your help," I told the Embassy. "My name is Marie Benjamin. My former husband, Frank Brown, has moved to Sydney with my two children, Peter and Sally. I'm desperate to find out their address."

I was informed due to the lack of information they didn't hold out much hope of tracing them. It was pointed out to me that Sydney was a big place even if they were living there. At least I was getting further with them in Australia than I'd with those in London. I was asked for my number, which I couldn't give, so I had to make the excuse I was staying with a friend so it was best I rang them again in a few days. At that moment the door was flung open. The office light was switched on.

"You can come out from hiding behind the desk, Benjamin," barked a male nurse."

He was a burly Brutus like man who had no trouble in hoisted me out of the office, like a piece of paper thrown into a paper basket, before locking the door.

"You're not allowed in there," he barked. "I shall have to report you for this."

"Oh please don't," I begged. "I wasn't doing any harm, honest."

"What was you doing in there?" he asked, his manner softening slightly.

"I'm trying to find out where my children are. Their father has taken them away from me, you see." I replied without revealing the full facts.

"That sounds tough. I wouldn't want to be parted from my kids." He paused for thought. "Look, go back to your ward, I won't report you this time but don't let me catch you in there again. Understood?"

I nodded and hurried back to my ward, relieved I wasn't going to be reported. Heaven knows what those Hitlers in authority would've done had they'd found out what I'd been up to. It was just my bad luck the nurse on night duty had returned from her fag break much earlier than usual. She told the male nurse, who happened to pass by, I was missing and guessed I might be in the office as I was always asking to make a phone call. I spent the next few weeks feeling thoroughly depressed because I couldn't see a way out and I was sure those in authority had it in for me. In fact I wasn't popular with any of the staff and it seemed the World was against me. I suppose from their point of view I was just a pest who didn't toe the line. They said I was always complaining and saying I didn't belong there. I wouldn't take no for answer when I kept asking to use the phone. They wanted patients who did as they were told and I was probably regarded as a potential bad influence on other patients. I was feeling sorry for myself but then, out of the blue, my luck change for the better.

I was walking in the grounds getting some fresh air and exercise which was something the medical staff encouraged. I always wandered close to the exit gate in the vain hope the security guard would take pity on me and let me out which, in reality, was never going to happen. I was about to return to my ward when suddenly Kenny came running up to the security guard, swearing like a trouper and in a blind panic, shouting Spider Trapman had set fire to the hedge. At first the guard dismissed Kenny's claims and told him not to tell tales. Within moments though he realised this wasn't just Kenny being Kenny but well and truly the hedge was on fire and it burning some. The flames were several feet high and rising steadily and smoke filled the air. The guard rushed to the scene and attempted to beat out the flames with his jacket but it was already too late to stop the hedge from being destroyed. Amongst all the mayhem I witnessed Spider Trapman running from the scene with a guilty look on his face. I'll never know if he started the fire deliberately and at the time I frankly didn't care. This was my chance. The gate was unguarded and without giving it a second thought I ran across the road to the street opposite. I noticed the obscured sign which read Kings Street but this wasn't the time to dwell on it and my only thought was getting as far away from the hospital as I could. I couldn't believe my luck and, had the opportunity arisen, I would've kissed Kenny and Spider Trapman for unwittingly helping me to escape. I knew though, this was only the beginning, I'd need Lady Luck to stay with me if I was to stay out of Hillbury.

I ran downhill in Kings Street which made it easier for an unfit person like me and the sheer elation and adrenaline allowed me to run that bit faster. My spirits took a bit of a nose dive when I glanced over my shoulder to see a male nurse in pursuit. He must have spotted me running away but damn him for not making the fire his priority. Why was he worrying about me for goodness sake? He should've been more concerned about the safety others and he should've been helping put out the fire. I managed to find some inner strength and I speeded up a little; I'd be damned if I was going to let him catch me. In front of me there'd been a few people walking up Kings Street but they'd crossed the road presumably wishing to avoid me. They probably thought I was a mad woman running from Hillbury and they didn't feel brave enough to confront me. They might have thought I was dangerous?

"I can't be caught now," I remember telling myself. "I may never get another chance."

I got to the bottom of the hill but I saw there was a steep climb in front of me. This was the last thing I wanted as I was already panting heavily for breath and I thought my chest was going to explode at any minute. Instinctively I turned right into an alleyway and this turned out to be a good move as I was running on flat ground. I glanced over my shoulder to see the nurse still in pursuit. Swine! I took some encouragement though as he hadn't appeared to have gained any ground on me. With any luck, I thought, he might not have realised I'd taken the alleyway but this was wishful thinking on my part. It then occurred to me this must be Spider Trapman's alley and if so the irony wasn't lost on me. Best look out for any barbed wire I thought, just in case. I ran along which I believed to be The Cut and I came to a road where I quickly crossed over to a grassed area. I got the impression I was in a new housing estate, judging by the buildings, certainly built more recently than those in King Street. Not that I'd the time to study the houses but my observing tendency kicked in automatically. Having run across the grass, I ran along a path parallel to some bungalows on my right but I had to dodge one elderly occupant who chose this precise moment to step out in front of me. Instinctively I took the road to my right but I found myself running slightly uphill which I could've done without. I'd long since been running only on adrenaline but I couldn't entertain the thought this wasn't going to sustain me for much longer. My body was demanding me to collapse but my mind wouldn't hear of it. I kept telling myself I couldn't be caught, I just couldn't.

I was gasping for breath and I thought my lungs were going to explode like a volcano erupting. My body was aching all over, each muscle felt like lead weights, my calves protested and I feared getting cramp at any moment. With each step I took, my knees threatened to lock if I persisted with this sadistic punishment. If only I'd taken athletics more seriously at school and joined a running club or something. I glanced over my shoulder once more to see the nurse on his way through The Cut. He was a persistent bugger, I had to give him that but why had he picked on me? He didn't pick on you, he was just doing his job. You ran away and he followed after you. Simple as that. It didn't feel like it at the time, I felt the World was against me. When I turned the corner to be confronted with a dead end road I felt nothing but despair. I was trapped, my legs were refusing to run anymore and my lungs could take no more. I'd made it so far but the nurse was sure to catch me and take me back to Hillbury. My legs buckled and my knees hit the ground but then I heard a voice cry out.

"Quick this way" shouted a man, I later learned to be Andrew, beaconing me down his driveway. "Come in, quick," he commanded.

What was I to do? Trust this man? You had to trust him otherwise you'd have been caught. Somehow I got up and I negotiated with my legs and lungs to allow me to run into Andrew's house. I stood in the hallway exhausted but I slowly began to get my breath back. I leant against a windowsill as my legs weren't willing to allow me to stand upright. It seemed like I'd have to consult The Legs Union before I could stand unaided once more. I watched Andrew, through net curtains, sweeping his driveway and moments later the nurse arrived on the scene. I listened intently and I could just about hear their conversation.

"Have you seen a woman come running this way?" the nurse asked.

"What woman would that be?" Andrew replied.

215

"She's escaped from Hillbury Hospital," the nurse told him. "She's one of those half casts. You know the sort. So if you've seen her?"

"No I don't know the sort," Andrew answered clearly unimpressed with his derogatory description of me. I did see a woman with dark skin run up that maisonette's garden path over there. The one with the high hedge. I think I saw her go into the back garden. You can get to it by going through the white painted gate."

The nurse thanked him and he made his way as Andrew had instructed. Andrew watched as he entered the maisonette's garden and when he was out of sight Andrew returned to the house and I heard him hurry upstairs. Moments later he came down again and handed me a long blonde wig.

"No time to lose," Andrew said. "Put this on. They won't be looking for a blonde."

I didn't know what Andrew intended to do but I was out options so I put the wig on. He led me through his kitchen, out of the back door, into his garage via its side entrance. I sat in his car whilst he opened the main garage door before he drove up his drive and onto the road.

"Keep your head down so no one can see your face," he told me.

"Your garage door, you've left it open," I gestured to him but still facing the floor.

"It'll be fine," he answered. "There's nothing worth nicking. I'm Andrew, by the way, what's your name?"

"Marie," I answered.

"Nice to meet you, Marie," smiled Andrew.

Andrew looked into his rear view mirror and began to laugh. I was still facing the floor and I asked him what he was laughing at. Andrew explained he'd not sent the nurse into just anybody's garden but none other than the fearsome Moany Groany's. She'd many confrontations with the kids, who played football and cricket on the green and, if a ball landed in her garden her front door was flung open and she came out foaming at the mouth. It was then a race between her and the kids to get to the ball first. Her accommodation was on the second floor which gave the kids an advantage but if she got there first she confiscated it and it took a parent to get it back. What used to annoy her the most was when the ball rolled up her path but rolled back down again before she could get hold of it. Whenever she appeared the boys used to sing *Moany Groany* to the tune of *Mony Mony* a song recorded by a sixties pop group called *Tommy James And The Shondells*.

Andrew caught sight of the nurse scurrying down the path with Moany Groany waving her fist. She was notorious for her scolding tongue and it looked like the nurse was getting a severe ear bashing. Andrew hoped so, anyway. He was still chuckling when he reached the edge of the village where he told me I could sit up. As he drove me out of the village he lit his pipe, puffed it gently out of one side of his mouth, still smiling out of the other. He was a middle aged man, his face was well lined, his brown eyes revealing a tint of sadness behind

217

those warm smiles. Obviously I was very grateful to him but I was curious to know why he'd helped me when many people wouldn't have done. Andrew revealed he'd been in his garden and, being on a corner, he could see across his neighbour's gardens and saw me running. It was clear to him I was running from someone and judging by the anguish on my face I was desperate not to get caught. At this point he didn't know if he was going to help me or not but he gave me benefit of the doubt until he'd discovered more. He candidly stated had I been running from the Police, having stolen something or if I'd been guilty of vandalism, he'd have handed me over without hesitation. Two reasons decided him to help me. I'd escaped from Hillbury and the nurses racist attitude towards me. I told him I'd been called worse and the nurse probably saw nothing wrong in what he said. Andrew said I shouldn't accept such derogatory remarks and he was right but things were different back then. The nurse's attitude wasn't the half of it though, he'd a score to settle with Hillbury.

I listened intently to Andrew's sad tale and why he held the hospital responsible for his wife's death. The coroner's verdict was suicide and he accepted this but it was their barbaric treatment of her which had driven her to it. Having had firsthand experience of Hillbury I'd no doubt he wasn't exaggerating when he described the anguish his wife had endured. He'd never forgive himself for not doing something about it before it was too late. He'd been persuaded to allow his wife to be admitted to the hospital for her depression but she constantly begged him to have the electric shock treatment stopped. He constantly had nightmares and restless nights going through his mind what he should and shouldn't have done. Whilst it was too late for his wife he'd made a promise to himself to help any poor unfortunate soul who'd become a victim of Hillbury. His tragic story left me in no doubt I'd done the right thing in escaping from Hillbury. I shuddered to think what might have happened had I'd remained and I told him how grateful I was for his kindness. I explained how Spider Trapman and Kenny had unwittingly helped me escape.

"I think it's no exaggeration to suggest they saved your life," Andrew said. "In my opinion these two are your unlikely heroes."

"Spider Trapman and Kenny, my heroes?" I paused for a moment to ponder his suggestion before nodding in agreement.

Then we both laughed. I hadn't laughed so far much in a long time and it made a change to experience tears of laughter rather than sorrow. They obviously hadn't intended to help me and they were both probably totally oblivious to the fact I'd escaped. It didn't matter though. I was eternally grateful to them and it was just a pity I wouldn't get the opportunity to thank them.

Andrew told me he'd two grown up sons and they'd both moved away but they met up on occasions. We'd travelled a number of miles and I hadn't asked him where we were going. I was about to do so when he pulled some cash from his pocket and placed it in my hands.

I gasped: "Fifty pounds! That's a lot of money, I can't accept this."

He shook his head: "Take it, I can afford it. I've more than enough money for my needs and my boys have well paid jobs so they don't need it."

"You always need money for a rainy day." I suggested.

"Don't worry, I've got plenty of money stashed away at home where no one can find it. Only my boys know where I keep my savings which they can share between them when I'm gone. So I don't have to worry about them. Before you say anything, I know I should put the money in a bank but I don't trust them and I don't want the tax man getting their hands on any of it after I've fallen off this mortal coil. Now I'm going to drop you off at a tube station. Buy a ticket to one of the mainline stations in London and get yourself as far away as possible. Don't tell me where you're going," he warned. "Then if someone should come knocking at my door, I won't be able to tell them where you've gone even if they try beating it out of me."

For the rest of the journey he continued to smoke his pipe and I stared aimlessly out of the window. Where would I go? Down towards Devon or Cornwall perhaps? Or maybe a shorter journey to Norfolk or Suffolk? How about up north somewhere? There were many possibilities and I felt quite excited by the fact. It seemed in no time at all we'd arrived outside the tube station.

"How can I ever repay you?" I asked.

"Make a success of your life and above all, don't get caught," he commanded.

I handed the wig back to him. He shook his head.

"You can keep it," he offered, "it's of no use to me."

"Thank you but no," I replied dropping the wig onto the passenger seat. "Without that wig I'm just another coloured girl. People expect folk like me to have dark hair. Wearing that wig I'm likely to stand out like a sore thumb. I need to blend in."

He nodded and smiled. He waived as he drove away.

"God bless you," I called out as I watched him pass through the traffic lights, round the corner and out of view.

Chapter 15

I bought a single ticket to Central London and I sat in one of the carriages towards the rear of the station. Suddenly it dawned on me. I'd escaped Hillbury but what the heck was I going to do now? The practicalities of going anywhere but London occupied my mind. If I went elsewhere whether it be south, west, east or north I didn't have a clue where to go. A large city? A small town? A pretty little village? I'd be lost. I concluded the only thing I could do was stay in the Capital where it was easy for me to blend in. In another place I might stand out in a crowd and the wrong thing said to the wrong person could lead a trail back to those at Hillbury. I couldn't risk that. The initial euphoria of escaping Hillbury faded rapidly when the realisation dawned on me I'd nowhere to stay. I couldn't go back to my flat as this would be the first place they'd come looking for me. I thought of a reconciliation with Mother but even if she did welcome me with open arms they'd surely come knocking at her door. I was a fugitive, no two ways about it. You were so desperate to escape Hillbury you hadn't given any real thought what you'd do afterwards. I'd have to live on the streets where I'd be invisible to those in authority. It hadn't dawned on me until then the temptation for the demon drink would rear its ugly head once more. The good thing about Hillbury, if there was anything good about Hillbury, was I didn't have access to alcohol. I was beginning to get the better of my addiction but I realised then there'd be no one to stop me having a drink. I knew I'd have to rely on a great deal of willpower if I was going avoid drinking again but this was going to be a challenge. Suddenly I wasn't looking forward to reaching London; I feared what the rest of seventies had in store for me.

The rest of my tube journey I sat deep in thought and formalising a plan for what lay ahead of me. If I was going to sleep rough I needed to buy a warm sleeping bag. As I got nearer to my destination I became more anxious and the time it took between each station seemed to lessen with every stop. I even thought about travelling around the tube network for as long as I could but I realised buying a sleeping bag was my immediate priority. Departing from the tube station I sought out the camping shops but the cost for any half decent bag was rather pricy I thought. I was reluctant to spend a lot on this one item as I wanted to make my money last as long as possible. My plan was to reserve some money for a night's accommodation for those particularly cold nights. A sleeping bag though was an essential item for me so I resigned myself to spend more than I wanted. I was about to purchase an expensive bag I'd seen in a shop window when I spied a second hand camping shop. With nothing to lose I ventured inside and scanned the shop hoping to spot what I was looking for.

"Can I help you, Madam?" the lady shop assistant enquired.

"Don't suppose you've got a sleeping bag for sale?" I asked looking round the shop but not seeing one.

"I think you're in luck there," she replied. "I've got one in the back of the shop. I'd put it aside for someone but they haven't come back for it. So if you want it?"

"I'd like to take a look at it." I countered.

She nodded and disappeared round the back but as I surveyed the shop I wasn't feeling too hopeful. The shop was dirty, the goods looked shabby at best and the place smelt of something none too pleasant. I decided to make a quick exit and buy the one I'd seen in the shop window opposite. All on offer in this place was bound to be dirty and smelly so I was wasting my time. As I turned to leave the lady returned with the sleeping bag and to my surprise it was in very good condition. Like new in fact.

"How much?" I asked.

"Five pounds," she replied.

I pulled a face. It was worth it but I still didn't want to spend this much so I fiddled around in my pockets as if I was searching for some cash. She looked at me and must have thought if I couldn't afford five pounds for such a good sleeping bag I must be hard up.

"Oh go on, give us a quid and it's yours," she said smiling. "And you can have this old ruck sack to carry it in. It's very tatty and I haven't been able to sell it but it'll do you turn."

I paid up at once and left the shop before she changed her mind. I hadn't thought about carrying the sleeping bag around with me and I soon realised I was glad of the ruck sack.

My bargain purchase perked me up a bit but before I could look for somewhere safe to stay I'd have to risk returning home just the once. I needed to pick up a few essential things such as some clothing and footwear. What I collected needed to fit in one bag so I had to choose carefully. My plan was to get my things when it was dark and hope the landlord hadn't re-let the flat and dumped my possessions out onto the street. Night had fallen when I stood in the shadows across the street from my flat. I was relieved to see the estate agents sign stating it was available for rent. My next thought was one of annoyance as clearly he wasn't expecting me to return and to continue my tenancy. I had to be thankful though for small mercies because if lights were blazing in the property I'd been stuffed. My keys had been taken from me when I was admitted to Hillbury but I'd hidden a front door key behind the drain pipe. Wherever I've lived I've always hidden a key outside in case I ever inadvertently locked myself out. I never did of course but it was a habit I'd picked up from Mother. Frank used to complain about this but it was a good job I hadn't listened to him.

The weather conditions couldn't have been better as I cautiously made way towards the front door and I continued to look over my shoulder. Thick fog was everywhere and it was difficulty to see more than ten yards in front of me. I was confident no one would see me entering my flat and

I could slip in and out undetected. Never-the-less I continued to be cautious as each step took me closer to my door but, having surveyed the area, I was satisfied nobody was watching. Having retrieved the key I opened the front door and entered quietly. I was relieved to get inside, it had occurred to me the landlord may have changed the locks, thankfully he hadn't. It was also fortunate he hadn't got rid of my things and I remained in the flat no longer than I needed to. I collected my things without turning on a light and I remembered I'd hidden twenty pounds in the bedroom, in case of emergency, in the false bottom of the chest of drawers. Hiding money in the house was another habit I'd picked up from Mother and sure enough the cash was still there. When I left I made sure the door was locked securely as I didn't want anyone to suspect I'd been there. Nobody was going to notice the few things I'd taken and I quickly scurried off into the night and vanished into the fog.

It was a sobering thought to realise home from then on was living on the Streets of London. I'd be lying if I said I wasn't scared but I'd have to prepare myself the best I could and try and make the best of it. I needed to remain positive and believe I was down but not out and things would get better. When and how I'd no idea; I'd got my freedom but I'd paid one hell of a price for it. Yet no matter how low things got I never regretted escaping from Hillbury. The only money I had was the cash I'd retrieved from my flat save what Andrew had generously given me less the tube fare and the cost of the sleeping bag. I didn't want anybody to know I'd some cash and risk being robbed or worse so I made sure I kept my money well hidden; tucked inside my knickers. You better make it clear to Peter and Sally you hadn't picked this habit up from Mother. I decided if anyone remarked on my nice new looking sleeping bag I'd tell them where I bought it and for how much. I could have claimed I'd stolen it, in a bid to impress, but I thought honesty was the best policy in this instance.

For my first night I slept in an alleyway which gave me shelter from the freezing wind. A fellow rough sleeper, a seasoned campaigner, known to everyone as Old Bill showed me where to stay. He'd seen me wondering around and guessed I was looking for somewhere to lay my head. It was pretty obvious, you'd a sleeping bag sticking out the top of your ruck sack so it didn't take a genius to work this one out.

"Looking for somewhere to spend the night?" Old Bill asked.

"Why do you ask?" I replied rather defensively.

"You look lost, dear. Come with me," he gestured.

He walked on a few paces but I wasn't sure what to do. I considered running off in the opposite direction but then he stopped and turned round.

"It's all right, dear. Don't be afraid. You're homeless just like me, aren't you?

"Yes." I nodded.

"Then come," he smiled, "you're safe with me."

I followed him but I kept my distance. He looked harmless enough but I needed to be on my guard.

"Park yourself there," he pointed to a corner in the alleyway. "I'll be kipping just here, if you need me. Stick close to me and nobody will bother you."

"Thanks," I said but still not sure of him.

Old Bill, bless him, kept his eye on me over the coming weeks but he kept his distance unless invited to come closer. Whenever the police moved us on he'd show me a different place to stay and the homeless community got to know me. He was a real gentleman; must have been in his seventies. When I got to know him better I let him know a few things about myself but I kept Hillbury out of the equation. I decided to trust him to some degree but all the same I didn't want risk telling him anything he didn't need to know. I was probably doing him a dis-service but I couldn't be certain he wouldn't tell on me if he thought he might gain from it. I was surprised to learn he once ran his own business dealing in exports and imports. Sporting a long grey beard and a skeleton like body, his eyes on fire, I'd never have guessed he was once a successful businessman. Unfortunately for him the three day a week arrived and his business ran into difficulties. His second wife divorced him and he ended up losing everything including his home.

As the weeks went by he continued to be very supportive to me until one day he said he was going to be out of town for a few days. I watched him head off on this cold, rainy morning but I never saw him again. To this day I often wonder what happened to him. Had he somehow found work and a place to stay or did he just die one night from the bitter cold? He may have just decided to move on to a different part of London but he didn't want to tell me. Perhaps I was an inconvenience to him? I'll never know.

I'd discovered a few squats and I go to one of them whenever it was too cold to sleep outside. Sometimes though these places were oversubscribed or there'd be someone there who didn't take kindly to my presence so I'd just move on. I saw no sense in confrontation. If all else failed or if I desired some comfort I'd afford myself the luxury of some run down bed and breakfast. There were a number of these establishments scattered around London and I used a different one each time. I knew though paying for accommodation would eat into my meal budget, although I must confess, I often used to beg or steal food.

On one occasion I'd heard about this B & B on the Old Kent Road which I'd been told was very cheap. A very cold night had been forecast so I thought a little more warmth would be very welcome. I made my way to this place and rang to the doorbell.

"Can I help you?" I heard a voice ask before a man's face appeared from around the door.

"Do you have a room for the night?" I tentatively enquired.

He nodded. A fag hung from his mouth like Andy Capp: "Two quid, in advance."

He held out his hand and I gave him two one pound notes. He pulled the door open and let me in before handing me a key.

"Straight up the stairs," he said," last door on your left down the corridor."

I took the key from him and as I made my way up the stairs I noticed each step creaked. I also observed the staircase carpet was threadbare and, judging by its condition, should've been replaced long ago.

"Watch out for the loose floorboards on the landing," he shouted.

He wasn't joking. There were loose floorboards leading all the way to my room and I stepped cautiously. I'd visions of the floorboards giving way leaving me with my head and upper body sticking out the floor and my legs dangling through the ceiling below. Oh do stop your silly giggling at this ridiculous notion. Honestly, you can't take yourself anywhere, can you? Don't go letting Peter and Sally think you crashed through the floorboards because you didn't. You might think it'd amuse them but stick to the facts and not some gag from an early black and white film. You walked along the landing and apart from the floorboards creaking you entered your room without incident. I did but the carpet in my room was so threadbare it served little purpose and more loose floorboards were evident. The carpet, what there was of it, only covered the centre of the room and the rest of the floor was bare boards. I like a wooden floor but I didn't dare walk bare foot for fear of splinters sticking into my feet. The room itself couldn't have been more than eight foot by eight foot and there was a distinctive lack of bedroom furniture. The only heat source was a small electric fire in the corner and I'm no electrician but it looked too dangerous to even risk plugging it in. The bed was on its last legs and the linen, what there was of it, may well have been infested with fleas. As a caution I removed the linen from the bed and slept on it in my sleeping bag. B & B's such as this were generally dirty and cold and this was no exception but it was a lot warmer than sleeping in an alleyway. This was the best I could say about this place but for two quid what else could I expect?

The next morning I awoke to the sound of noisy traffic coming from the Old Kent Road outside. The hum of cars, roar of motor bikes and impatient motorists sounding their horns all mixed together produced an almighty din. I ventured downstairs to the dining room but if I'd hoped breakfast was included in the price I would've been sorely disappointed. A sign though in the dining room stated breakfast cost fifty pence and I was feeling hungry I decided to opt for this optional extra. However when I saw the burnt offerings on other guests plates I started to have second thoughts. What sealed it though was when Andy Capp came in carrying a breakfast plate, his fag still hanging out of his mouth, ash dripping onto the food. Time to go, I decided. My hunger had to wait.

For food I often sought out the contents of hotel dustbins and I know this sounds appalling but I tended to pick up unused fresh fruit and vegetables somebody had discarded without a second thought. I found by cutting out the bad bits they were fine to eat and even in those days it was surprising to find perfectly edible food being thrown away just because they were less than perfect. I wasn't stupid enough to pick up any cooked or half eaten food and I never considered eating meat no matter how hungry I got.

On Thursdays a branch of the Salvation Army opened their doors for the community to come in for tea or coffee and maybe spot of lunch. The lady running it was very kind to me and I'd pay a few pence for a coffee but she let me have the food for free.

"Just the veg, dear?" she always asked.

Yes, please," I'd always reply.

The menu was very basic and other than veg there was nothing vegetarian on offer but I was grateful for what I was given.

There were other times when a sympathetic cafe owner took pity on me and I'd have beans on toast or even a jacket potato, if I was lucky, in exchange for washing the dishes. I'd pick out the independently run cafes as the Nationally known ones usually sent me packing. On one particular day I came across a newly opened cafe and a quick glance at the menu told me there were a few things I would eat. I went inside.

"Take a seat, Madam," invited the cafe owner, "I'll come and take your order in a moment."

"I was wondering if you could spare me some food and cup of coffee in exchange for me washing the dishes?" I asked, rather embarrassed.

She looked at me inquisitively: "I'm not looking for staff, I'm afraid."

"No," I answered. "Just this once. In exchange for me washing some dishes you give me the food."

"Free of charge?" she queried.

"Yes," I said, feeling awkward.

"I'm new to this area, is this normally the done thing?" she asked, still looking puzzled.

I decided I was probably going to get nowhere with this lady: "Sorry to trouble you." I turned to leave.

"Wait," she called out. "I don't need any dishes done but if you'll sweep the floor you can have some beans on toast with coffee. Is that okay?" she asked handing me a broom she'd got from a cupboard.

I nodded: "Thank you," I replied, taking the broom from her and I began sweeping the floor.

"What's your name?" she innocently asked.

"Dawn," I replied. "Dawn Baker."

I think you better explain. I will. I was so paranoid Hillbury could discover my whereabouts, I used a number of aliases and Dawn Baker was just one of them. After all, as far as I knew, Dawn Baker hadn't escaped from Hillbury and anyway I wasn't important so surely nobody was going to waste time and resources trying to find me? There were times though when paranoia kicked in and I'd flea a scene convinced I'd been spotted by someone from Hillbury. Yet on this particular day my cautious approach may well have been justified. I hadn't taken long sweeping the floor and I was soon sitting down to a generous portion of beans on toast and piping hot coffee. Having eaten every scrap, guilt overcame me, as I felt sweeping the floor was insufficient payment for my breakfast. I persuaded the cafe owner to let me wash up my dishes and as I was finishing drying my plate, she came into the kitchen.

"Dawn!" she said, "or whatever your name is?"

"Excuse me?" I replied innocently.

"It's none of my business but I'm guessing you're in some kind of trouble," she said and held up her hand to gesture to me not to reply. "The fact is I don't care and I don't want to know. I think you should know there's a fellow on the other side of the road who's been eyeing up this place for the past few minutes. Now he may be nobody or he might be looking for you? Perhaps he's just someone deciding whether or not he wants to come and eat here? I suggest you don't stay to find out. You can leave via the backdoor."

I did as she'd ordered and I took myself as far away from the scene as my legs would take me. I never did find out who the man watching the cafe was because I never went back to find out. That evening I slept in an alleyway near Oxford Street but I felt safe enough as I was just another homeless person like many others. This was my life and I could see no way back. I'd nobody to help me and not even the Big Issue existed back then. Even if they had, I don't think I could've turned to them for fear of those at Hillbury discovering my whereabouts. For the same reason signing on the dole or finding a job weren't options open to me and besides I'd no fixed abode, so I was screwed either which way. So surely if I'd disappeared from society nobody would care? If so, those at Hillbury wouldn't care either. Or would they? These thoughts constantly played on my mind but these fears were something I had to learn to live with.

Chapter 16

I'd been living on the streets for about six months when I first met Harry. Just as Old Bill had done before, Harry took me under his wing and I looked up to him for guidance and wisdom. Unfortunately he was also bad influence on me as he introduced me to the art of alcohol theft. Post Harry I'm ashamed to say I'd pinched the odd bottle of beer or spirit mostly from delivery vans but this was nothing compared to him. He'd seen what I was up to and he made it his business to teach me his profession as he saw it.

Harry was one of life's real characters but sadly he was an alcoholic and worse still, he didn't seem to care. His haggard face was consistently red and blotchy and I'm not exaggerating when I say he looked like a walking corpse. His thin, bonny frame suggested he cared more for the booze than he did for a meal. He never told me his age but as he fought in the war he had to be a good deal older than me and he certainly looked it. He always looked out for me and I was grateful to him when he invited me to stay in his squat. It didn't belong to him of course but everybody respected his claim to the property. Already in residence were Linda, Beryl, Mark, Dave and Tim who were all very friendly and immediately made me feel welcome. Both women I reckoned were about the same age as Harry and I remember Linda was at least six foot tall. In contrast Beryl was very short, five feet if that and they looked an odd pair when they stood next to each other. Mark and Dave were about the same age as me, rough and ready characters but they were always very polite to me. Tim I guessed was about ten years older who never said much but he seemed content to sit there smoking his pipe. I learned from Linda and Beryl a lady called Helen was, up until a couple of weeks before, staying in the squat but she suddenly left and hadn't come back. Compared to sleeping outside the squat felt like I'd won the Jackpot just like when Mother Superior had transferred me out of the Evil Witch's class to Sister Flanagan's.

The building was a derelict, tiny one bed flat with no running water or electricity and was of course devoid of a heating system. There was though an open fire and one of our tasks each day was to gather up some burning material. Linda and Beryl both said I was much friendlier company compared to Helen who kept herself to herself. We all mucked in but Harry didn't help with the chores as his role was to supply the booze. The rest of us did our fair share without complaint and we worked like a co-operative with no single one person in charge. On occasions one of us managed to bring home some coal which was usually nicked from someone's bunker. Otherwise we relied on paper, cardboard and bits of scrap wood to keep us warm. On cold nights we all huddled around the fire and we enjoyed each other's company; we were like a family and we looked out for each other. Harry frequently entertained us with his beautiful harmonica playing and if we knew the words we'd sing along or just hum if we didn't. Sing? You could hardly describe the wretched noise you all made as singing! It was like listening to a clowder of cats screeching as they fought each other for territory. All right, none of us could sing but it was for our own enjoyment, we weren't getting paid for it. Should think not! If anyone else had been in earshot they'd have paid for your silence or got down on their knees and begged you to stop.

Harry was a Beatles fan and he insisted their songs would last forever. Just like traditional folk songs which have been passed down generations their songs would prevail. Perhaps he was right? Their music is still popular today and have been reinterpreted by other artists. One of my favourite Beatle tunes he played was *Eleanor Rigby* and as we all sang along I was reduced to tears. Harry did the song full justice as far as I was concerned. As strange as it may seem this was one of the happiest periods of my life. None of us in the squat were blessed with material things but we had each other's support. As well as playing the harmonica, with a bit of encouragement and an offer of a few swigs of whisky, Harry entertained us with various stories. He'd about fifty all retained in his mind but he rarely strayed from the script. Yet no matter how many times I heard one his stories he always managed to make them sound fresh and interesting. It may seem odd I should recall the memories of another but Harry made them sound so real and personal they became my memories too. Many of his stories were his adventures during the war but they were probably figments of his imagination or at least grossly exaggerated. It didn't matter though, Harry kept me and others amused for hours. One evening he told his favourite story and the next day my life changed forever.

"Have I ever told you about my time spent in a German prison camp during the war?" he asked.

He told us this story at least once a week and I heard it so many times I learnt it off by heart. There was no point in telling Harry we'd heard it before because he'd tell it anyway so we just shook our heads and Harry began his spiel.

"It was the winter of 1943," he always began. "The Germans had taken me prisoner."

Harry was very vague about this. He said it was on the border between France and Belgium but he never stated where exactly. There was no point in trying to get him to be more precise as he'd just shrug his shoulders.

"I tell yer," Harry continued, "this squat we're living in is like Buckingham Palace compared to the dirty, cold, rat infested huts us prisoners were kept captive in. Geneva Convention? Huh! Bloody well didn't apply to that place, I can tell yer. I'm not exaggerating when I say life was Hell and fellow prisoners were dying daily from the cold or starvation. The Germans didn't care though, one less person to feed was probably the way they saw it. Not surprisingly a week didn't go by without someone planning or attempting to escape, even though if they got caught, they risked facing the firing squad depending on the Commandant's mood. In any event security was very tight and even if anyone did manage to escape their journey ahead was very treacherous. The few that did escape probably died of the cold before they could cross the border. Captain Bolton was the one in charge of escape attempts. He was an all right guy but he was a bit of a twit. He couldn't organise a drinking session in a brewery."

Gary piped in: "You mean, a p..."

"Ah, Ah, Ah," Harry said, preventing Gary from finishing his sentence. "I know what I mean but there's ladies present."

"We've heard a lot worse, Harry. For a start, you've just used the word bloody in our presence." Beryl pointed out.

"Bloody's all right. The other word isn't." Harry answered.

This was Harry for you. What he considered a swear word depended on what mood he was in. Besides, the women living on the streets swore just as much if not more than the men. Not only that, Harry's principles went out of the window when he was drunk and then he swore like a trouper women present or not.

"Why didn't they wait 'til summer?" I asked with a degree of logic.

I asked this question every time so it became part of the story and I always got the same answer.

"That's a good question," Harry answered. "I suppose they thought that Jerry wouldn't expect them to try escaping in winter which would give

240

them an element of surprise. They were mad to try, I certainly didn't have any intention of risking it. As bad as conditions were, I'd every intention of taking my chances in the prison camp. I'd make it my business to keep out of Captain Bolton's way whenever he was looking for volunteers for an escape attempt.

"But you did escape?" I queried, keeping to the script.

"Yes, I did," Harry confirmed, "but all in good time."

Harry gestured he wanted a drop of whisky and I handed him a bottle of single malt which I'd found earlier in an alley way. It was probably left behind by a drunk thinking the bottle was empty and Harry was more than happy to finish it off. He was smiling as he swallowed his drink in one go and he then licked his lips in satisfaction.

"Lovely drop of whisky that," Harry declared, "good job you had some, Marie. I'm currently out of stock and this just won't do. I'll shall have to go shopping tomorrow."

"Going on one of your trips then?" Linda asked.

Harry nodded: "I think I'll try the Liverpool Street area, not frequented those parts for a while. There's a couple of places where I can get a few donations.

"You nick it, you mean," Mark suggested.

Harry tutted: We don't use such language around here. Let's just say I purchase some spirits on indefinite credit."

241

"Will you take me with you," I asked hopefully.

Harry shook his head: "Not this time."

"But I won't get in your way. I promise. I'll just watch, like I always do," I pleaded.

Harry shook his head again. I wasn't giving up though.

"You can have the rest of the whisky." I bartered.

By the look on Harry's face I could see he was tempted. I was hopeful for a positive answer.

"I dunno," he replied but still considering my offer.

"The next bottle of whisky I get is yours" I offered.

"All right but you stay out of my way." Harry demanded. "Now where was I?"

"You were going to tell us how you managed to escape," I replied.

"Oh that's right," said Harry taking another swig of whisky. "I swear to you this is true."

Harry's face took on a serious demeanor as he continued his story. We all listened intently although we already knew what was coming, we enjoyed the suspense just the same.

"German guards came into our hut one early morning and me and Johnny Smart, a good mate of mine, were hurled out of bed and told to get dressed quickly. Have I ever mention Johnny to you before?" he asked.

We all rolled our eyes. Hardly a day went by when Harry didn't mention Johnny Smart.

242

Harry continued: "Johnny and I looked at each other. What the Hell had we done? Was this it for us? Were we about to face the firing squad? This occurred to both of us but we were too scared to mention it. We both wet ourselves. We were taken outside where there were other prisoners from other huts all looking scared and bemused. Sergeant Cork was there, who'd already been briefed, put us out of our misery. We'd been selected to work in a mine near the Swiss border and we'd be away from the camp for a few days. We were told Captain Williams was coming with us on and he'd look out for our wellbeing. He was a good sort was Captain Williams. We all breathed a sigh of relief and we began to feel positive about the work we'd been assigned. We all felt it couldn't be any worse than the conditions in the camp.

We were bundled into the back of a truck with a couple of armed guards who had orders to shoot if we stepped out of line. Our journey to the mine was a bumpy one and it was a relief when we got there. We were put to work immediately and I'm telling yer, the work was so tough we barely had the energy to crawl to bed and this was before we'd erected our tent. It was pretty tatty and had more holes in it than you could imagine and there were twelve of us crammed into such a tight space we could hardly move. Bit of a bugger if one of us needed a wee and if anyone farted death threats followed. Farts aside, raw sewage couldn't compare with the stench of twelve mucky, smelly men after a day spent in a dirty mine. It was so bad it's a wonder we didn't all pass out and Sergeant Cork said we should all come with a health warning. In addition to the horrible smell, Billy Brown's snoring was so loud you'd have thought they'd been an earthquake. Even New Zealander Larry Dickens remarked on it and earthquakes were second nature to him."

Harry never failed to make us all howl with laughter when he spoke about the farting and snoring. It wasn't so much what he said, it was the way he said it and his facial expressions which made things so funny. He was a naturally funny man and his comic timing was impeccable. Whenever I think of him it reminds me what a tragedy it was he lived his life the way he did. Wasting his life as an alcoholic was sad enough but I'm not exaggerating to suggest he could've gone down as one of the World's great comics. He could've been a household name, lived a life of luxury, instead of the pitiful one he did have.

Harry continued: "We had to be thankful for small mercies it wasn't raining otherwise with all the holes in the tent we'd have surely got soaked. It was also fortunate for us there were enough bodies to keep us from freezing to death because we'd little in the way of bedding. I suppose we had to consider ourselves lucky we were given a tent to sleep in and not been told to kip in the mine. For this we'd Captain Williams to thank as he'd persuaded the Germans all of us were likely die from an overdose of gas fumes if we spent the night in the mine. Not that the Germans cared about our welfare but they needed us to stay alive to complete the work. True, replacing us was easy enough but it would've caused a delay which they didn't want. Due to his rank, Captain Williams was given his own tent with a half decent sleeping bag but I'd immeasurable respect for him when he not only insisted on erecting it by himself but lent a hand with ours as well."

Harry took another swig of whisky; his eyes shining with contentment. It didn't take much to satisfy him. If he'd plenty of whisky he'd everything he needed and he craved for nothing else. Although I'm sure much of the content of Harry's stories were pure fantasy I believe the next part of this one actually happened. I state this with a degree of certainty as his description of events was so horrific he couldn't have made it up. He took a deep breath and tears swelled up in his eyes as he continued his story.

"At the end of the second day's shift we came out of the mine and we were greeted by a howling blizzard with six feet of snow in places. I looked at Johnny and I could tell what he was thinking. How the Hell were we going to survive the night in these conditions even if the tent was still standing? Maybe the Germans would take pity on us and let us sleep in the truck? They'd surely realise we couldn't spend the night in the tent? Maybe though, they wouldn't care less? We set off back to camp with heavy hearts. I think everyone was thinking the same but nobody muttered a word. I looked at Captain Williams who was putting on a brave front but his face told a different story. If anyone was going to persuade the Germans to keep us safe it was going to be Captain Williams. That's what I kept telling myself. Captain Williams would save the day for us."

Tears rolled down Harry's cheeks as he prepared to recount the next part. This surprised me as I hadn't been witness to these tears before. A little watering in the eyes he'd allow but not tears like this. Harry was giving the performance of his life.

"The next course of events became more frightening than I could possibly have imagined as the truck suddenly went into a terrifying skid. The brakes squealed and screamed as we were tossed around like beads in a baby's rattle. Then the truck turned over on its side and we slid down an embankment at such a great speed it would've surely rivalled the fastest of any toboggan. Only one thought crossed my mind. We'd had it. I don't remember what happened next as I must have passed out. The next thing I was aware of was Johnny pulling me away from the truck just as it burst into flames. We could hear screams coming from the truck but there was nothing we could do," he said with tears pouring from his eyes like a river which had burst its banks. "These were some of our mates, poor buggers and even the German guards didn't deserve that."

We all felt concerned for Harry as he sat sobbing his heart out. There was an awkward silence as we all looked at each other. These tears weren't part of the usual script I reasoned and I'm sure the others thought the same. I decided to move the story on by asking a question I already knew the answer to.

"I suppose as you were near the Swiss Border you were able to escape?"

Harry nodded. He wiped the tears from his eyes with a dirty hanky and regained his composure. I was never convinced there was much truth to the rest of this story and at best I believe Harry exaggerated a lot of it.

"There was no way of us getting back to the prison camp even if we'd wanted to. Although we were still in shock we saw an opportunity to escape from Germany and get back to Blighty. Much as anything, we owed it to Captain Williams, Sergeant Cork and the rest of the lads to at least try. Harry and I were in full agreement with this. As difficult as conditions were, we made our way to the border. Luckily Johnny had a compass to help us and more fortunately he was familiar with the area having worked in the region before the war. Johnny hadn't mentioned this to me before but then he was always full of surprises. He surprised me even more when he suggested we should travel only at night. It was his view we stood a better chance of not being caught if we travelled under the protection of darkness. I could see his logic but I suggested the journey would be hard enough in daylight let alone at night. I agreed to his suggestion when he pointed out we were still wearing our Davy Lamps which the Germans had given us to work in the mine. Again we'd Captain Williams to thank as he'd

247

persuaded the Germans we'd get more work done if we didn't have to carry hand oil lamps.

To preserve our fuel, as we headed towards the border, Johnny and I took it turns to use our Davy Lamps. We were cold, tired and hungry but giving up was never an option. The Germans would just shoot us anyway and neither of us wanted our friends horrific deaths to be in vain. We had to succeed for them.

I think I can just about believe they'd Davy Lamps. Does sound a bit convenient though and it's a wonder both lamps survived the accident.

"Come the break of dawn we knew we'd have to find somewhere to take sanctuary. We came across a farm and we sited a barn which would offer us the shelter we needed. We approached it cautiously and we constantly looked out for any persons in the vicinity. Johnny tentatively went inside whilst I kept watch but I did my best to make sure I couldn't be seen by anyone. Moments later Johnny whispered it was okay for me to enter and we quickly concealed ourselves behind some haystacks. We reasoned as long as the farmer hadn't any plans to remove the haystacks that day we'd be fine. How wrong we were. We'd only been resting for about a half an hour when it was just our luck a young child wandered in with her pet dog. Naturally the dammed hound blooming well went and sniffed us out and we were confronted with this dog yapping and the little girl looking at us curiously. Fortunately Johnny spoke fluent German which was another thing that took me by surprise. Apparently only Captain Williams was aware of his language skills and Johnny passed on anything useful he heard the Germans discuss."

It was clear to us all Harry was in awe of Johnny and no doubt he worshipped him. Thinking about it, this may have been the catalyst to Harry's fall from grace? In his eyes, did he believe he couldn't live up to Johnny so he gave up on himself? If this was the case, damn Johnny Smart!

"Johnny explained to this little girl we were haystack fairies and she shouldn't tell anyone about us. She nodded and walked away with her dog trotting by her side. We didn't hang about though and we scarpered as fast as our legs would carry us and headed towards some woods. After a few miles our legs insisted we stopped running and we had to settle for a steady walking pace. We looked behind us and we couldn't see anyone in pursuit so we were hopeful the little girl had told no one. I told Johnny his haystack fairies story was a stroke of genius because who'd believe her? Anybody would think the little girl's imagination was running wild, wouldn't they? What if they realised somebody had been in the barn? Would they contact the authorities or would they prefer to ignore it? After all, having soldiers traipsing over your land could prove very inconvenient to a farmer. They might not even be pro Hitler and they may have every sympathy for British soldiers? Besides, they wouldn't know who'd been in their barn, it could've been a couple of vagrants. The uncertainty troubled us which made us more determined to get out of Germany as fast as possible. We were though exhausted and German soldiers on our trail or not we had to rest."

Haystack fairies? This sounds so ridiculous maybe it's true?

"Finding somewhere safe to rest in the woods until dark was going to be challenging. We looked around looking for inspiration and then Johnny spotted with his eagle eye a tree house high up, almost concealed behind the branches. This was a stroke of luck for us especially as someone had carved out footholds into the tree all the way up. We found the tree house to be in good condition and by placing a few extra branches in the right places we were able to conceal it from view. Why and who ever had built it we could only speculate but we were grateful for the sanctuary it offered and we slept until dark."

I've always thought finding a tree house in those woods was a very unlikely scenario. I mean, what would be the chances?

"When night fell we climbed down from the tree house and continued our journey. Visibility in the woods was limited even with both Davy Lamps switched on. We had to take care not to trip over a tree stump or a branch as we could've easily had a nasty accident. It was a relief when the woods gave way to open farmland and Johnny said we were within touching distance of the Swiss border. He cautioned the final hurdle could prove to be the most difficult and how right he was. Before we could reach the safety of Switzerland we were spotted by a German patrol and although we were both exhausted we weren't going give up now. From somewhere we found the strength to start running across a field but it was so dark we switched both Davy Lamps on. As we ran we could almost feel the German bullets as they flew passed our ears and one brushed my shoulder. It seemed likely one of us would be hit.

Harry paused again for another drop of whisky. I looked at the bottle and noticed it was almost empty.

"I'll show you the bullet wound later," Harry promised. "Every winter that bullet wound gives me gip".

He pulled a handkerchief from his pocket to clear his airways. All part of his act. He never showed us the bullet wound I might add.

"When it seemed we'd be either caught or killed the bullets stopped. We didn't understand why but we weren't hanging around to find out. Freedom was within our grasp and we could almost taste it but we didn't stop running until we made it to Switzerland. I asked Johnny if he was sure and he nodded citing it was an area of Switzerland he was very familiar with. We collapsed to the ground, exhausted, laughing our heads off and frankly we were too tired to move another inch. It was though a freezing cold night and after a while I said to Johnny we really needed to keep moving. He agreed but he needed to rest for just five more minutes but then we both fell asleep which could've been fatal. Luckily a farmer found us and he somehow got us to our feet and virtually carried us to his farm house.

Huddled around a blazing fire, we were given hot food and warm clothing and whilst we sat recovering from our ordeal we reflected on how lucky we'd been. The farmer said it was fortunate it was he who'd found us as and not one of his neighbours as he was sure they were German collaborators. Johnny and I agreed it was a miracle we weren't killed in the accident and how a German bullet didn't get us we'll never know. The question we kept asking ourselves was why had Jerry had suddenly stopped their gun fire and given up on pursuing us? Johnny suggested they may have lost sight of us but I wasn't convinced. When it had all sunk in and we reflected on what had happened to our mates we bawled like babies."

We were all surprised when Harry started crying once again and I was particularly troubled and concerned for him. However, another drop of whisky put him back on track.

"The farmer said he'd do what he could to help us get back to Blighty and in the meantime we were happy to help out on the farm. His tractor needed some repairs so he appreciated our help and I think he enjoyed having us around."

I shan't repeat the antics Harry and Johnny got up to. The farmer may have enjoyed and appreciated their company but I'm sure he could've done without them behaving like naughty school children at times. No doubt it was Johnny who put Harry up to it all. From what I gathered Harry would've done anything Johnny told him to do.

Except giving up the drink, he never succeeded with that.

"As the weeks went by we started to wonder if we were any nearer getting home but he assured us things were happening but it was taking time. Eventually we decided we'd try and make our own way but just as we were about to leave a car drew up outside the farmhouse. Instinctively Johnny and I hid in the coal bunker until we learned it was a British Diplomat no less who'd come for us. We were full of our self-importance as we sat into the back of the vehicle. We said our farewells to the farmer and we told him we couldn't thank him enough for all he'd done. We were taken to the British Embassy in Zurich to give our account of how we'd escaped and a few days later we were flown back to England."

I'd always thought this part of Harry's story was implausible. How could a simple Swiss farmer manage to arrange for a British Diplomat to come all the way from Zurich and take Harry and Johnny back with him? It wasn't as if they were high ranking officers or essential to the war effort.

"Back in Blighty we were asked to give our account to British Intelligence as according to them things didn't make sense. Johnny was indignant. Why were they disputing our version of events? After all, he could pinpoint the exact field we'd run across."

This bit always made me smile. Johnny must have been some kind of Superman. He may well have known the area well but the exact field? Really?

"The Intelligence Officers shook their heads; we couldn't be remembering things accurately. It couldn't possibly have been this particular field and they explained why. To have run across a minefield without being blown up was surely impossible but Johnny insisted he was right and I did my best to back him up. They decided to send us to hospital where we were examined for both physical and mental defects and, after several tests, they concluded we were suffering mental trauma. Blow me if some idiot doctor didn't conclude we were mentally unstable and had us discharged from the army. We were put to work at Handley Page for the rest of the war. That's a laugh to start with. If they really believed we were mentally unstable surely to God they wouldn't have let us near the war planes. Still, I wasn't complaining, it meant I didn't have to go back to the front line and I liked working at Handley Page."

Harry drank the last drop of whisky before picking up his harmonica and played another of his favourite Beatles' tunes. It struck me there was a sadness I hadn't witnessed before. I still to this day can't make up my mind how much of it is true. Having encountered these events so many times could he no longer hold back his emotions and the tears just flowed? Would he tell it again? I never got the chance to find out due to the events that unfolded the next day.

Hang on. You're getting ahead of yourself, aren't you? There's a sequel to this story. Oh I can't expect Peter and Sally to listen to another of Harry's yarns. Why not? Be honest, you want to them so just go ahead and tell them. Don't forget both of these stories are part of your memories of your life as a homeless person. Well, if you think so but if they look bored I'll shut up. Fair enough.

"We were handy men, able to turn our hands to most things, so we were set to work in Handley Page's workshop." Harry always began. "Obviously the skilled stuff was left to the experts but we were useful to them as labourers. We took digs in Radlett so we'd be close to work and Mrs Harrison, the landlady, looked after us very well. She took a shine to me and I think she enjoyed mothering me. She tended to give me a bigger breakfast which made Johnny grumble. In the evenings Johnny and I used to frequent the local pubs and we got to know a lot of people who lived in Radlett. There was a Scot called Ewan who'd moved down from Glasgow after the First World War. He could get us anything we wanted off the Black Market. At a price, that is. Blow me if he couldn't get bananas when most people could only dream of eating. We usually found him sitting on his favourite stool in the Red Lion where he alternated between a glass of whisky and a beer, whilst smoking strong non filtered cigarettes. He always wore a pin striped suit and ash from his cigarettes frequented the lapel on his jacket. It didn't seem to bother him, it didn't occur to him to use an ash tray."

I was amused by his description of Ewan. He reminded me of Old Tom whom I used to serve when I worked in the pub.

"If we weren't having a drink with Ewan we'd often venture into London by catching a train to St Pancreas from Radlett Station. I've a hundred and one stories I could tell about our nights out in London but there's one in particular which sticks out in my mind. We were at Piccadilly Station waiting to catch the tube back to St Pancras when we heard the air raid siren go off and we ended up spending the night in the station. There were a lot of children with their mother's as well as the elderly and we all had to make ourselves as comfortable as possible. I happened to have my harmonica in my pocket so I started to play a few tunes just to pass the time. I was soon joined by an old guy playing a violin. From what I could gather he was a professional musician on his way home from a gig. I bowed to his superior musicianship and followed his lead and I hoped my amateur playing wouldn't stand out too much. I was relieved when some lady got hold of a couple of drum sticks from somewhere and began tapping the wall. She was clearly an amateur so I wasn't feeling so self-conscious playing with the professional violinist and I really started to enjoy myself. We were starting to make a half decent sound and things went up a notch when a school girl, who could only have been about fourteen, began playing her recorder rather beautifully I thought. When a middle aged lady joined in with some delightful singing everyone around us stopped what they were doing to listen. We had a great night and I wished it could've been recorded but technology was much more basic then. Then again, it probably didn't sound as good as I remembered so it's probably just as well. One things for sure, it lifted everyone's spirits."

I think it would've sounded great had it been recorded. Harry was a better musician than he gave himself credit for and I bet the professional violinist thought so too.

"After the war Johnny and I kept in touch for a while but the demon drink was beginning to take ownership of me. Johnny tried to help me but I wouldn't admit I'd a drink problem so I rejected his help. What a fool I was. In the end he lost patience with me and I can't say I could blame him. Inevitably we lost contact. Last I heard he was running a successful car dealership business in North London specialising in German imports, would you believe? At least he did all right for himself and I'm glad about that. Johnny was one of the good guys."

Chapter 17

The next day I set off with Harry on his shopping trip and he reminded me I was to remain outside to keep watch. If I sited a policeman I was to hurry into the off-licence and call out if anyone knew where the Red Lion was. Harry would then offer to show me where it was and as soon as we'd left the shop we were to scarper as fast as our legs would carry us. Harry explained it was the most common name for a pub and there was likely to be a Red Lion nearby. Sounded simple enough to me, what could go wrong? Harry always choose his off-licence with care but there was always a chance a copper would come by. We arrived at his chosen off-licence and he waited until they'd several customers before making his move. With the shop keeper preoccupied serving a customer Harry was in and out, like a flash, armed with as many bottles as he could carry.

"It was a cinch," Harry declared. "There's only an old dear in there and she doesn't know what time of day it is. Poor cow. I don't think she was aware I was even there. Wish they were all that easy."

"Can I have a go?" I asked cockily thinking I could easily pull it off.

"Not yet, when you've watched me a few more times we can talk about it then," he answered.

"But we could double our takings if I went in there and you said yourself it was easy." I argued.

258

"It's not worth the risk, leave it, you're not ready for it yet." He countered. "There's plenty of drink here for all of us."

Trouble was I wasn't listening and before he could stop me I was inside the off-licence along with several other customers. I observed the old lady serving a customer and I quickly grabbed a couple of bottles of whisky off the shelf near the door. My heart was pounding. It was then I realised pinching some booze from an unguarded van was one thing but this was something else. I wasted no time in running out of the off-licence but in my haste I tripped on the pavement. I was quickly on my feet with the bottles of whisky still in each hand and for a moment I thought I'd get away with it. Unfortunately for me a policeman on his beat happened by and he grabbed hold of my collar as I attempted to run away.

"Gotcha!" he shouted with some satisfaction.

"Let go of me," I shouted back. "I've done anything wrong."

Pleading my innocence was futile and I knew I was in trouble. I looked across the street and Harry was gone. I felt such a fool. The thought of being sent back to Hillbury flashed through my mind. I'd risked everything and for what? A couple of bottles of whisky. Basically, you were a bloody idiot. Don't I know it?

"Not done anything wrong, huh? What are you doing with those bottles of whisky then?" he scorned.

259

"I've just bought them," I replied knowing he wasn't likely to believe me.

"Show me your receipt," he demanded.

"I wasn't given one," I answered, continuing with this ridiculous lie.

"Come with me," he ordered.

He marched me into the off-licence before asking the old lady if she'd served me. She shook her head and I was escorted to the Police Station in handcuffs. I felt so humiliated with handcuffs on, I thought they were reserved for hardened criminals and not a pathetic wretch like me. Once at the station I was so embarrassed and it seemed everyone was looking at me. Other than the Arresting Officer and the Duty Sergeant nobody was looking at you. It was just your imagination. Be honest, you felt a fool because you knew you wasn't getting away with this one and you wasn't going to see Harry and the others again. I felt physically sick. I cursed myself. How could I have been so stupid? You didn't need those bottles of whisky but you just wanted to impress Harry and show off to the others. So it served you right.

I was detained in a cell for the next two weeks with only the walls as company save the prison guard who brought me food each day. Not that the guard was any company. Apart from "Here's your food" she said nothing else to me. She'd hardly have won a Chatterbox Of The Year Award if there was such thing. During this virtually solitary confinement it gave me time to think and reflect on how I'd got myself into this mess. I took a hard look at myself and I didn't like what I saw. I'd become a drunk and a petty thief. I just hoped to God Mother knew nothing of what I'd become. I felt so ashamed.

I didn't mind too much being on my own and, I had to be honest, the prison cell was preferable to the damp squat and a million miles better than sleeping out in the streets. Although I missed Harry and the gang I realised I didn't want to go back to the squat. I needed somehow to turn my life around and I feared what would become of me. I'd been caught stealing and I realised I could be given a prison sentence but my biggest fear was being sent back to Hillbury. I spent sleepless nights worrying about this and on the night before my trial I was feeling terrified. If this wasn't bad enough, the lawyer I'd been assigned didn't fill me with much confidence. Robert Kane was his name and right from the start he behaved indifferent towards me. He never gave me the impression he cared what sentence I was going to get. It seemed to me he was just going through the motions and I'm sure he thought I was stupid and a blight on society. So I wasn't fancying my chances.

As I was led into Court you could've knocked me down with a feather when I looked up to see the same man who'd awarded Frank the children. He'd treated me so abysmally when our paths last crossed, how was going to treat me now I'd committed a crime? My first thought was he was going to crucify me and worst of all he was going to send me back to Hillbury. The injustice of it all, raced through my mind. He was responsible, as far as I was concerned, for the mess I was in. Come now. He didn't help but you did a whole lot of it yourself.

I feared my chances of a good outcome seemed somewhat remote. The trial was soon at a close and I stood in the dock resigned to the fact I was condemned before he began his summing up.

"Marie Benjamin," he said sternly. "You have been found guilty of attempting to steal spirits from Robertson's off-licence in the Old Kent Road on 21st December 1976. Before I pass sentence have you anything to say?"

"I'm very sorry for the trouble I've caused," I muttered ashamedly.

"Very well," he continued. "This is your first offence and I will take this into consideration. I must also consider the psychiatric report recommending you be detained in a mental institution to undergo treatment."

"Please don't send me back there." I pleaded. There were so may tears rolling down my face you'd have thought the River Thames had burst its bank.

"Silence!" he shouted as he slammed his hammer down on the bench. "Anymore outbursts like that and I'll hold you in contempt of court. The privilege of medical treatment was given to you but you chose to reject it by running away. Instead you elected to live a homeless existence and you've become a blight on society. So send you back to conclude the medical treatment? In my opinion it'd be a waste of public money. Punishment is the only answer. I sentence you to three years in prison."

I punched the air in triumph. He gave me a dirty look but I didn't care. So relieved was I to hear he wasn't sending me back to Hillbury the prison sentence had no sting. He continued his summing up but, to be honest, most of his words went in one ear and out the other. It was only afterwards it occurred to me my name would be in the papers and I just hoped Mother wouldn't learn of the prison sentence. I couldn't bear the thought of Mother finding out I was guilty of petty theft. It had been a long time since I last saw her but reconciliation had always been on my mind if she was willing. Kane told me afterwards he felt the sentence was harsh and he'd appeal on my behalf. This was the first time he'd shown any concern for me and if he'd tried harder I might have got off with a warning? Well, probably not! I didn't seem to care though and I resolved to do my time and then I'd be free. In the meantime at least I'd have a roof over my head, I'd have a bed to sleep in and I'd be given regular meals. However when everything had sunk in the euphoria of not going to Hillbury gave way to other fears. How would I be treated by the prison staff? Would my fellow inmates be hostile towards me? Would the colour of my skin determine how I'd be treated? I felt sick to the stomach and for a while I wished I was back with Harry and the others. I needn't have worried. The prison staff and inmates treated me okay and whilst prison was no picnic, I learned if I kept my nose clean I'd be all right.

I was in prison as punishment but from the first day I was determined to be as positive as I could. There were group therapy sessions for alcoholics and I willingly attended these. I wasn't the only alcoholic who'd ended up in prison for stealing booze and once I knew this I felt a little better about myself. It was such a relief to know I wasn't the only one and I wasn't such a bad person after all. I felt confident I could turn my life around. I was fortunate the prison governor recognised alcohol could easily turn respectable, honest people into petty thieves and he'd the foresight to invest time and money into addressing this problem. Even so it'd taken all the courage I could muster to walk through the door in the first place and bear my soul to strangers. I began nervously but once I got going there was no stopping me.

"My name's Marie Benjamin and I'm an alcoholic."

Everybody applauded and I relaxed considerably. People I didn't know were being so supportive and I felt a mixture of pride, relief and gratitude. Finally I'd admitted I was an alcoholic not only to myself but also to others and it was so good to be in the company of people who didn't judge or criticise me. They were, after all, the same as me; each one an alcoholic determined to be rid of this illness. I felt there and then this was a turning point in my life and I was determined from then on never to drink again.

I spoke of my arrest trying to steal from an off-licence in the Old Kent Road. Someone was kind enough to suggest I got a harsh sentence for a first offence but I made it clear to everyone present I'd no complaints. I confessed that sooner or later I would've ended up in prison; a slap on the wrist wouldn't have deterred me from stealing again.

"Look at me," I said to the class. "I'm shaking. Not just because I'm nervous but because I haven't had a drink. I'm sure you're all familiar with this feeling. Thing is, I've got to stop drinking. I know I can't be tempted whilst I'm banged up in here but when I leave I've got to make sure I stay sober. Stay away from the booze."

They applauded me again and I felt more encouraged. I was on a roll and it all came out.

"If I don't stop, it's going to kill me. I can't let that happen. I've got to get out of here and regain my self-respect. I've got two children in Australia and they're with their father. I've got to find them. Thanks. That's all I wanted to say."

It was a weight off my shoulders making this little speech; just sharing my thoughts with others helped. They were all very kind and sympathetic and they wanted to know about my children. I told them the whole story and whilst I went on a bit nobody seemed to mind and they all genuinely felt aggrieved for me. I was determined make a success of my rehabilitation. Oh I knew it was going to be hard, there was no use pretending otherwise and some days were better than others.

After a few weeks in prison I'd got used to the routine and I never minded the jobs I had to do. There were days when I'd be given a mop to clean the floors which set my mind back to the Glebe. At least O'Neil wasn't around to verbally abuse me and in many ways I thought prison was preferable to working at the Glebe. Not that I didn't have my bad days and none more so when I was admitted to the hospital ward with abdominal pains. I was administered a course of IV antibiotics which over a few days seemed to do the trick. For the first couple of days I wasn't allowed any food and only a few sips of water. Not that I felt like eating or drinking anyway but I must admit my mouth could've done with a little more moisture.

On my first night the hospital ward had been thankfully very quiet and I managed to get some sleep. This was not to last. The relatively peace and quiet at night was well and truly shattered with the arrival of Patricia and Kelly. What was physically the matter with either of them I never found out but in my humble unqualified medical opinion they weren't sane. My first reaction was they belonged in Hillbury but I immediately reprimanded myself for wishing this on other human beings. Kelly was well and truly away to the fairies but I know I shouldn't make fun. No, you shouldn't! I felt desperately sorry for these ladies; losing your mind is a terrible thing but I needed rest. When Kelly wasn't snoring or talking in her sleep, she'd burst into spontaneous song and whilst there was a familiarity to the words I couldn't comprehend what she was singing. It certainly wasn't Irish but I surmised it may well have been Scottish Gaelic or perhaps another Celtic language. Patricia, meanwhile, I believe, had dementia and she was constantly wandering around the ward and going to every bed but her own. At these times the nurses were often noted for their absence and I found myself having to get up and guide Patricia back to her own bed. Then there was an old lady, whose name I didn't discover, who was sick everywhere when four nurses attempted to get her onto a trolley and fit her with a neck brace. Eventually they got the job done and the old lady was wheeled off for an Xray never return. What happened to her I never found out. The noise and commotion which had accompanied all this made Piccadilly Circus seem like a ghost town, so when I'd sufficiently recovered I was glad to return to the relative normality of prison life.

I continued to talk about my problems and share thoughts with the other inmates but it seemed to me it was only those who'd a drink problem themselves who fully understood. Those who weren't addicts expressed sympathy for sure but with other alcoholics I shared a common bond. Mavis was the person I most preferred to talk to and, as she was a worse case than I was, I didn't feel so bad about myself. Mavis, before prison intervened, was on a bottle of whisky a day and apart from the shakes her physical presence told its own story. I was witness to her progress which in turn gave me the encouragement and belief to rid myself of my drinking habit. I admit there were times when the constant shakes half scared me to death and I'd try and hide my embarrassment by jiving and humming *Rock Around The Clock*. I wasn't fooling Mavis who knew exactly where I was at. My jiving amused some of the other prisoners and I think they thought I was just larking around. I don't think they realised I was just trying to hide my embarrassment. You couldn't really blame them for laughing at your dancing efforts, could you? Let's face it, a member of Pans People, you wasn't. You'd a lack of any sense of rhythm and your singing sounded like a fog horn.

During my stay in prison I spent as much time as I could in their library where I could indulge myself in learning and the pleasure of literature. I'd left the convent at fifteen with no qualifications and with no expectation to make anything of my life in the World of Commerce. The prison library had opened my eyes to learning and suddenly I craved knowledge and books became my new addiction. I'd read everything I could lay my hands on. Novels by distinguished authors such as Charles Dickens and Agatha Christie, Shakespeare's plays, auto biographies and biographies, magazines. I'd read them all. I was making up for lost time having wasted my time at school. In my defence the Evil Witch didn't help matters but even in Sister Flanagan's class I never really knuckled down despite my interest in History. Spending a lot of time in the prison library earned me brownie points with authority and I came to be regarded as a model prisoner. The governor in particular recognised my enthusiasm and gave me jobs to do in the library which I loved doing.

After I'd been in prison about six months my useless lawyer, who turned out not to be so useless, came to tell me an appeal date had been granted. At my hearing I nervously stood in the dock; the possibility of being sent free dominated my mind. I tried not to get my hopes up too much even though my lawyer was confident of a successful outcome. I was relieved the man who'd decide my fate I hadn't faced before and I felt encouraged as his demeanour seemed more kindly. I crossed everything I could cross as I held my breath as he spoke.

"Miss Benjamin, I have re-examined your case and I have reached a decision. Firstly I must commend you on your attitude whilst you've been in prison. The prison governor has reported you've made great progress in tackling your alcoholism and you've been making every effort to improve your education, making full use of the library facilities. Well done."

I glanced at my lawyer's face and he was smiling. My heart was racing. Was I about to be set free? I told myself to keep calm, there may be a but."

He continued: "I also understand you have been keeping yourself fit by the using the gymnasium regularly. As a young man I used to frequent the gymnasium myself but mine was for the purpose of

269

boxing. Something I wouldn't expect a lady such as yourself to be indulging in."

By now the suspense was killing me. Surely he wouldn't deliver a cruel blow now?

He concluded: "Given your circumstances it seems to me you shouldn't have been sent to prison in the first place. You've been candid about your spell in Hillbury and I'm going to order an inquiry. Be assured, if what you've told me can be substantiated the necessary action will be taken. It was wrong your children were taken from you and I can't imagine the heartache this must've caused you. You must have been devastated to learn your husband had taken them to Australia and I pray it's not too late for you to be reunited with them. I hope either the British or Australian Embassy can assist you in this matter. You've been punished and suffered enough and, in view of this, I'm exercising my powers to quash you prison sentence. You are free to go although I strongly recommend you join Alcoholics Anonymous and I don't expect to see you in a court again."

It took a few moments for his words to sink in. Was I really free to go? Another glance at my lawyer's face as he was grinning from ear to ear confirmed it. I struggled to control my emotions as tears of joy flowed down my face. I felt so happy, so relieved. At last a judge who understood. A judge with a heart. I hadn't realised one existed. It was July 1977. The nation celebrated the Queen's Jubilee and there was a feel good factor following Virginia Wade's women's singles title win at

270

Wimbledon. Good for her, I thought, but for me my joy was greater. I had my freedom.

Chapter 18

Once out of prison I had to find somewhere to live and get a job. The prison service provided me with a list of low rent bedsits and I settled for one in Central London. The room was tiny but it was clean and tidy and the other people who lived in the same building seemed pleasant enough. I'd enough money to cover two weeks rent but I needed to find a job quickly. I'd also been given a list of potential employers who'd look kindly on someone who'd been in prison. As it turned out I didn't need this list as I learned from a fellow resident there was a job vacancy in a baker shop not five hundred yards from my accommodation. This was encouraging as I knew I could do that job. After all, I'd experience of working in a bakers in Dublin so I knew about the different types of bread. I wasted no time in taking myself down to the baker shop feeling confident of success. When I arrived outside the shop I could hardly believe it as I thought the lady inside the shop, busily serving a customer, bared an uncanny resemblance to O'Neil. Those unpleasant memories came flooding back when the horrible O'Neil treated me so badly when I was just a servant girl. For one bizarre moment I considered whether or not it was her. This woman, serving cakes, looked identical and I could've been fooled into believing O'Neil had come across from Ireland just to spite me. I closed my eyes for a few moments and I tried to calm myself. I told myself to clear my head of all emotions and consider this with common sense and logic. You were such a daft cow, you'd taken your paranoia to another level with those idiotic thoughts. O'Neil wouldn't have looked that way after all those years; she'd be an old woman if indeed she was still alive. Apart from anything else, O'Neil wouldn't have left Ireland and taken an English job. A hypocrite she may have been but the very thought was ridiculous. I was being ridiculous I know and when I opened my eyes I realised this woman wasn't identical to O'Neil after all. There you are you see, paranoia. All right, smart arse!

I took a deep breath and made my way into the shop. The smell of freshly baked bread wafted up my nostrils and for a few moments I was transported back in time to the bakery in Ireland. I thought of the friends I'd made there and if I'd my time again and with hindsight I could've made different decisions. My thoughts of Ireland were broken by the sound of a lady's voice I soon learned to be Mrs Walsh.

"Can I help you?" she asked with a smile.

I relaxed a little. Her manner was much more kindly than O'Neil's so this was a good start.

"I've come about the vacancy", I replied trying to look confident.

"Oh yes," she said still smiling. "My name is Mrs Walsh and I'm the proprietor. What's your name?"

"Marie Benjamin," I replied extending my hand and was relieved when she took it.

"Nice to meet, Marie", she said still keeping her smile. "Tell me a bit about yourself. Have you had any experience in this line of work?"

I nodded: "I worked in a bakery in Ireland when I was in my teens", I said gleefully.

"Oh good," her smile now beaming. "Tell me more?"

I decided to be completely honest with Mrs Walsh. I thought this to be the best policy.

"I must be honest. There's no way of dressing this up. I've recently spent six months in prison and I'm a recovering alcoholic."

"Oh," she said, only a glimmer of a smile remained.

"I was sentenced to three years but after six months I was freed on appeal. I don't want to offer any excuses but I'll not drink again. I determined about that."

"What was you in prison for?" she asked which sounded more out of curiosity than in judgement.

"Petty theft," I answered, "stealing some booze from an off-licence."

I explained the circumstances which led me down this path and I assured her this was all behind me. Mrs Walsh thanked me for my honesty and I could sense she'd some sympathy for me. Would this be enough though? Would she disregard my past and just consider my ability to do the job. I felt sick. My whole future could depend on what she decided. She smiled again, which was encouraging.

"My father was an alcoholic too but nobody gave him a second chance when he needed it and he eventually died of liver failure."

"I'm sorry to hear that", I said not knowing what else to say.

It then crossed my mind she wouldn't be giving me a second chance. Nobody had helped her father so why would she help me?

"I liked to think I'm a good judge of character,' she continued, "My instincts tell me you're a good person but you've been treated badly by others. I think you deserve another chance, Marie."

I was so relieved when she agreed to give me a chance and I was to work in the shop on a week's trial. If I came up to scratch she'd consider offering me the job on a permanent basis. I thanked her and I left the shop with a big smile on my face. I knew instinctively things would get better from now on and I could hold my head up high. I think I must have skipped all the way home like an eager school child.

I started work in the shop the following day having made sure I arrived a little early. I worked hard that week and I soon made a good impression with the regular customers. After only a few days Mrs Walsh offered me the job on a permanent basis and I readily accepted. I'd earn ten pounds a week which meant there was just enough to pay the rent and feed myself.

As much as I enjoyed my job at the bakers the highlight of the week for me was Wednesday afternoons when it was half day closing and I'd visit the local library. It was on one of these visits there was to be another turning point in my life. I'd been working at the bakers for about ten months and as usual I'd selected a couple of books from the library to read for the coming week. I always chuckle when I remember that day. Actually you usually end up in hysterics when you relay this story to anyone. Me? No! Yes, you do. Well, perhaps a little chuckle when I recall waiting in the queue and in front of me was a rather stupid woman trying the poor library assistant's patience. I must confess I thought at the time the woman even looked rather stupid which was very unkind of me and I'm ashamed to say I nicknamed her Gormless. There you go, you're starting to giggle already. Tell it straight faced. Okay? All right but when the woman spoke it did nothing to change my perception of her.

"Oh dear it's so difficult," said Gormless. "I just can't make up my mind. The question is shall I take "*Wuthering Heights*" or plump for one of these Agatha Christie's.

"It's all a matter of choice, madam," the library assistant told Gormless. "It all depends on what your prefer. All of these are excellent novels."

"Yes but which one?"

"That's up to you, madam. Why not take them all?"

"Take them all but just go." I muttered under my breath.

"I couldn't possibly take them all," Gormless explained to the assistant. "I'm not a very fast

276

reader, you see. One book is more than enough at a time. Will you choose for me?"

"If you wish, madam. May I suggest this one," the assistant suggested picking up the first book in the pile.

"Oh! *A Caribbean Mystery*" said Gormless reading the book title. "I'm not so sure. Thoughts of the Caribbean will have me pining for a holiday."

"Well how about *They Do It With Mirrors?*" Suggested the assistant hopefully.

"It's not kinky, is it? I mean, it's not filth, is it. I mean, I'm not a prude but I can't be doing with that type of thing."

The assistant assured her it was perfectly acceptable reading material for anyone. Gormless then momentarily selected *Dead Man's Folly* before settling on *Cat Amongst The Pigeons* declaring she was an animal lover. The assistant quickly stamped the book before she changed her mind and ushered her towards the exit citing a queue had built up. As Gormless exited the library the assistant and I collapsed in fits of laughter.

"You had a right one there," I said momentarily regaining my composure.

The assistant nodded in agreement: "It's always the same with her. She always picks up half a dozen books before deliberating on which one she'll have. I'm sure she doesn't actually read them." She stamped the books I'd selected. "I'm afraid I haven't managed to get a copy of the book you wanted. The one about your father's regiment, I mean, but I'll keep trying. You've tried Somerset House, I take it?"

"Yes, I've reached a dead end," I replied. "With a name like Benjamin you wouldn't think I'd have such a problem, would you? Perhaps it's because my Father was born in Africa I'm having so much difficulty."

I started to make my way towards the exit when a grey haired, elderly man, smartly dressed in a pin stripped suit approached me. He told me his name was Vaughan and he couldn't help but overhear my conversation with the library assistant. He asked me to confirm my name was Benjamin and I was immediately suspicious. After all he could be anyone and a thought crossed my mind he may have been one of Frank's associates or even some gangster after Frank. Frank has crossed swords and had dealings with all sorts of dodgy people so nothing would've surprised me. These people would know all they needed to know about Frank, including his ex-wife. So if Mr Vaughan did have a connection with Frank what did he want with me? I decided to remain in the safety of the library whilst the conversation continued.

"You wouldn't in any way be related to Isaac Benjamin, by any chance?" Mr Vaughan asked casually.

"Yes, he was my father," I replied. I relaxed a little. I was relieved Frank's name hadn't been mentioned.

"I thought so, I can see the likeness," Mr Vaughan said with a smile.

"You knew my father?" I asked excitedly.

"I knew your father very well." Mr Vaughan continued. "I fought alongside him during the war. He was a very brave man."

"Thank you," I said graciously.

"He saved my life, your father did," Mr Vaughan added. "A Jerry badly wounded me and left me for dead. Your father came to my aid. Without any concern for his own safety he carried me back to the trenches. There I received some initial lifesaving first aid before being carted off to the nearby makeshift hospital for treatment. I lay in a hospital bed for several weeks before I was strong enough to be brought back to England to begin a long term recovery. I have a lot of people to thank. The doctors and nurses who nursed me back to health, the first aider in the trenches but most of all I have your father to thank. It was an extremely brave thing what he did for me and I wouldn't be here if it wasn't for him. I was very sorry when he was killed in battle."

"Thank you. I don't remember much about my father," I said, offering my hand in friendship. It's a pleasure to meet you, Mr Vaughan."

"Please, call me Brian," he replied shaking my hand.

"I'm Marie," I smiled.

Mr Vaughan invited me to join him for afternoon tea in a pleasant tea room in the high street. It was a traditional tea shop with spotless white table cloths, shiny cutlery and quality crockery. It had attractive oak beams decorated with

279

polished brass ornaments and antique chairs to sit on. It was a joy to be in such a place but most of all I was so thrilled to be talking to someone who knew Father. I learned so much from Mr Vaughan; details Mother didn't know or if she did she never told me. Mr Vaughan described Father's life in the army and how he used to carry a photo of me wherever he went. I spoke frankly about my life and Mr Vaughan was most sympathetic and not in the least bit judgmental. He told me he was a solicitor and he was looking for someone to help him with his paperwork. He asked if I'd be interested but if I was offended by his offer, he'd apologise. I said I wasn't in the least offended but was he sure he wanted to employ me? After all, he knew nothing about me and whether or not I was capable of doing the job. He said I was Isaac Benjamin's daughter and that was good enough for him. I was delighted to accept his job offer. My pay was to commence at fifteen pounds a week which was a lot more than I was earning at the bakery. I told Mr Vaughan I'd have given notice to Mrs Walsh but he said he was content to wait.

As much as I was delighted to accept Mr Vaughan's job offer I was dreading going into work the next day. What was I going to say to Mrs Walsh? I felt so guilty. She'd given me a chance when many others wouldn't have and now I was going to leave. I felt like a traitor.

"My dear, girl," said Mrs Walsh, "you've got nothing to apologies for. Of course you should take the job, it's wonderful opportunity for you. In fact, if you'd told me you'd turned down an opportunity like that I'd been disappointed in you. I soon realised you wouldn't be with me long. You've got ability Marie and you deserve this chance. It's going to be tough for the girl I employ to take your place because she'll have to measure up to you, so she'll have to be good. I hope you'll keep in touch, Marie."

"Most definitely, Mrs Walsh. I shall come in regularly to buy my bread from you." I promised.

For the next ten years I continued to buy my bread from Mrs Walsh and she was always interested to know how I was getting on. When she retired she sold the business on to another lady but it was never the same. The shop's no longer there and in its place is a block of flats.

Having worked my notice I set off to Mr Vaughan's office in Covent Garden for my first day in my new employment. I was excited but also terrified I wouldn't be up to the job but I took to it immediately. I soon got a system going and Mr Vaughan was thrilled with what I was doing and he confessed he didn't know how he'd ever managed without me. He admitted admin was never his strong point and he was impressed whatever paperwork he wanted I was able to find it immediately. I kept a close tabs on things and I must admit I became very possessive over my filing system to the point I told Mr Vaughan he was not to take any file without my knowledge. He laughed: "Yes, Boss" he said. I felt embarrassed and apologised but he said this was absolutely fine and he needed someone to organise him. He assured me the office was running so much more efficiently and he was able to take on more cases.

It was at this time I decided I'd try and make peace with Mother. I'd lost count of the years I hadn't seen her and I didn't know whether I'd left it too late for a reconciliation. I couldn't be certain if she was still alive although I felt sure she still was.

I was hoping she wasn't aware of my recent past as it would've disappointed her so much. Frankly, I'd been too ashamed to contact her up until then but I'd turned my life around and I was able to hold my head up high. I promised myself to tell her what a fool I was to cut myself off from her. That is, of course, if she was willing to see me again? If I turned up at her door she might slam the door in my face? I had to be prepared for this possibility. I plucked up the courage to knock her door only to discover she'd moved on and none of the neighbours said they'd a clue where she was living. If they did, they weren't saying. Then I thought of Father Kelly. If anyone knew where she was it'd be him. I hadn't seen him for years either and we never exactly hit off so would he help me? It also occurred to me he may have moved on from the church or passed away? There was only one way to find out so off I trotted to the church and fortunately I found him in the grave yard. I don't mean he was buried there, he was just attending to some graves. There you go again, stop this silly giggling. What will Peter and Sally think if you start giggling when you mention Father Kelly in the grave yard? You're right, I mustn't laugh so I'll just say he didn't recognise me but he admitted I'd the same skin complexion as the Marie he remembered. I was able to confirm enough facts about Mother to reassure him. He agreed to take me to Mother's flat but he stressed if she didn't want to see me I was to walk away without a fuss. I agreed.

Arriving at Mother's he knocked her door and I stood behind him so she wouldn't see me. I wanted to see her before she saw me and to be brutally honest if she was to throw something it would more likely hit Father Kelly rather than me.

"Why Father Kelly, what can I do for you?"

"I hope I've done the right thing, Mrs Benjamin, for I've brought someone to see you."

He stepped out of the way leaving me in full view. She gasped and her mouth dropped.

"Oh, Father Kelly," she cried. "You have indeed done the right thing."

I fell into Mother's arms and we both sobbed uncontrollably. Father Kelly made a discreet retreat. Hugging each other, Mother led me into her sitting room where we talked for hours. I brought Mother up to speed regarding Frank and the children and she took this news very hard.

"This is all my fault," she cried. "If I'd been the mother I should've been none of this would've happened."

"No, Mother, it's not your fault. Frank was determined to part me from Peter and Sally. There was nothing you could've done."

283

"But I should have lent you that money for the rent. Can you ever forgive me?"

"There's nothing to forgive. It's me who needs forgiveness."

"It's all in the past, Marie, let's look forward. I've got some money saved. Enough I think to get you to Australia."

"Thanks, Mum, but Australia is a big place. Unless I can trace their address I haven't got a cat in hell's chance."

"Don't give up hope. Promise me that. Guí mé lá amháin a bheidh do leanaí a bheith ar ais le leat áit a mbaineann siad."

"I pray this will be so too, Mother."

"You haven't forgotten it, then?"

"How could I ever forget the beautiful Irish language?"

Mother smiled: "Bless you but as I say, don't give up hope."

"I won't give up hope. Hope is all I've got right now. I've got a new job working in a solicitor's office," I said changing the subject.

"Oh very posh!"

"I'm working for a Mr Vaughan. He knew Father during the war. Did Father ever mention a Mr Vaughan to you?"

"Can't say he did but then your father never said much about the war."

"Mr Vaughan said Father saved his life."

"Really? I'd like to meet this Mr Vaughan."

"You would?"

"You sound surprised, Marie?"

I hesitated. I was reluctant to say this reaction wasn't like the mother I knew. Having just reconciled with her, I didn't want to upset the apple cart. Luckily Mother answered her own question.

"I know what you're thinking, Marie. It's not like me to take a positive interest in your friends and acquaintances and you'd be right to think this. I realise now what a terrible mother I was to you."

"No Mother, you weren't" I said interrupting.

"Don't argue with your mother."

"No Mother," I replied, accepting defeat.

"I've had years to think about this and there hasn't been a day when I haven't longed for the opportunity to put things right. I've now got this chance and I'm not going to mess it up. Besides, this Mr Vaughan knew your father. So I'll be thrilled to meet him."

"And so you shall Mother."

Mother got her wish a couple of weeks later when I introduced to her to Mr Vaughan. I could tell Mother was charmed by Mr Vaughan and she was overjoyed when he spoke of Father so fondly. She listened intently to his recollections of the times he spent in Father's company. Mother hardly said a word; she was content listening to Mr Vaughan. I have to say I'd never known Mother to be so quiet. She told me she was very proud of me when he told her what a great job I was doing for him. This was another first for me. Mother had never told me she was proud of me before. The new Mother I now had made me very happy.

Chapter 19

I'd only been working at the solicitors office for about six months when Mr Vaughan quite casually asked me if I'd be interested in studying to become a solicitor. I laughed but he never battered an eyelid. Was he serious? He assured me he was. I was gobsmacked. Me? A solicitor? The mere thought of me becoming a solicitor seemed like a fairy tale to me. Not to him it wasn't. He'd every faith in me and he was prepared to put his money where his mouth is and pay for me to go to evening classes. If I was interested, that is. I said I'd like to discuss it with my mother. Mr Vaughan was perfectly okay with this and understood why I needed some reassurance this was right for me.

"Why on Earth are you asking me, my girl?" Mother asked, looking astonished.

"I value your opinion." I replied.

Mother chuckled: "When I think of all the times I wished you'd asked me for my opinion you never did. There were so many times when you never considered the value of my experience and yet now you've been offered a golden opportunity you want my opinion? For goodness sake, Marie, tell that nice Mr Vaughan you are most certainly interested before he changes his mind. Work hard, study hardy and make me the proudest Mother on Earth."

Once I'd heard Mother's views and the challenge of making her the proudest Mother on

Earth, I had to do it as much for her as myself. So when it was time to begin my studies I went along full of enthusiasm. I wasn't kidding myself though, I knew it was going to be hard but I didn't realise how hard it would be. I was flooded with a mindful of information and I thought at times I'd drown in the sheer volume of it all. Mr Vaughan had warned me it would be tough. Tough it certainly was. For a start I didn't have a degree. Anyone with a law degree certainly had the best head start but if I'd one in any subject I could've completed a one year Graduate Diploma in Law. Instead I had go down the Chartered Legal Executive route and this was a long process. For years I studied hard, pulled my hair out many times when the learning got tough but I stuck at it. I wasn't going to give up. Studying in my bedsit posed its problems but I managed. I soon realised I wasn't just doing it for myself and for Mother but all those who had helped me up until then. I had to succeed for Mr Vaughan, of course, who'd invested so much in me. Mrs Walsh was thrilled when she learned of my studies and she gave me a chance when many wouldn't have. I had to do it for her. I had to do it for the judge who'd set me free and quashed my conviction. For all those who'd been so supportive in prison, for my friends at the squat for their companionship and even the lady who'd sold me the sleeping bag for next to nothing. When things got tough I'd think of Andrew who'd stuck his neck out and hid me from authority and the lovely Mr Jennings who was so nice to me. Then of course there was dear Mrs Houseman,

Mother Superior and Sister Flanagan. I couldn't let any of these people down. I also drew determination by sticking two fingers up at those who'd been so horrible to me. The Evil Witch, the nasty O'Neill, the rotten judge who separated me from my children and not to mention all those Hitlers at Hillbury. Above all others, two fingers up at Frank. Damn him and damn them all if I was going to fail.

The day came when I eventually qualified as a solicitor and I felt extremely relieved and proud. Mother was as proud as she said she'd be and she wasted no time in telling everyone in the church of my success. She didn't just leave it at that as she also told the postman, the milkman, the dustmen and anyone else who came to her door. All her neighbours knew within minutes of me sharing my news with her plus anyone she met at the bus stop as well as the bus conductors. All the staff in every shop she went in were also informed and within a few days I think half of London knew I'd qualified.

It was my lucky day when I went up before that judge for my appeal against my prison sentence and I know he's pleased I haven't let him down. I did though, many years later, appear in front of him but this time I was in Court assisting a barrister I'd engaged to make a plea for one my clients. Quite incredible when I think about it but then again my life has been incredible. He remembered my face but he couldn't place where he'd seen me before and when I explained he nearly fell off his chair. What he said to me that day I've never forgotten.

"I'm so glad I set you free that day. I congratulate you. Seeing you today, a respectable solicitor, has reminded me why I do what I do. You have shown me how worthwhile this profession can be. You must be very proud."

Two weeks after I'd qualified my joy turned to sadness when Mother died of a massive heart attack. Father Kelly came for me and I got to the hospital just in time and I was grateful to him for the comfort and support he gave me. We'd had our differences in the past but he was there for me when I needed it. I won't hear a word against him now. I sobbed as I tenderly held Mother's hand and I laid my head on her lap. With her other hand Mother gently stroked my hair which she hadn't done since I was a child. Quietly she slipped away but in no pain I was assured.

I knew Mother had a heart problem and I was aware she was taking a lot of pills but I didn't realise the extent of it. The specialist said he was amazed Mother had lasted so long given her heart condition. There are several theories why she lasted longer than she ought to have done but I believe he hadn't taken into account Mother's stubbornness. Before she died she was going to see me qualified and no matter how grim the prognosis this was the terms she made with God.

I didn't realise or more accurately I didn't admit to myself, until she was dying, how much

Mother meant to me. Damn it, she was so infuriating but for all her faults, I loved her so much. I was full of remorse but I could never get back the years we'd lost. What haunts me the most is I never told her I loved her. I never blinking well said it. I'd been a cow, there's no two ways about it. Aren't you being a little hard on yourself? Not in the least! I'd blamed so much on Mother when in reality most of it was my own doing. There are many people who don't see it this way and they can't understand why Mother turned her back on you when you needed her help. Yes, this is true but for all that's been said I always find myself defending her. It's difficult to explain but Mother couldn't help doing what she did; it was the way she'd been brought up. It was just the way she was. We were both very stubborn, I realise it now. Just one more of my life's regrets.

After Mother died I went to her flat to sort things out. Much of her stuff I gave to Father Kelly for him to distribute as he saw fit. Not that she'd much of any value but some of her clothes would've done someone a good turn. She did have several pairs of stiletto heels of various bright colours. That was a thing about Mother. She could be dressed like she'd been dragged through a hedge backwards but her shoes always looked immaculate.

Over the years I received offers from bigger solicitors firms wanting me to work for them. On several occasions I was told I could name my own salary but I can honestly say I was never tempted although Mr Vaughan always made it clear he wouldn't stand in my way. I knew I'd always remain loyal to Mr Vaughan and I'd no hesitation in turning them all down. I was rewarded for my loyalty when, after his death, he left the business to me in his will.

I never remarried. I enjoyed a few relationships with men but I never considered marrying any of them. My marriage had been a disaster and after that Hellish experience I wasn't going to trust a man again. Not even Bill Baxter? Ah now, Bill Baxter was and is a wonderful man. Last summer, a chance in a billion, I ran into Bill in a department store in London and we both did a double take before we recognised each other. After all we hadn't seen each other for many years but for Bill's part he was looking very sprightly for his age. He was always very fond of sport and he was in town to take in some tennis at Wimbledon. He was astonished to learn Frank had emigrated to Australia, as Frank was so Pro-Britain, Bill could never imagine him emigrating.

Back then Frank told him we'd parted company and I'd moved back to Dublin with my mother. He found this hard to believe because he knew how much the children meant to me. Suspicious, Bill called at the only address he had for me but of course I'd already been evicted. Information Frank hadn't shared with him. Although Bill didn't believe I'd moved back to Dublin he didn't have the time or the means to try and trace me. He was very disappointed and saddened to discover, when he was next in town, Frank had moved on again but Bill had no idea where he'd moved to. He never heard from Frank again. Bill believes Frank had decided to sacrifice their lifelong friendship rather than risk his old friend passing on his address to me.

Bill had never married which surprised me somewhat because he was a good looking man. In fact, he still is rather dashing I have to say. He was very kind and he held down a well-paid job so who wouldn't want to marry him? As they say, what's not to like? From what I understand there were a lot of women in his life at one time or other but perhaps he just didn't meet the right one? Perhaps there was no woman worthy of him although he'd never have suggested this. He'd remained in Brighton all his life and last August he invited me to his home for a holiday. He was the perfect host showing me the sites of Brighton including the famous Lanes. We've met up a couple of times since but purely as friends. Are you sure? I'm sure. Back in the early seventies I would've jumped at the chance of becoming Mrs Baxter but it wasn't to be. I certainly married the wrong best friend. When I telephoned and informed him of Frank's death he was sorry to hear it but he said he'd lost his old friend a long time ago.

Whilst I'd never given up completely on contacting my children my hopes had faded over the years. I'd made many fruitless visits to the Australian Embassy in London but the answers were always the same. Frank had disappeared and there was no trace of him. They suggested he was probably living under a new name somewhere and Australia was a big country so sorry they couldn't help. They also suggested to me he may not even be living in Australia and hadn't that occurred to me? They said they sympathised with me but as far as they were aware Frank hadn't committed a crime and it was all a question of resources. These were the hard facts and they didn't want to offer me false hope. I told them hope was all I had and I'd hang onto that. I had to keep telling myself I would see my children again even if I found this hard to believe.

So this is my life in a nutshell. A big nutshell you should add. Is this all you're going to say about your life as a solicitor? What else is there to say? It's the second half of your life; you achieved so much you ought to be proud. Should I? Of course you should and don't be modest. You helped a lot of people; you made a difference. Surely Peter and Sally would want to hear about your many achievements? Perhaps but I'll tell them about this part of my life another time. After all, I'm going to spend as much time with them as I can from now on.

You keep looking at your watch? Peter and Sally should be here any minute so I need to be clear in my mind what I'm going to say. You've just spent the last hour or so going through what you're going to say as you've done many times before. It's important to me they learn the lot, good, bad and indifferent. I want to know everything about them as well, we've got a lifetime to catch up on. Peter has assured me he and Sally had a happy upbringing and although their father was away a lot he treated them well when he was at home. I'm glad about that. I'm glad he turned out to be a half decent father so perhaps he'd an ounce of goodness in him after all. I must admit when Peter phoned to tell me Frank had died I had to stop myself from screaming with delight. I felt like a footballer must feel like and doing a lap of honour around Wembley after winning the cup with his team. I'd visions of Frank burning in Hell for eternity along with Evil Witch and O'Neil. You better not tell Peter and Sally this. I won't and anyway I realised almost immediately these were wicked thoughts and I slapped my wrists. I even offered my sympathy even though it wasn't sincere. Yet he was their father and they grieved for him so I had to respect that. I was also pleased to learn their stepmother treated them like her own and, although she was the Other Woman, I have to be honest and say she didn't cause my marriage break up. Frank and I did this all on our own so if it hadn't been her it would've been someone else. I bear her no grudge and I honestly hope she'd a better life with Frank than I ever did. I'd be happy to meet her. I'm looking forward to flying to Australia with them next month where I shall spend a few months in lovely and warm sunshine, far away from the cold British winter. I'm excited at the prospect of getting to know my four grandchildren and of course my son-in-law and daughter-in-law.

Before all this though, I'm charged with showing Peter and Sally some of the best Britain has to offer. Firstly though, I shall show them where they lived when they were little and Mother's old home. I'll give Hillbury a miss though, not that I know where it is anyway or if indeed it's still there. Next week we're off to Ireland which will be somewhat of a nostalgic trip for me. I'm looking forward to returning to the location of Uncle Michael's farm, Lord knows who runs it now. Whether I can face going back to the convent, if indeed it's still there, I shall have to see. According to the internet the Glebe is now open to the public so this will be interesting. O'Neill aside I have some found memories of this place and I do hope the pond's still there. It will bring back some happy memories. I'll be interested to see if the bakery is still there but it wouldn't surprise me if they've built a block of flats in its place. Or perhaps a car park? What an awful thought!

The waiter is beckoning you to him. This is it, old girl, the moment has arrived. I'm terrified. Come on now, pull yourself together, file all those nerves away. This is no time for your legs to turn to jelly, so get a grip, you daft bitch. They're going to love you so stop worrying. Do you think so? Of course. They're probably just as nervous about meeting you. No doubt they're hoping they'll be met with your approval. I suppose you're right. Now put one foot in front of the other and start walking towards the restaurant. I didn't see them come in. They must have come in the other entrance. The waiter is pointing to them but he doesn't need to do that, I know my children when I see them. My legs are still like jelly. All three of us are smiling and crying at the same time. We're bawling like babies as we hug each other tightly.

In my minds-eye I see Mother standing beside me with a beaming smile. I hear her say: "Peter agus Sally ar ais le leat áit a mbaineann siad."

THE END